The Light Fantastic

The Light Fantastic

Edited by Harry Harrison

Science Fiction Classics from the Mainstream

Introduction by James Blish

New York
Charles Scribner's Sons

Printed in the United States of America
Library of Congress Catalog Card Number 76-140772
SBN684–10228–5

Acknowledgments

"The Muse," by Anthony Burgess, copyright © 1968 by Anthony
Burgess; reprinted by permission of the author and his agents,
International Famous Agency, Inc.

"The Unsafe Deposit Box," by Gerald Kersh, copyright © 1962 by the
Curtis Publishing Company; reprinted by permission of
Mrs. Gerald Kersh.

"Something Strange," by Kingsley Amis, copyright © 1956 by
Kingsley Amis; reprinted by permission of the author.

"The End of the Party," by Graham Greene, copyright © 1947 by
Graham Greene; reprinted by permission of The Viking Press, Inc.

"The Circular Ruins," translated by James R. Irby, is from LABYRINTHS
by Jorge Luis Borges, copyright © 1962 by New Directions Publishing
Corporation; reprinted by permission of New Directions Publishing
Corporation.

"The Shout," by Robert Graves, copyright © 1950 by Robert Graves;
reprinted by permission of Collins-Knowlton-Wing, Inc.

"The Door," by E. B. White, copyright © 1939, 1967 by E. B. White.
Originally appeared in *The New Yorker* and reprinted by permission of
Harper & Row, Publishers.

"The Machine Stops," by E. M. Forster, from THE ETERNAL
MOMENT AND OTHER STORIES by E. M. Forster, copyright © 1928
by Harcourt Brace Jovanovich, Inc.; copyright © 1956 by E. M. Forster.
Reprinted by permission of the publisher.

"The Mark Gable Foundation," by Leo Szilard, copyright © 1961 by
Leo Szilard; reprinted by permission of Simon & Schuster, Inc.

"The Enormous Radio," by John Cheever, copyright © 1953 by
John Cheever, from THE ENORMOUS RADIO AND OTHER STORIES
by John Cheever; reprinted by permission of the publisher,
Funk & Wagnalls.

"The Shoddy Lands," by C. S. Lewis, from OF OTHER WORLDS by
C. S. Lewis, copyright © 1966 by The Executors of the Estate of
C. S. Lewis. Reprinted by permission of Harcourt Brace Jovanovich, Inc.

Contents

The Light Fantastic

Introduction
The Function of Science Fiction

by James Blish

Not every man would have the daring to title a story of his own "The Finest Story in the World," but Rudyard Kipling knew exactly what he was doing. If there is any short story in English which deserves to be called the finest on all counts — for characterisation, for perfection of language and structure, for emotional power and depth of implication, and in many other departments — I would nominate James Joyce's "The Dead" as the front-runner; but this is not at all what Kipling meant to claim by his title, which I think he would have retained even had he been in a position to know Joyce's piece and share my assessment of it. He was talking about Story as Tale — the kind of story which is so intensely interesting in itself that it hardly matters how it is told, and the best examples of which have survived many retellings and will survive many more.

It should not be surprising, as C. S. Lewis points out in *An Experiment in Criticism,* that almost all such stories are fantasies; nor should it be surprising that Kipling's exemplar of the type is a science fiction story. Many readers and almost all writers in this field know that Kipling was one of the finest of all science fiction writers.

1

What *should* be surprising, but unhappily is not, is that this fact about Kipling is unknown to the vast majority of teachers and scholars of English literature — and to the few that do know it, it is a source of embarrassment.

This is a specific example of a general situation. In the nineteenth century, virtually every writer of stature — and many now forgotten — wrote at least one science fiction story. This book includes two examples from the period. Edgar Allen Poe wrote several; so did Ambrose Bierce, and Fitz-James O'Brien, and Edward Everett Hale, and Jack London, and many others. As an example of such a production from an author unknown now, let me cite *The Last American* by J. A. Mitchell, which was published in 1889 by Frederick A. Stokes & Brother, and went through ten editions in the succeeding four years. Additional examples from this period may be found in a volume edited by Sam Moskowitz called *Science Fiction by Gaslight.*

Jules Verne, in short, was just plain wrong in assuming that he had invented a whole new kind of story. It had been in existence for decades; indeed, it was almost commonplace, and widely accepted. Poe's life, let it be remembered, was cut short in 1849. By about 1860, the science fiction story was a fully formed and highly visible literary phenomenon in English; Verne was merely the first author working in the form in another language to catch the public eye.

These writers did not call what they did "science fiction", or think of it as such; the term was not invented until 1929. When H. G. Wells published his early samples of it in the 1890's — and in the process showed that such pieces could also be works of art — he first called them "fantastic and imaginative romances", and, later, "science fantasy" (a term which has now been degraded to cover a sub-type in which the science content is minimal, and what little of it is present is mostly wrong). Most of its producers, however, never bothered to give it a label, nor did editors feel the lack; it was considered to be a normal and legitimate interest for any writer and reader of fiction. Indeed, the Utopian romance, such as Butler's *Erewhon* and Bellamy's *Looking Backward,* was a prominent feature of that literary landscape.

This assumption crossed smoothly into the twentieth century and gave every sign that it was going to continue undisturbed. Guy de Maupassant wrote science fiction; so did Joseph Conrad; so did Lord Dunsany (especially in his five Jorkens books). Science fiction novels, mostly by Carl H. Claudy, appeared regularly in *Boy's life* — which was not an innovation either, but only a continuation of the dime novel tradition established by the Frank Reade series. There was so much of such work about by 1926 that when *Amazing Stories,* the world's first science fiction magazine, appeared in that year, it sailed for a considerable time almost entirely upon reprints, including some from German sources.

And it is still possible in 1970 to say that there are few writers of stature, from Robert Graves all the way down to Hermann Wouk, who have not published at least one science fiction story, even if one rules out of the definition of "writers of stature" all those who have made their reputations almost entirely inside the field itself (e.g., Isaac Asimov, Ray Bradbury, Arthur C. Clarke, Robert A. Heinlein). Were it necessary, Mr. Harrison could have produced a book to this effect a good ten times the size of this one, but I think the case already proven by inversion: that is, by the fact that this volume excludes science fiction stories by mainstream writers which are already known to most readers (Stephen Vincent Benet's "By the Waters of Babylon", for example) — and by the additional fact that it is impossible to find any such story by Franz Kafka and Karel Capek, to say nothing of Sir Arthur Conan Doyle, which has not been reprinted to the point of outright unavoidability.

Yet there has been a significant change in attitude toward such material, which I have exemplified by the ignorance of or embarrassment toward Kipling's science fiction which is endemic among most teachers and scholars who are not specialists in science fiction. An even more specific example of the new attitude may be found in this book, in Graham Greene's "The End of the Party". This story is science fiction in an almost chemically pure state — though its subject, telepathy, is still regarded by most scientists as being too unlikely to reward serious study — but Greene goes out of his way, inside the story itself, to reject the label, as though his tale would somehow seem less plausible did he not repudiate the form in which it is cast. The attempt, of course, only calls attention to the fact Greene wanted to sweep under the rug, and in this he is fortunate, for if people interested in pigeon-holes (and there are people with legitimate professional interests in pigeon-holes, such as librarians) cannot call the story science fiction, they will have to call it fantasy, which would be *more* destructive of its credibility.

Greene is not alone. Consider the case of Kurt Vonnegut, Jr. He has been published in science fiction magazines; he has attended one of the ten-day sessions of the annual Milford (Pennsylvania) Science Fiction Writers' Conference; he was for a while a member of Science Fiction Writers of America, the field's sole professional organization; he has testified to his admiration for science fiction, and his attendance at Milford, in one of his novels (*God Bless You, Mr. Rosewater, or, Pearls Before Swine*); and almost all of his work is science fiction. But both he and his publishers now take the most elaborate public pains to deny and/or ignore these plain facts, as though they were somehow pejorative, like a criminal record.

Another case: When Walter M. Miller Jr.'s *A Canticle for Liebowitz* achieved hard-cover publication, his publishers denied on the flap copy that it was science fiction, a tack that was obediently followed by most of its reviewers. (That is to say, by reviewers in the American press, most of whom still will not review a science fiction book unless they are so assured that it is somehow some other kind of thing.) Yet it had been first published, serially, in a science fiction magazine; all of Miller's prior and subsequent production has been science fiction, and has appeared in those same magazines; and the novel itself won a "Hugo" award (which it deserved) as the best science fiction novel of its year, an award accepted by Mr. Miller with no show of protest.

Still more recently, both Thomas M. Disch and Brian W. Aldiss, science fiction writers virtually since birth and important innovators in the field, have shown preliminary signs of repudiating their crèche at their first success outside it, as though, again, their past work was somehow discreditable. One of America's most recent major publishers of science fiction will not actually label their books science fiction because they fear the label will limit sales; another tries to have the best of both worlds by describing it coyly as "partly science, partly fiction, and just a little beyond tomorrow's headlines".

These examples could be multiplied, but I think the point is clear. Most mainstream reviewers and critics seem happy to follow its lead, which has, indeed, become a sort of critical syndrome. Kingsley Amis has struck it off in an epigram:

"Sf's no good," they bellow till we're deaf.

"But this looks good." — "Well then, it's not sf."

And Theodore Sturgeon has summarized the situation in more usual critical language, though just as tersely:

Never before in literary history has a field been judged so exclusively by its bad examples.

To this, I will add, never before in literary history has so sharp a change in critical attitude taken place without anyone's taking any notice of it, let alone wondering how it came about.

#

Yet had anyone thought that question worth asking, the answer would have been immediately to hand. One needs only to look at the dates, and to think, briefly and indeed quite superficially, about the recent history of any kind of genre fiction.

The villain of the story, as any political theoretician could have postulated *a priori*, is a social invention; in this case, the invention (by the American publishing firm of Street & Smith) of the specialized fiction magazine, that is, the kind of magazine which publishes only love stories, or only detective stories, or only cowboy stories. This invention, as it turned out, was malign; in literature, it is almost a pure obverse of Mussolini's discovery that the way to raise the birth rate is to fail to supply electricity to housing projects. Every such magazine ghetto — with one highly significant exception — killed off the literary sub-type it attempted to exploit. The first such to die was the love story, which had been rendered superfluous by magazines like *True Confessions* (though these were not to last much longer). The sports story followed; by 1944 there were pulp magazines so specialized as to publish nothing but stories about a single sport — baseball, mostly, but football, hockey and even basketball also had their monomaniacal journals, as I remember only because I wrote for them, out of financial desperation and in an agony of boredom. The sports story is now utterly dead. The Western or cowboy story was the next victim, followed by the formal detective story. There are hardly any such magazines any more, except for a few detective magazines and a lot of science fiction magazines; indeed, there are no longer any other magazines of specialized fiction, for the penultimate member of the line, the "women's magazine," survives today only upon recipes, interior decoration and sex advice, and publishes as little fiction as it can possibly manage.

The significant exception, as noted, is the magazine devoted to science fiction (and marginally, to fantasy), of which there are still quite a number, though they are now threatened by another social invention, the paperback book. These magazines have managed to change with the times, and indeed offer a startling example of adaptation to social invention which brings one back directly to Mussolini's discovery. During their early history, they thrived side by side with magazines devoted to what the literary historian would call the Gothic tale (though it was quite unlike the product now being marketed under that label, such as the works of Daphne du Maurier): magazines with titles like *Weird Tales, Horror Stories* and *Terror Tales.* The once-enormous popularity of ghost stories now seems puzzling until one realizes that they were utterly dependant for their effect upon the uncertainty and shadowiness of all sources of artificial light prior to the general installation of electricity, which did not become universally available in the West, even in the United States, until well after World War I. Once one can dispell a shadow by touching a button, belief in ghosts is doomed, and with it the literature of ghosts. (There is, to be sure, a vigorous modern revival of interest in witchcraft and demonology, but its roots lie in eschatological realms which have almost no bearing upon this argument.) Today, magazine fantasy is chiefly allegorical; the brief Gothic excursion is almost forgotten, although the nerve, as *Rosemary's Baby* showed, can still sometimes be touched by invoking much more powerful and essentially irrelevant fears. (For example, Ira Levin's novel is much closer to the women's-magazine convention than it is to the Gothic; its two central fears are "Suppose my baby should be born deformed?" and "I think the neighbors don't like me". The witchcraft is only a paranoid top-dressing. Fritz Leiber's *Conjure Wife,* a much better book and one much more knowledgeable about the essentials of magic, nevertheless is also paranoid at bottom; it exploits the common fear of the ineffective male that women are members not only of a sex, but of a conspiracy.)

For the survival of its specialized magazines, however, science fiction paid a heavy price. An all-fiction periodical — and all one kind of fiction, at that — demands to be filled periodically; if good material is not available, bad must be published. (Television is now suffering the same kind of attrition.) The pulps, furthermore, never did pay well, and the rates for science fiction were particularly low up to about twenty-five years ago; Horace Gold, a veteran of that era and later one of the field's best editors, once described them as "microscopic fractions of a cent per word, payable upon lawsuit". As a result, the field became dominated by high-production hacks, so that what was to be found beneath the lurid covers was often quite as bad as the covers suggested it was. (In mitigation, it should also be noted that new writers raised in this school did learn one art which is almost extinct in mainstream fiction today: tight plotting.)

How seriously this segregation has hurt the field may be seen in almost any of the critical excursions into it undertaken by mainstream critics, for it invariably turns out that what they are discussing in such excursions is the pulp era, not modern science fiction. One such article which appeared in *The Saturday Review of Literature* (before that title was truncated) about a decade ago was even illustrated with magazine covers from the early 1930's; and an article by the eminent French critic Michel Butor which was published in the Fall, 1967 issue of *Partisan Review* mentioned not a single living author of science fiction but Ray Bradbury (whose work offers a splendid example of what we now mean by "science fantasy").

This, however, may be no more than an example of cultural lag, like the familiar one between painting and music. In his significantly titled *A Century of Science Fiction,* Damon Knight, who is almost the inventor of serious criticism in science fiction, wrote in 1962:

> By and large, the hostile critics have fallen silent. When s.f. is mentioned by a respected literary figure today, his comments are likely to be informed and friendly — an unheard-of thing twenty years ago.

At the time, this was really only a hope, for if challenged to cite such friends, the only ones Mr. Kinght could have adduced were Kingley Amis and C. S. Lewis (and the later was after all virtually an insider, having written three science fiction and eight fantasy novels, and published short stories in one of the U. S. science fiction magazines). But it was an informed hope, for it was based in large part upon another social change which Knight, like all his colleagues, had long known to be absolutely inevitable: the advent of space flight. How great an influence this has had toward making science fiction respectable can be estimated from the fact that of the many millions who watched the first lunar landing on television or heard it on the radio, hardly any could have escaped exposure to two or three interviews with science fiction writers.*

But the reason for the trend back toward respectability goes much deeper than this. Let us recall to mind that, in the teeth of modern critical scorn, science fiction has been popular with readers *and writers* over a long period — more than a century —

---

*This was an international phenomenon. I was in Venice at the time, where I heard myself being quoted over Rome Radio.

during which the very possibility of space flight, atomic energy and other staple subjects of such stories was discounted by almost everyone.*

What explains this popularity, under such handicaps? Knight suggests (in the same preface quoted earlier):

Science fiction is distinguished by its implicit assumption that man can change himself and his environment. This alone sets it apart from all other literary forms. This is the message that came out of the Intellectual Revolution of the seventeenth and eighteenth centuries, and that has survived in no other kind of fiction.

This is a valid and critically useful insight; but were the factor it describes the only one in operation, readers could obtain the message equally well from the accounts of actual space flights and other wonders which they find in newspapers. (And this is in fact now a fairly widespread assumption: All of us in the field have now been asked, "Now that they've really landed on the Moon, what do you guys have left to write about?" One writer confronted with this question replied with justifiable irritation, "For Christ's sake, lady, there hasn't been a moon landing story published in fifteen years"; but though the question does show the usual ignorance of science fiction, what is more important is that it shows a rather frightening continued ignorance of the boundlessness of the realm opened by the Eagle landing.) Yet sales figures for science fiction last year were at their highest in history.

In addition, therefore, I propose that — in an age which has seen the decline of religion as an important influence on the intellectual and emotional life of Western man — science fiction is

---

*When Robert H. Goddard began his rocket experiments in the early 1920's, he was rebuked editorially by the *New York Times* for wasting his university's money. The possibility of space flight was rejected with scorn alike by theoreticians like H. Spencer Jones, the then Astromomer Royal (in a book with the misleadingly science-fictional title *Life on Other Worlds),* and practical engineers like Lee de Forest, inventor of the thermionic valve without which radio and television alike would have been impossible. These examples, too, could be multiplied, *ad nauseam*

the only remaining art form which appeals to the mythopoeic side of the human psyche.

#

This proposal brings us full circle back to what Kipling meant by a Story. In *Fiction and the Unconscious,* Simon O. Lesser makes the point formally:

> Like some universally negotiable currency, the events of a well-told story may be converted effortlessly, immediately and without discount into the coinage of each reader's emotional life.

A related argument is proposed by Susanne K. Langer in *Philosophy in a New Key,* that music calls to our attention a class of conceptual relationships which also includes, and therefore is usefully analogous to, the emotions (a most difficult idea to paraphrase, but luckily not without helpful antecedents, particularly in the work of Kenneth Burke). Later, in *Feeling and Form,* she proposes more generally that art, like science, is a mental activity whereby we bring certain contents of the world into the realm of objectively valid cognition, and that it is the particular office of art to do this with the world's emotional content.

In comment on this latter proposal, George Richmond Walker adds:

> Even scientific theories are accepted or rejected because of what can only be called an aesthetic preference for clarity, simplicity, elegance and generality. It is the function of the arts to make us widely and deeply aware of our affective experience, to help us to know and to understand what we feel.

In support of Walker's first point, it is useful to remember that the fundamental aesthetic rule by which scientific ideas are judged, which is usually put as "The simplest theory which accounts for all the facts is the preferable one," was formulated by William of Occam as "One must not multiply entities without reason;" it is a product of the logic of medieval scholasticism and therefore vastly antedates the scientific enterprise *per se*; it is often called "Occam's Razor." The obverse of his second point is that science concentrates on helping us to know and order our sensory and operational experience – the external rather than the affective.

There has always been some overlap between the two. The mathematician Michael Polanyi notes:

> The affirmation of a great scientific theory is in part an expression of delight. The theory has an inarticulate component acclaiming its beauty, and this is essential to the belief that the theory is true.

This is not, perhaps, very happily put, but the meaning shines through. More colloquially, C. P. Snow has testified that the act of scientific discovery includes an aesthetic satisfaction which seems exactly the same as the satisfaction one gets from writing a poem or novel, or composing a piece of music. I don't think anyone has succeeded in distinguishing between them.

Most psychiatric theories, the Freudian most markedly, seem to depend for their continued life almost entirely upon their effectiveness as artistic constructs, since none of them makes a good match with sensory and operational experience, and their record of medical effectiveness is no better (and no worse) than that of other forms of faith-healing – and we shall see below that faith is also a question of some importance.

Science fiction at its best serves all three of these avenues to reality, and in this it is unique:

(1) It confronts the theories and data of modern science with the questions of modern philosophy, to create "thought experiments" like that of Einstein's free-falling elevator which may in themselves advance science. The most striking example of this, of course, is space flight itself, for which science fiction both provided the impetus and prepared the public; but scientists themselves have lately turned to using science fiction to propose thought experiments dealing with the social effects of what they do, as may be seen in the story in this book by the late Leo

Szilard. Obversely, most such thought experiments posed by to-day's philosophers unconsciously falls into science fiction form. Here is an example by George Richmond Walker:

Suppose there were beings on another planet who were organized differently from us, with different sense organs, different brains, and different logic and mathematics. Their views of the universe would necessarily be very different from ours. Would the universe then be what they say it is or what we say it is?

(2) Like all the arts, science fiction adds to our knowledge of reality by formally evoking what Lord Dunsany called "those ghosts whose footsteps across our minds we call emotions". This is what makes it an art; as Walker says, a true knowledge of understanding of affective experience is the basis of wisdom; it is what distinguishes the civilized man from the savage, the adult from the child, and the sane from the mentally ill. But unlike any other art, science fiction evokes for the non-scientist the basic scientific emotions: The thrill of discovery, the delight in intellectual rigor, and the sense of wonder, even of awe, before the order and complexity of the physical universe.

(3) Science fiction creates myths in which, because the authority of modern science is invoked to back them, modern man can believe (though whether or not they are worthy of belief is the subject of another essay altogether). As the world-wide reaction showed, the emotional experience of watching the first lunar landing was primarily a numinous one, thoroughly secular though the facts of the event might be described to be. Again, too, there is a supporting obverse phenomenon: Whereas the mass psychoses of the past derived their assumptions and their trappings from religion (for example, the chiliastic panic of 999 A.D., or the witch-craze of the sixteenth and seventeenth centuries), today their form is science-fictional (the Church of Scientology, the flying saucer mania). It will be observed that this mythopoeic function is one which cannot be fulfilled by even the very best fantasy, for here there can be no question of belief; indeed, of all the arts, fantasy requires the greatest suspension of disbelief, a sophisticated intellectual exercise which is outright inimical to

the will to believe.

If this hypothesis is valid — as necessarily I believe that it is — then we are unlikely to see any decline in the popularity of science fiction in the forseeable future. It further follows that the appearance of any such decline would have implications reaching far beyond the apparently tiny corner of recent literature occupied by science fiction. As Robert Conquest put the heart of the matter in *For the 1956 Opposition of Mars:*

> Pure joy of knowledge rides as high as art.
> The whole heart cannot keep live on either.
> Wills as of Drake and Shakespeare strike together;
> Cultures turn rotten when they part.

[I am indebted to Brain W. Aldiss, Harry Harrison and Robert A. W. Lowndes for suggestions and citations.]

Harpsden (Henley)
Oxon., England
1970

The Muse

by Anthony Burgess

"You're quite sure," asked Swenson for the hundredth time, "you want to go through with this?" His hands ranged over the five manuals of the instrument console and, in cross-rhythm, his feet danced on the pedals. He was a very old man, waxed over with the veneer of rejuvenation chemicals. Very wise, with a century of experience behind him, he yet looked much of an age with Paley, the twenty-five-year-old literary historian by his side. Paley grinned with undiminished patience and said:

"I want to go through with it."

"It won't be quite what you think," said Swenson. (This too he had said many times before.) "It can't be absolutely identical. You may get shocks where you least expect them. I remember taking Wheeler that time, you know. Poor devil, he thought it was going to be the fourteenth century he knew from his books. But it was a very different fourteenth century. Thatched cottages and churches and manors and so on, and lovely cathedrals. But there were polycephalic monsters running the feudal system, with tentacles too. Speaking the most exquisite Norman French, he said."

14

"How long was he there?"

"He was sending signals through within three days. But he had to wait a year, poor devil, before we could get him out. He was in a dungeon, you know. They got suspicious of his Middle English or something. White-haired and gibbering when we got him aboard. His jailers had been a sort of tripodic ectoplasm."

"That wasn't in System B303, though, was it?"

"Obviously not." The old man came out in Swenson's snappishness. "It was a couple of years ago. A couple of years ago System B303 was enjoying the doubtful benefits of proto-Elizabethan rule. As it still is."

"Sorry. Stupid of me."

"Some of you young men," said Swenson, going over to the bank of monitor screens, "expect too much of Time. You expect historical Time to be as plastic as the other kinds. Because the microchronic and macrochronic flows can be played with, you consider we ought to be able to do the same thing with—"

"Sorry, sorry, *sorry*. I just wasn't thinking." With so much else on his mind, was it surprising that he should be temporarily ungeared to the dull realities of clockwork time, solar time?

"That's the trouble with you young—Ah," said Swenson with satisfaction, "that was a beautiful changeover." With the smoothness of the tongue gliding from one phonemic area to another, the temporal path had become a spatial one. The uncountable megamiles between Earth and System B303 had been no more to their ship than, say, a two-way transatlantic flipover. And now, in reach of this other Earth—so dizzyingly far away that it was the same as their own, though at an earlier stage of their own Earth's history—the substance vedmum had slid them, as from one dream to another, into a world where solid objects might subsist, so alien as to be familiar, fulfilling the bow-bent laws of the cosmos. Swenson, who had been brought up on the interchangeability of time and space, could yet never cease to marvel at the miracle of the almost yawning casualness with which the *Nacheinander* turned into the *Nebeneinander* (there was no doubt, the old German words caught it best!). So far the monitor screens showed nothing, but tape began to whir out from the crystalline corignon

machine in the dead centre of the control-turret—cold and accurate information about the solar system they were now entering.
Swenson read it off, nodding, a Nordic spruce of a man glimmer-
ing with chemical youth. Paley looked at him, leaning against the
bulkhead, envying the tallness, the knotty strength. But, he
thought, Swenson could never disguise himself as an inhabitant of
a less well-nourished era. He, Paley, small and dark as those far-
distant Silurians of the dawn of Britain, could creep into the
proto-Elizabethan England they would soon be approaching and
never be noticed as an alien.

"Amazing how insignificant the variants are," said Swenson.
"How finite the cosmos is, how shamefully incapable of formal
renewals—"

"Oh, come," smiled Paley.

"When you consider what the old musicians could do with a
mere twelve notes—"

"The human mind," said Paley, "can travel in a straight line.
The cosmos is curved."

Swenson turned away from the billowing mounds of tape, saw
that the five-manual console was flicking lights smoothly and
happily, then went over to an instrument panel whose levers
called for muscle, for the blacksmith rather than the organist.
"Starboard," he said. "15.8. Now we play with gravities." He
pulled hard. The monitor screens showed band after band of
light, moving steadily upwards. "This, I think, should be—" He
twirled a couple of corrective dials on a shoulder-high panel above
the levers. "Now," he said. "Free fall."

"So," said Paley, "we're being pulled by—"

"Exactly." And then, "You're quite sure you want to go
through with this?"

"You know as well as I do," smiled Paley patiently, "that I
have to go through with it. For the sake of scholarship. For the
sake of my reputation."

"Reputation," snorted Swenson. Then, looking towards the
monitors, he said, "Ah. Something coming through."

Mist, swirling cloud, a solid shape peeping intermittently out
of vapour porridge. Paley came over to look. "It's the earth," he

said in wonder.

"It's *their* earth."

"The same as ours. America, Africa—"

"The configuration's slightly different, see, down there at the southern tip of—"

"I can't see any difference."

"Madagascar's a good deal smaller."

"The cloud's come over again." Paley looked and looked. It was unbelievable.

"Think," said Swenson kindly, "how many absolutely incomputable systems there have to be before you can see the pattern of creation starting all over again. This seems wonderful to you because you just can't conceive how many myriads upon myriads of other worlds are *not* like our own."

"And the stars," said Paley, a thought striking him; "I mean, the stars they can actually see from there, from their London, say—are they the same stars as ours?"

Swenson shrugged at that. "Roughly," he said. "There's a rough kinship. But," he explained, "we don't properly know yet. Yours is only the tenth or eleventh trip, remember. What is it, when all's said and done, but the past? Why go to the past when you can to to the future?" His nostrils widened with complacency. "G9," he said. "I've done that trip a few times. It's pleasant to know one can look forward to another twenty years of life. I saw it there, quite clearly, a little plaque in Rostron Place: *To the memory of G. F. Swenson, 1963—2084.*"

"We have to check up on history," said Paley, mumbling a little. His own quest seemed piddling: all this machinery, all this expertise in the service of a rather mean enquiry. "I have to know whether William Shakespeare really wrote those plays."

Swenson, as Paley expected, snorted. "A nice sort of thing to want to find out," he said. "He was born just five hundred years this year, and you want to prove that there's nothing to celebrate. Not," he added, "that that sort of thing's much in my line. I've never had much time for poetry. Aaaaah." He interposed his own head between Paley's and the screen, peering. The pages of the atlas had been turned; now Europe alone swam towards them.

"Now," said Swenson, "I must set the exactest course of all." He worked at dials, frowning but humming happily, then beetled at Paley, saying: "Oughtn't you to be getting ready?"

Paley blushed that, with a huge swathe of the cosmos spent in near-idleness, he should have to rush things as they approached their port. He took off his single boiler-suit of a garment and drew from the locker his Elizabethan fancy-dress. Shirt, trunks, cod-piece, doublet, feathered French hat, slashed shoes—clothes of synthetic cloth that was an exact simulacrum of old-time weaving, the shoes of good leather hand-made. And then there was the scrip with its false bottom; hidden therein was a tiny two-way signaller. Not that, if he got into difficulties, it would be of much use: Swenson was (and these were strict orders) to come back for him in a year's time. The signaller was to show where he was and that he was still there, a guest of the past, really a stowaway. Swenson had to move on yet further into space; Professor Shimmins to be picked up in FH78, Dr. Guan Moh Chan in G210, Paley collected on the way back. Paley tested the signaller, then checked the open and honest contents of his scrip: chief among these was a collection of the works of William Shakespeare—not the early works, though: only six of the works which, in this B303 year of A.D. 1595, had not yet been written. The plays had been copies from a facsimile of the First Folio in fairly accurate Elizabethan script; the paper too was a goodish imitation of the tough coarse stuff that Elizabethan dramatists wrote on. For the rest, Paley had powdered prophylactics in little bags and, most important of all, gold—angels fire-new, the odd portague, dollars.

"Well," said Swenson, with the faintest twinge of excitement, "England, here we come." Paley looked down on familiar river-shapes—Tees, Humber, Thames. He gulped, running through his drill swiftly. "Count-down starts now,"s said Swenson. A synthetic voice in the port bulkhead began ticking off cold seconds from 300. "I'd better say good-bye then," gulped Paley, opening the trap in the deck which led to the tiny jet-powered very-much-one-man aircraft. "You should come down in the Thames estuary," said Swenson. "*Au revoir,* not good-bye. I hope you prove whatever it is you want to prove." 200–199–198. Paley went down, settled himself in the seat, checked the simple controls. Waiting took, it seemed, an age. He smiled wryly, seeing himself, an Elizabethan, with his hands on the wheel of a twenty-first-century miniature jet aircraft. 60—59—58. He checked his Elizabethan vowels. He went over his fictitious provenance: a young man from Norwich with stage ambitions ("See, here have I writ a play and a goodly one"). The synthetic voice, booming here in the small cabin, counted to its limit. 4—3—2—1.

Zero. Paley zeroed out of the belly of the mother-ship, suddenly calm, then elated. It was moonlight, the green countryside slept. The river was a glory of silver. His course had been pre-set by Swenson; the control available to him was limited, but he came down smoothly on the water. What he had to do now was to ease himself to the shore. The little motor purred gently as he steered in moonlight. The river was broad here, so that he seemed to be in a world all water and sky. The shore neared—it was all trees, sedge, thicket; there was no sign of habitation, not even of another craft. What would another craft have thought, sighting him? He had no fears about that: with its wings folded, the little air-boat looked, from a distance, like some nondescript barge, so well had it been camouflaged. And now, to be safe, he had to hide it, cover it with greenery in the sedge. But, first, before disembarking, he must set the time-switch that would, when he was safe ashore, render the metal of the fuselage high-charged, lethally repellent of all would-be boarders. It was a pity, but there it was. It would automatically switch off in a year's time, in twelve months to a day. In the meantime, what myths, what madness would the curious examiner, the chance finder generate, tales uncredited by sophisticated London?

And now, London, here he came.

#

Paley, launched on his night's walk up-river, found the going easy enough. The moon lighted field-paths, stiles. Here and there a small farmhouse slept. Once he thought he heard a distant whistled tune. Once he thought he heard a town clock strike. He had no idea of the month or day or time of night, but he guessed that it was late spring and some three hours or so off dawn. The year 1595 was certain, according to Swenson. Time functioned here as on true Earth, and two years before Swenson had taken a man to Muscovy, where they computed according to the Christian system, and the year had been 1593. Paley, walking, found the air gave good rich breathing, but from time to time he was made uneasy by the unfamiliar configurations of the stars. There was Cassiopoeia's Chair, Shakespare's first name's drunken initial, but there were constellations he had not seen before. Could the stars, as the Elizabethans themselves believed, modify history? Could this Elizabethan London, because it looked up at stars unknown on true Earth, be identical with that other one that was only now known from books? Well, he would soon know.

London did not burst upon him, a monster of grey stone. It came upon him gradually and gently, houses set in fields and amid trees, the cool suburbs of the wealthy. And then, like a muffled trumpet under the sinking moon, the Tower. And then came the crammed houses, all sleeping. Paley breathed in the smell of this summer London, and he did not like what he smelled. It was a complex of old rags and fat and dirt, but it was also a smell he knew from the time he had flipped over to Borneo and timidly penetrated the periphery of the jungle: it was, somehow, a jungle smell. And, as if to corroborate this, a howl arose in the distance, but it was a dog's howl. Dogs, man's best friend, here in outer space; dog howling to dog across the inconceivable vastness of the cosmos. And then came a human voice and the sound of boots on the cobbles. "Four of the clock and a fine morning." He instinctively flattened himself in an alleyway, crucified against the dampish wall. The time for his disclosure was not quite yet. He tasted the vowel-sounds of the bellman's call—nearer to American than to present-day British English. "Fowrrr 'vth' cluck." And then, at last knowing the time and automatically feeling for a stopped wristwatch that was not there, he wondered what he should do till day started. Here were no hotels with clerks on all-night duty. He tugged at his dark beard (a three months' growth) and then decided that, as the sooner he started on his scholar's quest the better, he would walk to Shoreditch where the Theatre was. Outside the City's boundaries, where the play-hating City Council could not reach, it was, history said, a new and handsome structure. A scholar's zest, the itch to see, came over him and made him forget the cool morning wind that was rising. His knowledge of the London of his own century gave him little help by way of street-orientation. He walked north—the Minories, Houndsditch, Bishopgate—and, as he walked, he retched once or twice involuntarily at the stench from the kennel. There was a bigger, richer, filthier, obscener smell beyond this, and this he thought must come from Fleet Ditch. He dug into his scrip and produced a pinch of powder; this he placed on his tongue to quieten his stomach.

Not a mouse stirring as he walked, and there, under rolling cloud all besilvered, he saw it, he saw it, the Theatre, with something like disappointment. It was mean wood rising above wooden paling, its roof shaggily thatched. Things were always smaller than one expected, always more ordinary. He wondered if it might be possible to go in. There seemed to be no night-watchman protecting it. Before approaching the entrance (a door for an outside privy rather than a gate to the temple of the Muses) he took in the whole moonlit scene, the mean houses, the cobbles, the astonishing and unexpected greenery all about. And then he saw his first living animals.

Not a mouse stirring, had he thought? But those creatures with long tails were surely rats, a trio of them nibbling at some trump of rubbish not far from the way in to the Theatre. He went warily nearer, and the rats at once scampered off, each filament of whisker clear in the light. They were rats as he knew rats—though he had only seen them in the laboratories of his university—with mean bright eyes and thick meaty tails. But then he saw what they had been eating.

Dragged out from a mound of trash was a human forearm. In some ways Paley was not unprepared for this. He had soaked in images of traitor heads stuck on Temple bar, bodies washed by three tides and left to rot on Thames shore, limbs hacked off at Tyburn (Marble Arch in his day) and carelessly left for the scav-

engers. (Kites, of course, kites. Now the kites would all be roost-
ing.) Clinically, his stomach calm from the medicine he had
taken, he examined the gnawed raw thing. There was not much
flesh off it yet: the feast had been interrupted at its beginning.
On the wrist, though, was a torn and pulpy patch which made
Paley frown—something anatomically familiar but, surely, not ref-
erable to a normal human arm. It occured to him for just a
second that this was rather like an eye-socket, the eye wrenched
out but the soft bed left, still not completely ravaged. And then
he smiled that away, though it was difficult to smile.

He turned his back on the poor human relic and made straight
for the entrance-door. To his surprise it was not locked. It
creaked as he opened it, a sort of voice of welcome to this world
of 1595 and its strange familiarity. There it was—tamped earth
for the groundlings to tamp down yet further; the side-boxes; the
jutting apron-stage; the study uncurtained; the tarrass; the tower
with its flagstaff. He breathed deeply, reverently. This was the
Theatre. And then—

"Arrr, catched ye at it!" Paley's heart seemed about to leap
from his mouth like a badly fitting denture. He turned to meet
his first Elizabethan. Thank God, he looked normal enough,
though filthy. He was in clumsy boots, goose-turd-coloured hose,
and a rancid jerkin. He tottered a little as though drunk, and, as
he came closer to peer into Paley's face, Paley caught a frightful
blast of ale-breath. The man's eyes were glazed and he sniffed
deeply and long at Paley as though trying to place him by scent.
Intoxicated, unfocussed, thought Paley with comtempt, and as
for having the nerve to sniff . . . . Paley spoke up, watching his
vowels with care:

"I am a gentleman from Norwich, but newly arrived. Stand
some way off, fellow. Know you not your betters when you see
them?"

"I know not thee, nor why tha should be here at dead of
night." But he stood away. Paley glowed with small triumph, the
triumph of one who has, say, spoken home-learnt Russian for the
first time in Moscow and has found himself perfectly understood.
He said:

"Thee? *Thee?* I will not be thee-and-thou'd so, fellow. I would speak with Master Burbage."

"Which Master Burbage, the young or the old?"

"Either. I have writ plays and fain would show them."

The watchman, as he must evidently be, sniffed at Paley again. "Gentleman you may be, but you smell not like a Christian. Nor do you keep Christian hours."

"As I say, I am but newly arrived."

"I see not your horse. Nor your traveller's cloak."

"They are—I have left them at mine inn."

The watchman muttered. "And yet you say you are but newly arrived. Go to." Then he chuckled and, at the same time, delicately advanced his right hand towards Paley as though about to bless him. "I know what 'tis," he said, chuckling. " 'Tis some naught meeting, th'hast trysted ringading with some wench, nay, some wife rather, nor has she belled out the morn." Paley could make little of this. "Come," said the man, "chill make for 'ee an th' hast the needful." Paley looked blank. "An tha wants bedding," the man said more loudly. Paley caught that, he caught also the significance of the open palm and wiggling fingers. Gold. He felt in his scrip and produced an angel. The man's jaw dropped as he took it. "Sir," he said, hat-touching.

"Truth to tell," said Paley, "I am shut out of mine inn, late-returning from a visit and not able to make mine host hear with e'en the loudest knocking."

"Arrr," said the watchman put his finger by his nose, a homely Earthly gesture, then scratched his cheek with the angel, finally, before stowing it in a little purse on his girdle, passing it a few times in front of his chest. "With me, sir, come."

He waddled speedily out, Paley following him with fast-beating pulse. "Where go we, then?" he asked. He received no answer. The moon was almost down and there was the first intimations of summer dawn. Paley shivered in the wind; he wished he had brought a cloak with him instead of the mere intention of buying one here. If it was really a bed he was being taken to, he was glad. An hour or so's sleep in the warmth of blankets and never mind whether or not there would be fleas. On the streets nobody was astir, though Paley thought he heard a distant cat's concert—a painful courtship and even more painful copulation to follow, just as on real Earth. Paley followed the watchman down a narrow lane off Bishopgate, dark and stinking. The effects of the medicine had worn off; he felt his gorge rise as before. But the stink, his nose noticed, was subtly different from before: it was, he thought in a kind of small madness, somehow swirling, redistributing its elements as though capable of autonomous action. He didn't like this one little bit. Looking up at the paling stars he felt sure that they too had done a sly job of refiguration, forming fresh constellations like a sand tray on top of a thumped piano.

"Here 'tis," said the watchman, arriving at a door and knocking without further ado. "Croshabels," he winked. But the eyelid winked on nothing but glazed emptiness. He knocked again, and Paley said:

" 'Tis no matter. It is late, or early, to drag folk from their beds." A young cock crowed near, brokenly, a prentice cock.

"Neither one nor t'other. 'Tis in the way of a body's trade, aye." Before he could knock again, the door opened. A cross and sleepy-looking woman appeared. She wore a filthy nightgown and, from its bosom, what seemed like an arum lily peered out. She thrust it back in irritably. She was an old Elizabethan woman, about thirty-eight, grey-haired. She cried:

"Ah?"

"One for one. A gentleman, he saith." He took his angel from his purse and held it up. She raised a candle the better to see. The arum lily peeped out again. All smiles, she curtseyed Paley in. Paley said:

" 'Tis but a matter of a bed, madam." The other two laughed at that "madam." "A long and wearisome journey from Norwich," he added. She gave a deeper curtsey, more mocking than before, and said, in a sort of croak:

"A bed it shall be and no pallet nor the floor neither. For the gentleman from Norwich where the cows eat porridge." The watchman grinned. He was blind, Paley was sure he was blind; on his right thumb something seemed to wink richly. The door closed on him, and Paley and the madam were together in the rancid hallway.

"Follow follow," she said, and she creaked first up the stairs. The shadows her candle cast were not deep; grey was filling the world from the east. On the wall of the stairwell were framed pictures. One was a crude woodcut showing a martyr hanging from a tree, a fire burning under him. Out of the smiling mouth words ballooned: *AND YETTE I SAYE THAT MOGRADON GIUETH LYFE.* Another picture showed a king with crown, orb, sceptre and a third eye set in his forehead. "What king is that?" asked Paley. She turned to look at him in some amazement. "Ye know naught in Norwich," she said, "God rest ye and keep ye all." Paley asked no further questions and kept his wonder to himself at another picture they passed: "Q. Horatius Flaccus" it said, but the portrait was of a bearded Arab. Was it not Averroes?

The madam knocked loudly on a door at the top of the stairs. "Bess, bess," she cried. "Here's gold, lass. A cleanly and a pretty man withal." She turned to smile at Paley. "Anon will she come. She must deck herself like a bride." From the bosom of her nightgown the lily again poked out and Paley thought he saw a blinking eye enfolded in its head. He began to feel the tremors of a very special sort of fear, not a terror of the unknown so much as of the known. He had rendered his flying-boat invulnerable; this world could not touch it. Supposing it were possible that this world was in some manner rendered invulnerable by a different process. A voice in his head seemed to say, with great clarity: "Not with inpunity may one disturb the—" And then the door opened and the girl called Bess appeared, smiling professionally. The madam said, smiling also:

"There then, as pretty a mutton-slice as was e'er sauced o'er." And she held out her hand for money. Confused, Paley dipped into his scrip and pulled out a clanking dull-gleaming handful. He told one coin into her hand and she still waited. He told another, then another. She seemed satisfied, but Paley seemed to know that it was only a temporary satisfaction. "We have wine," she said. "Shall I—?" Paley thanked her: no wine. The grey hair on her head grew erect. She curtseyed off.

Paley followed Bess into the bedchamber, on his guard now. The ceiling beat like a pulse. "Piggesnie," croaked Bess, pulling her single garment down from her bosom. The breasts swung and the nipples ogled him. There were, as he had expected, eyes. He nodded in something like satisfaction. There was, of course, no question of going to bed now. "Honeycake," gurgled Bess, and the breast-eyes rolled, the long lashes swept up and down, up and down coquettishly. Paley clutched his scrip tightly to him. If this distortion—likely, as far as he could judge, to grow progressively worse—if this scrambling of sense-data were a regular barrier against intrusion, why was there not more information about it on Earth? Other time-travellers had ventured forth and come back unharmed and laden with sensible records. Wait, though: had they? How did one know? There was Swenson's mention of Wheeler, jailed in the Middle Ages by chunks of tripodic ectoplasm. "White-haired and gibbering when we got him aboard." Swenson's own words. How about Swenson's own vision of the future—a plaque showing his own birth and death dates? Perhaps the future did not object to instrusion from the past. But (Paley shook his head as though he were drunk, beating back sense into it) it was not a question of past and future, it was a question of other worlds existing *now*. The now-past was completed, the now-future was completed. Perhaps that plaque in Rostron Place, Brighton, showing Swenson's death some twenty years off, perhaps that was an illusion, a device to engender satisfaction rather than fear but still to discourage interference with the pattern. "My time is short," Paley suddenly said, using urgent twenty-first-century phonemes, not Elizabethan ones. "I will give you gold if you will take me to the house of Master Shakespeare."

"Maister—?"

"Shairkspeyr."

Bess, her ears growing larger, stared at Paley with a growing montage of film battle-scenes playing away on the wall behind her. "Th'art not that kind. Women tha likes. That see I in thy face."

"This is urgent. This is business. Quick. He lives, I think, in Bishopgate." He could find out something before the epistemological enemies took over. And then what? Try and live. Keep sane with signals in some quiet spot till a year was past. Signal

Swenson, receive Swenson's reassurances in reply; perhaps—who knew?—hear from far time-space that he was to be taken home before the scheduled date, instructions from Earth, arrangements changed . . . .

"Thou knowest," said Paley, "what man I mean. Master Shakespeare the player at the Theatre."

"Aye aye." The voice was thickening fast. Paley said to himself: It is up to me to take in what I wish to take in; this girl has no eyes on her breasts, that mouth forming under her chin is not really there. Thus checked, the hallucinations wobbled and were pushed back temporarily. But their strength was great. Bess pulled on a simple dress over her nakedness, took a worn cloak from a closet. "Gorled maintwise," she said. Paley pushed like mad, the words unscrambled. "Give me money now," she said. He gave her a portague.

They tiptoed downstairs. Paley tried to look steadily at the pictures in the stairwell, but there was no time to make them tell the truth. The stairs caught him off his guard and changed to an escalator of the twenty-first century. He whipped them back to trembling stairhood. Bess, he was sure, would melt into some monster capable of turning his heart to stone if he let her. Quick. He held the point-of-day in the sky by a great effort. There were a few people on the street. He durst not look on them. "It is far?" he asked. Cocks crowed, many and near, mature cocks.

"Not far." But nothing could be far from anything in this cramped and toppling London. Paley strained to keep his sanity. Sweat dripped from his forehead and a drop caught on the scrip which he hugged to himself like a stomach-ache. He examined it as he walked, stumbling often on the cobbles. A drop of salty water from his pores. Was it of this alien world or of his own? If he cut off his hair and left it lying, if he dunged in that foul jakes there, from which a three-headed woman now appeared, would this B303 London reject it, as a human body will reject a grafted kidney? Was it perhaps not a matter of natural law but of some God of the system, a God against Whom, the devil on one's side, one could prevail? Was it God's club-rules he was pushing against,

not some deeper inbuilt necessity? Anyway, he pushed, and Elizabethan London, in its silver dawn, steadied, rocked, steadied,
held. But the strain was terrific.

"Here, sir." She had brought him to a mean door which
warned Paley that it was going to turn into water and flow down
the cobbles did he not hold its form fast. "Money," she said. But
Paley had given enough. He scowled and shook his head. She held
out a fist which turned into a winking bearded man's face, threatening. He raised his own hand, flat, to slap her. She ran off,
whimpering, and he turned the raised hand to a fist that knocked.
His knock was slow in being answered. He wondered how much
longer he could maintain this desperate holding of the world in
position. If he slept, what would happen? Would it all dissolve
and leave him howling in cold space when he awoke?

"Aye, what is't, then?" It was a misshapen ugly man with a
row of bright blinking eyes across his chest, a chest left bare by
his buttonless shirt. It was not, it could not be, William
Shakespare. Paley said, wondering at his own ability to enunciate
the sounds with such exact care:

"Oi ud see Maister Shairkespeyr." He was surlily shown in, a
shoulder-thrust indicating which door he must knock at. This,
then, was *it*. Paley's heart martelled desperately against his breast-
bone. He knocked. The door was firm oak. threatening no lique-
faction.

"Aye?" A light voice, a pleasant voice, no early morning cross-
ness in it. Paley gulped and opened the door and went in. Bewildered, he looked about him. A bedchamber, the clothes on the
bed in disorder, a table with papers on it, a chair, morning light
framed by the tight-shut window. He went over to the papers; he
read the top sheet (". . . giue it to him lest he raise all hell again
with his fractuousness"), wondering if there was perhaps a room
adjoining whence came that voice. Then he heard the voice again,
behind him:

" 'Tis not seemly to read a gentleman's private papers lacking
his permission." Paley spun about to see, dancing in the air, a
reproduction of the Droeshout portrait of Shakespeare, square in
a frame, the lips moving but the eyes unanimated. He tried to call

but could not. The talking woodcut advanced on him—"Rude, mannerless, or art thou some Privy Council spy?"—and then the straight sides of the frame bulged and bulged, the woodcut features dissolved, and a circle of black lines and spaces tried to grow into a solid body. Paley could do nothing; his paralysis would not even permit him to shut his eyes. The solid body became an animal shape, indescribably gross and ugly—some spiked sea urchin, very large, nodding and smiling with horrible intelligence. Paley forced it into becoming a more nearly human shape. His heart sank in depression totally untinged by fear to see standing before him a fictional character called "William Shakespeare," an actor acting the part. Why could he not get in touch with the *Ding an sich,* the Kantian noumenon? But that was the trouble—the thing-in-itself was changed by the observer into whatever phenomenon the categories of time-space-sense imposed. He took courage and said:

"What plays have you writ to date?"

Shakespeare looked surprised. "Who asked this?"

Paley said, "What I say you will hardly believe. I come from another world that knows and reveres the name of Shakespeare. I believe that there was, or is, an actor named William Shakespeare. That Shakespeare wrote the plays that carry his name—this I will not believe."

"So," said Shakespeare, tending to melt into a blob of tallow badly sculpted into the likeness of Shakespeare, "we are both to be unbelievers, then. For my part, I will believe anything. You will be a sort of ghost from this other world you speak of. By rights, you should have dissolved at cock-crow."

"My time may be as short as a ghost's. What plays do you claim to have written up to this moment?" Paley spoke the English of his own day. Though the figure before shifted and softened, tugging towards other shapes, the eyes changed little, shrewd and intelligent eyes, modern. And now the voice said:

"Claim? *Heliogabalus, A Word to Fright a Whoremaster, The Sad Reign of Harold First and Last, The Devil in Dulwich* .... Oh, many and many more."

"Please." Paley was distressed. Was this truth or teasing, truth or teasing of this man or of his own mind, a mind desperate to control the *données*, the sense-data, make them make sense? On the table there, the mass of papers, "Show me," he said. "Show me somewhat," he pleaded.

"Show me your credentials," said Shakespeare, "if we are to talk of showing. Nay," and he advanced merrily towards Paley, "I will see for myself." The eyes were very bright now and shot with oddly sinister flecks. "A pretty boy," said Shakespeare. "Not so pretty as some, as one, I would say, but apt for a brief tumble of a summer's morning before the day warms."

"Nay," said Paley, "nay," backing and feeling that archaism to be strangely frivolous, "touch me not." The advancing figure became horribly ugly, the neck swelled, eyes glinted on the backs of the approaching hands. The face grew an elephantine proboscis, wreathing, feeling; two or three suckers sprouted from its end and blindly waved towards Paley. Paley dropped his scrip the better to struggle. The words of this monster were thick, they turned into grunts and lallings. Pushed into the corner by the table, Paley saw a sheet of paper much blotted ("Never blotted a line," did they say?):

> I haue bin struggling striuing? seeking? how I
> may compair
> This jailhouse prison? where I liue unto the
> earth world
> And that and for because

The scholar was still there, the questing spirit clear while the body fought to keep off those huge hands, each ten-fingered. The scholar cried:

"*Richard II*! You are writing *Richard II*?"

It seemed to him, literatures's Claude Bernard, that he should risk all to get that message through to Swenson, that *Richard II* was, in 1595, being written by Shakespeare. He suddenly dipped to the floor, grabbed his scrip and began to tap through the lining at the key of the transmitter. Shakespeare seemed taken by surpise by this sudden cessation of resistance; he

put out forks of hands that grasped nothing. Paley, blind with
sweat, panting hard, tapped: "R2 by WS." Then the door opened.

"I did hear noise." It was the misshapen ugly man with eyes
across his bare chest, uglier now, his shape changing constantly
though abruptly, as though set on by silent and invisible
hammers. "He did come to attack tha?"

"Not for money, Tomkin. He hath gold enow of's own. See."
The scrip, set down before so hurriedly, had spilt out its gold on
the floor. Paley had not noticed; he should have transferred that
gold to his—

"Aye, gold." The creature called Tomkin gazed on it greedily.
"The others that came so brought not gold."

"Take the gold and him," said Shakespeare carelessly. "Do
what thou wilt with both." Tomkin oozed towards Paley. Paley
screamed, attacking feebly with the hand that held the scrip.
Tomkin's claw snatched it without trouble.

"There's more within," he drooled.

"Did I not say thou wouldst do well in my service?" said
Shakespeare.

"And here is papers."

"Ah, papers." And Shakespeare took them. "Carry him to the
Queen's Marshal. The stranger within our gates. He talks
foolishly, like the Aleman that came before. Wildly, I would say.
Of other words, like a madman. The Marshal will know what to
do."

"But," screamed Paley, grabbed by strong shovels of hands, "I
am a gentleman. I am from Norwich. I am a playwright, like
yourself. See, you hold what I have written."

"First a ghost, now from Norwich," smiled Shakespeare,
hovering in the air like his portrait again, a portrait holding
papers. "Go to. Are there not other worlds, like unto our own,
that sorcery can make men leave to visit this? I have heard such
stories before. There was a German—"

"It's true, true, what I tell you!" Paley clung to that, clinging
also to the chamber-door with his nails, the while Tomkin pulled
at him. "You are the most intelligence man of these times! You
can conceive of it!"

"And of poets yet unborn also; Drythen, or some such name, and Lord Tennis-balls, and a drunken Welshman and P. S. Eliot? You will be taken care of, like that other."

"But it's true, true!"

"Come your ways," growled Tomkin. "You are a Bedlam natural." And he dragged Paley out, Paley collapsing, frothing, raving. Paley raved:

"You're not real, any of you! It's you who are the ghosts! *I'm* real, it's all a mistake, let me go, let me explain!"

" 'Tis strange he talks," growled Tomkin. And he dragged him out.

"Shut the door," said Shakespeare. Tomkin kicked it shut. The screaming voice went, over thumping feet, down the passage-way without. Soon it was quiet enough to sit and read.

These were, thought Shakespeare, good plays. Strange that one of them was about, as far as he could judge, an usurious Jew. This Norwich man had evidently read Marlowe and seen the dramatic possibilities of an evil Lopez-type character. He, Shakespeare, had toyed with the idea of a play like this himself. And here it was, ready done for him. And there were a couple of promising-looking histories here, too. About King Henry IV. And here a comedy called *Much Ado About Nothing*. Gifts, godsends. He smiled. He remembered that Aleman, Doctor Schleyer or some such name, who had come with a story like to this madman (mad? Could madmen do work like this? "The lunatic, the lover, and the poet": a good line in that play about fairies that Schleyer had brought. Poor Schleyer had died of the plague). Those plays Schleyer had brought had been good plays, but not, perhaps, quite so good as these.

Shakespeare furtively (though he was alone) crossed himself. When poets had talked of the Muse, had they perhaps meant visitants like this, now screaming feebly in the street, and the German Schleyer and that one who swore, under torture, that he was from Virginia in America, and that in America they had universities as good as Oxford or Leyden or Wittenberg, nay better? He shrugged, there being more things in heaven and earth

&c. Well, whoever they were, they were heartily welcome so long as they brought plays. That *Richard II* of Schleyer's was, perhaps, in need of the emendations he was now engaged on, but the earlier work, from *Henry VI* on, had been popular. He read the top sheet of this new batch, stroking his auburn beard silvered, a fine grey eye reading. He sighed and, before crumpling a sheet of his own work on the table, read it. Not good, it limped, there was too much magic in it. Ingenio the Duke said:

> Consider gentlemen as in the sea
> All earthly life finds like and parallel
> So in far distant skies our lives be aped,
> Each hath a twin, each action hath a twin,
> And twins have twins galore and infinite
> And e'en these stars be twinn'd. . . .

Too fantastic, it would not do. He threw it into the rubbish-box which Tomkin would later empty. He took a clean sheet and began to copy in a fair hand:

THE MERCHANT OF VENICE

Then on he went, not blotting a line.

The Unsafe Deposit Box

by Gerald Kersh

You have a sharp eye, sir, a very sharp eye indeed, if you recognize me by those photographs that used to appear in the newspapers and the sensational magazines about 1947. I fancy I must have changed somewhat since then; but yes, I am Peter Perfrement, and they did make a knight of me for some work I did in nuclear physics. I am glad, for once, to be recognized. You might otherwise mistake me for an escaped convict, or a lunatic at large, or something of that sort; for I am going to beg you to have the goodness to sit in this shadowy corner and keep your broad back between me and the door. Have an eye on the mirror over my head and you will in due course see the reflections of a couple of elbows who will come into this cozy little bar. Those men will be looking for me. You will perceive, by the complete vacuity of their expressions, that they are from Intelligence.

They'll spot me, of course, and then it will be, "Why, Sir Peter, how lucky to find you here!" Then, pleading business, they'll carry me off. And evading those two young men is one of the few pleasures left me in my old age. Once I got out in a laundry basket. Tonight I put on a workman's suit of overalls over my dinner suit and went to a concert. I intend to go back home to the Center after I've had my evening, but I want to be left alone a bit. Of course, I have nobody but myself to blame for any slight discomfort I may at present suffer. I retired once and for all, as I thought, in 1950. By then the inwardness of such atom bombs as we let off over, say, Hiroshima was public property. My work, as it seemed, was done.

So I withdrew to a pleasant little villa at the Cap des Fesses just outside that awful holiday resort Les Sables des Fesses in the south of France. Fully intended to end my days there, as a matter of fact—set up library and study there, and a compact but middling-comprehensive laboratory. I went to all the music festivals, drank my glass of wine on the *terrasse* of whatever café happened to take my fancy, and continued my academic battle with Doctor Frankenburg. This battle, which was in point of fact far less acrimonious than the average game of chess, had to do with the nature of the element fluorine. I take it that esoteric mathematics are, mercifully, beyond your comprehension; but perhaps you were told at school something of the nature of fluorine. This is the *enfant terrible* of the elements.

Fluorine, in temperament, is a prima donna and, in character, a born delinquent. You cannot keep it pure; it has such an affinity for practically everything else on earth, and what it has an affinity for, it tends to destroy. Now I had a theory involving what I can only describe to a layman as tame fluorine—fluorine housebroken and in harness. Doctor Frankenburg, whose leisure is devoted to reading the comic papers, used to say concerning this, "You might as well imagine Dennis the Menace as a breadwinner." However, I worked away not under pressure nor under observation, completely at my leisure, having access to the great computer at Assigny. And one day I found that I had evolved a substance which, for convenience, I will call fluorine 80+.

I do not mean that I made it merely in formula. The nature of the stuff, once comprehended, made the physical production of it really absurdly simple. So I made some—about six ounces of it, and it looked rather like a sheet of hard, lime-colored gelatin. And potentially this bit of gelatinous-looking stuff was somewhat more potent than a cosmic collision. Potentially, mark you—only potentially. As it lay in my hand, fluorine 80+ was, by all possible calculations, inert. You could beat it with a sledge hammer or burn it with a blowlamp, and nothing would happen. But under certain conditions—conditions which seemed to me at that time quite impossible of acheivement—this morsel of matter could be unbelievably terrible. By unbelievably, I mean immeasurably. Quite beyond calculation.

The notebook containing my formula I wrapped in paper with the intention of putting it in the vault of the Banque Maritime des Sables des Fesses. The sheet of fluorine 80+ I placed between two pieces of carboard; then I wrapped it likewise and put it in my pocket. You see, I had a friend in the town with whom I often had tea, and he had a liking for the weird and the wonderful. Like the fool that I am, I proposed to amuse myself by showing him my sample and telling him that his inoffensive little thing, in a suitable environment, might cause our earth to go *psss!*—in about as long as it takes for a pinch of gunpowder to flash in a match flame. So in high spirits I went into town, paid my visit to the bank, first having got a pot of Gentlemen's Relish and a jar of Oxford Marmalade for tea, and so called on Doctor Raisin.

He was another old boy who had outlived his usefulness, although time was when he had some reputation as an architect specializing in steel construction. "Something special for tea," I said and tossed my little package of fluorine 80+ on the table.

"Smoked salmon?" he asked.

Then I brought out the marmalade and the relish, and said, "No," chuckling like an idiot.

He growled, "Evidently you have just paid a visit to the Café de la Guerre Froide," and sniffed at me.

"No, I've just come from the bank."

"So," he said, "that's a parcel of money, I suppose. What's it to me? Let's have tea."

I said, "I didn't go to the bank to take something out, Raisin. I put something in."

"Make me no mystifications, if you please. What's that?"

"That," I said, "is proof positive that Frankenburg is wrong and I am right, Raisin. What you see there is half a dozen ounces of absolutely stable fluorine eighty-plus and a critical mass, at that!"

Dry as an old bone, he said, "Jargon me no jargons. As I understand it, an atomic explosion takes place when certain quantities of radioactive material arrive, in certain circumstances, at what you call 'critical mass.' This being the case, that little packet may, I take it, be considered dangerous?"

I said, "Rather so. There's about enough fluorine eighty-plus there to vaporize a medium-sized planet."

Raisin said, "A fluorine bomb, an ounce of nitroglycerin—it's all the same to me." Pouring tea, he asked nonchalantly, "How do you make it go off? Not, I gather, by chucking it about on tables?"

I said, "You can't explode it—as you understand an explosion—except under conditions difficult to create and useless once created; although, perhaps, while valueless as a weapon, it could be put to peaceful uses."

"Perhaps me no perhapses. A fighting cock *could* be used to make chicken broth. What did you want to bring it here for, anyway?"

I was a little put out. Raisin was unimpressible. I told him, rather lamely, "Well, neither you nor anyone esle will ever see fluorine eighty-plus again. In about fourteen hours that piece there will—as you would put it—have evaporated."

"Why as I would put it? How do you put it?"

"Why, you see," I explained, "in point of actual fact, that stuff is exploding now. Only it's exploding very, very gradually. Now, for this explosion to be effectual as an explosion, we should have to let that mass expand at a temperature of anything over sixty-degrees Fahrenheit in a hermetically sealed bomb case of at least ten thousand cubic feet in capacity. At this point, given suitable pressure, up she'd go. But when I tell you that before we could get such a pressure under which my fluorine eighty-plus would undergo certain atomic alterations, the casing of our ten-thousand-cubic-foot bomb would need to be at least two or three feet thick."

Being a Russian, Raisin stirred marmalade into his tea and

interrupted. "It is a chimera. So let it evaporate. Burn your formula. Pay no further attention to it.... Still, since you have brought it, let's have a look at it." He undid the little parcel, and said, "I knew all along it was a joke." The paper pulled away, there lay nothing but a notebook.

I cried, "Good heavens—that ought to be safe in the bank! That's the formula!"

"And the bomb?"

"Not a bomb, Raisin—I've just told you that fluorine eighty-plus can't possibly be a bomb of its own accord. Confound it! I must have left it at the grocer's shop."

He said, "Is it poisonous?"

"Toxic? I don't think so.... Now wait a minute, wait a minute! I distinctly remember—when I left the house I put the formula in my right-hand coat pocket and the fluorine eighty-plus in the left. Now first of all I went to the Epicerie Internationale to get this marmalade and stuff, and so as not to crowd my left pocket I transferred.... Oh, it's quite all right, Raisin. There's nothing to worry about, except that this is not the kind of notebook I like to carry about with me. The sample is safe and sound in the bank. It was a natural mistake—the packages are very much alike in shape and weight. No cause for anxiety. Pass the Gentlemen's Relish, will you?"

But Raisin said, "This horrible little bit of fluorine—you left it in the bank, did you?"

"You bank at the Maritime?"

"Yes, why?"

"So do I. It is the safest bank in France. Its vaults—now follow me carefully, Perfrement—its vaults are burglarproof, bombproof, fireproof, and absolutely airtight. The safe deposit vault is forty feet long, thirty feet wide and ten feet high. This gives it a capacity of twelve thousand cubic feet. It is maintained at a low humidity and a constant temperature of sixty-five degrees Fahrenheit. The walls of this vault are of hard steel and reinforced concrete three feet thick. The door alone weighs thirty tons, but fits like a glass stopper in a medicine bottle. Does the significance of all this sink in?"

"Why," I said, "why—"

"Yes, why? You can say that again. What you have done, my irresponsible friend," said Doctor Raisin, "is put your mass of fluorine eighty-plus in its impossible casing. That's the way with the likes of you. It would never dawn on you that a bomb might be an oblong thing as big as a bank. Congratulations!" I said, "I know the manager, Mr. le Queuz, and he knows me. I'll go and see him at once."

"It's Saturday. The bank's closed by now."

"Yes, I know, but I'll ask him to come over with his keys."

Raisin said, "I wish you luck."

A telephone call to M. le Queux's house got me only the information that he was gone for the weekend to Laffert, about eighty miles inland, up the mountain, where he had a bungalow. So I looked about for a taxi. But it was carnival weekend, and there was nothing to be got except one of those essentially French machines that have run on coal gas and kerosene, and have practically no works left inside them, and yet, like certain extremely cheap alarm clocks, somehow continue to go, without accuracy, but with a tremendous noise. And the driver was a most objectionable man in a beret, who chewed whole cloves of raw garlic all the time and shouted into one's face as if were a hundred yards distant.

After a disruptive and malodorous journey, during which the car had twice to be mended with bits of wire, we reached Laffert, and with some difficulty found M. le Queux.

He said to me, "For you—anything. But to open the bank? No, I cannot oblige you."

"You had better," I said to him, in a minatory tone.

"But Sir Peter," said he, "this is not merely a matter of turning a key and opening a door. I don't believe you can have read our brochure. The door of the vault is on a time lock. This means that after the lock is set and the door closed, nothing can open it until a certain period of time has elapsed. So, precisely at 7:45 on Monday morning—but not one instant before—I can open the vault for you."

I said, "Then as I see it, you had better send for the locksmith and have the lock picked."

M. le Queux laughed. He said, "You couldn't open our vault without taking the door down." He spoke with a certain pride.

"Then I'm afraid I'll have to trouble you to have the door taken down," I told him.

"That would necessitate practically taking down the bank," M. le Queux said; and evidently he thought that I was out of my mind.

"Then," I said, "there's nothing for it *but* to take down the bank. Of course, there'll be compensation, I suppose. Still, the fact remains that, by the sheerest inadvertence, for which I hold myself greatly at fault, I have turned your bank-vault into a colossal bomb—a bomb compared with which your Russian multimegaton bombs are milk-and-water. Indeed, you would no more weigh or measure my fluorine eighty-plus in terms of mere megatons than you'd buy coal by the milligram or wine by the cubic centimeter."

"One of us is going crazy," said M. le Queux.

"Call a Hiroshima bomb a megaton," I said. "Dealing with my fluorine eighty-plus we have to make tables. So a million megatons equal one tyrranoton. A million tyrranotons equal one chasmaton. A million chasmatons make one brahmaton. And after a million brahmatons we come to something I call an ultimon, because it is beyond even the scope of mathematical conjecture. In a certain number of hours from now—and we are wasting time talking, M. le Queux—if you don't get that vault of yours open, the universe will experience the shock of half a chasmaton. Please let me use your telephone."

So I called a certain branch of Security, and after that told a minister, who shall be nameless, to be so kind as to get a move on—referring him, of course, to several other nuclear experts, in case my own name was not enough for him. Thus I was able, within twenty minutes, to tell M. le Queux, "It's all arranged. Army and police are on the way. So are some colleagues of mine. The Custodia Safe Company, who installed your vault, are flying their best technicians into Fesses. We'll have your vault open in a couple of hours or so. I'm sorry if this inconveniences you, but it's got to be done, and you must put up with it."

He could only say, "Inconveniences me!" Then he shouted, "After this, Sir Peter Perfrement, you will kindly take your banking business elswhere!"

I was sorry for him, but there was no time for sentiment just now, for I found myself caught in a sort of whirlpool of giddy activity. Accompanied by the usual quota of secret police from Security, four highly regarded nuclear physicists were rushed to Fesses. I was pleased to see among them my dear old enemy Frankenburg, who would have to admit that in the matter of fluorine he was totally confuted. There was also, of course, a swarm of policemen, both uniformed and in plain-clothes, and, goodness knows why, two doctors, one of whom kept talking and talking without rhyme or reason about fluorine being found in relatively high concentration in the human embryo and how good it was for children's teeth. An expert from the quiet old days of the high-explosive blitzes said that since one invariably evacuated the area surrounding an unexploded bomb until it was defused, it would be wise to evacuate Sables des Fesses.

At this the *maire* went into ecstasies of Gallicism. To evacuate this place at carnival weekend would be to ruin it—death rather than dishonor, and so forth. I said that if my fluorine 80+ blew, the problem of evacuation need not arise; for nobody anywhere, ever, would be any the wiser. The chief of police, giving me a suspicious look, said that the present danger was only hypothetical; but the panic that must attend a mass alarm would be inevitably disastrous. It would be necessary only to surround the block in which the bank was situated. This being in the business district of the town, and most of the offices shut up for the weekend, the matter might be accomplished—a hairsbreadth this side of impossibility.

So said the chief of police, filling a pipe as a pioneer fills his muzzle-loader with his last hard-bitten cartridge, and pointing it right at me. He made it clear, without speaking, that he thought this was all a put-up job, to get that bank vault open.

M. le Queux said, "But the armored car has been and gone,

and the bank is just about empty of cash until Monday." Still the chief of police wasn't satisfied. Watching him tamp down the charge in his pipe, I could not help reciting a hunting proverb of my grandfather's: *Ram tight the powder, leave loose the lead, if you want to kill dead.* He made a note of that. Meanwhile, Frankenburg and the others were poring over my notes, which I had been compelled to hand over.

Frankenburg growled, "I want to check, and double-check. I want a computer. I want five days."

But little Doctor Imhof said, "Come, we must grant the possibility that what we read here is valid. Even for the sake of argument we must grant it."

"Well, for the sake of argument," said Frankenburg.

"So," said Imhof, "*any* relaxation of pressure must render Perfrement's so-called fluorine eighty-plus harmless, must it not? This being the case, a hole drilled in the vault door should be an ample measure of precaution. This hole made, why, let the matter wait until Monday."

"So be it," said I. "He talks sense."

So now the engineers from the Custodia Company, having come in by plane, unloaded their massive paraphernalia in the bank. And among the cylinders and eye shields and other gear I noticed a number of gas masks. "What are they for?" I asked le Queux.

Frankenburg, unwilling to be convinced, was complaining, "Yes, yes, bore holes—leave Perfrement's thing until Monday. But unless I misread this formula, his so-called fluorine eighty-plus will by that time have ceased to exist."

A certain Doctor Chiappe said in a glum voice, "Metaphysics: If we leave it, it ceases to exist; if we don't leave it, it ceases to exist; but, as I read Perfrement's notes, if we leave fluorine eighty-plus, we shall be involved with it in a state of co-nonexistence. Better bore holes."

I said, "I asked you, M. le Queux, what are those gas masks for?"

He said, "Why, when the door is in any way interfered with, the alarm automatically goes off. We omit no precautions, none whatsoever. As soon as the alarm goes off, the vault fills with tear gas from built-in containers."

"Did you say tear gas?" I asked.

"In a high concentration."

"Then," I cried, "get away from that door at once!" I appealed to Frankenburg. "You hate every word I say, old fellow, but you're an honest man. Conceding that my notes are right—and I swear they are—you'll see that my fluorine eighty-plus has one affinity. One only. That is with C_8H_7C10—chloroacetophenone. And that, damme, is the stuff tear gas is made of!"

Frankenburg nodded. Chiappe said, "Slice it as you like—we've had it!"

And old Raisin grumbled, "This, I believe, is what the dramatists call a perfectly damnable impasse. Correct me if I'm wrong."

It was little Imhof who asked, "Is there no part of this place at all that's not guarded by alarm, and what not?"

Le Queux said, "Technically, there is only one part of our vault that's reachable from the outside—if you can call it the outside. The back of our vault abuts on the back of the jeweler's, Monnickendam's, next door. His vault, you see, is itself two feet thick. Hence—"

"Aha!" said the chief of police.

"Get Monnickendam," said the minister of Security, and that famous jeweler and pawnbroker was duly produced.

He said, "I'd open my vault with pleasure, but I have a partner, Warmerdam. Our vault opens by two combination locks which must be operated simultaneously. These locks are so placed that no one can operate both at the same time. I have my own secret combination and Warmerdam has his. We must both be present to open the vault."

"That's how one gets rich," old Raisin muttered.

Monnickendam corrected him, "That is how one *stays* rich."

"Where's Warmerdam?" they asked.

"In London."

London was telephoned, and Secret Service agents dragged poor Warmerdam shrieking from a dinner table and rushed him to a jetport and fired him over to Sables des Fesses with such dispatch that he arrived in a state of semiobfuscation, with a napkin still tucked under his chin.

But now, by the chief of police's expression, it was evident that the whole matter was an open-and-shut case to him. I was some sort of master criminal, a Moriatry, and my real objective was the jewelers' strong room. He strengthened the police cordon, and Monnickendam and Warmerdam opened their vault.

The men from Custoida went to work—but not before the two jewelers had got a signed and witnessed indemnity from the president of the bank; they wouldn't trust the minister—and so the heavy steel and concrete of the strong room cut through, we began to bite into the back of the bank.

"Time runs out," I said.

Raisin irritated everybody by saying, "Imagination, my friends, and nothing but imagination, is making us all sweat. All things considered, do you think that a megaton, a tyrannoton, or an ultimon could do us—us personally—more harm than, let us say, a pound of dynamite?"

The chief of police said, "Ha! You know a lot about dynamite, it seems."

"I should hope so," said Raisin. "I was sabotaging Nazis, my friend, when you were swinging a truncheon for the *Deuxieme Bureau.*"

I had better be brief, however. At about five in the morning we broke through.

I said, "Fine. You can take it easy now. Fluorine eighty-plus can't blow." And when I then suggested a hot cup of tea, M. le Queux tried to strangle me.

But the men worked on, until the hole was about two feet in diameter; and then one of the smallest of them took my key, wriggled through, and came back with the contents of my safe-deposit box—the little paper package of fluorine 80+.

I pointed out to Frankenburg how greatly it had diminished. "By George, we had a close call then!" I said.

And that, as you might think, was that. Ah, but you'd be wrong. For you see, in the course of that mad night, when every policeman in Sables des Fesses and its environs was mounting guard at the bank and at Monnickendam's, a gang of thieves broke into the Prince of Mamluk's Galleries, said to contain one of the four finest art collections in the world.

They stripped the place at their leisure. They took a priceless collection of antique jewels, three Rembrandts, four Holbeins, two Raphaels, a Titian, two El Grecos, a Vermeer, three Botticellis, a Goya and a Greuze. Greatest art burglary of all time, I'm told. They say that Lloyds would rather have lost a fleet of transatlantic liners than what they underwrote those pictures and things for.

Taking it by and large, I suppose it's for my own good that I was shipped back to England and put under guard.

If I'd had any sense, of course, I'd have kept quiet about that confounded fluorine 80+. As it is, I've made a prisoner of myself. They regard me—of all people!—as a compulsive chatterbox. As if fluorine 80+ is anything to chatter about. Why, you could make it yourself. Take 500 grams of fluorspar—

Oh-oh! Here come my two friends, I'm afraid. I will take my leave of you now, sir. . . . Good night to you.

Good evening, gentlemen!

Something Strange

by Kingsley Amis

Something strange happened every day. It might happen during the morning, while the two men were taking their readings and observations and the two women busy with the domestic routine: the big faces had come during the morning. Or, as with the little faces and the coloured fires, the strange thing would happen in the afternoon, in the middle of Bruno's maintenance programme and Clovis's transmission to Base, Lia's rounds of the garden and Myri's work on her story. The evening was often undisturbed, the night less often.

They all understood that ordinary temporal expressions had no meaning for people confined indefinitely, as they were, to a motionless steel sphere hanging in a region of space so empty that the light of the nearest star took some hundreds of years to reach them. The Standing Orders devised by Base, however, recommended that they adopt a twenty-four-hour unit of time, as was the rule on the Earth they had not seen for many months. The arrangement suited them well: their work, recreation and rest seemed to fall naturally into the periods provided. It was only the prospect of year after year of the same routine, stretching farther into the future than they could see, that was a source of strain.

Bruno commented on this to Clovis after a morning spent repairing a fault in the spectrum analyser they used for investigating and classifying the nearer stars. They were sitting at the main observation port in the lounge, drinking the midday cocktail and waiting for the women to join them.

"I'd say we stood up to it extremely well," Clovis said in answer to Bruno. "Perhaps too well."

Bruno haunched his fat figure upright. "How do you mean?"

"We may be hindering our chances of being relieved."

"Base has never said a word about our relief."

"Exactly. With half a million stations to staff, it'll be a long time before they get round to one like this, where everything runs smoothly. You and I are a perfect team, and you have Lia and I have Myri, and they're all right together—no real conflict at all. Hence no reason for a relief."

Myri had heard all this as she laid the table in the alcove. She wondered how Clovis could not know that Bruno wanted to have her instead of Lia, or perhaps as well as Lia. If Clovis did know, and was teasing Bruno, then that would be a silly thing to do, because Bruno was not a pleasant man. With his thick neck and pale fat face he would not be pleasant to be had by, either, quite unlike Clovis, who was no taller but whose straight, hard body and soft skin were always pleasant. He could not think as well as Bruno, but on the other hand many of the things Bruno thought were not pleasant. She poured herself a drink and went over to them.

Bruno had said something about its being a pity they could not fake their personnel report by inventing a few quarrels, and Clovis had immediately agreed that that was impossible. She kissed him and sat down at his side. "What do you think about the idea of being relieved?" he asked her.

"I never think about it."

"Quite right," Bruno said, grinning. "You're doing very nicely here. Fairly nicely, anyway."

"What are you getting at?" Clovis asked him with a different kind of grin.

"It's not a very complete life, is it? For any of us. I could do with a change, anyway. A different kind of job, something that isn't testing and using and repairing apparatus. We do seem to have a lot of repairing to do, don't we? That analyser breaks down almost every day. And yet—"

His voice trailed off and he looked out of the port, as if to assure himself that all that lay beyond it was the familiar star-scape of points and smudges of light.

"And yet what?" Clovis asked, irritably this time.

"I was just thinking that we really ought to be thankful for having plenty to do. There's the routine, and the fruits and vege-tables to look after, and Myri's story. . . . How's that going, by the way? Won't you read us some of it? This evening, perhaps?"

"Not until it's finished, if you don't mind."

"Oh, but I do mind. It's part of our duty to entertain one another. And I'm very interested in it personally."

"Why?"

"Because you're an interesting girl. Bright brown eyes and a healthy glowing skin—how do you manage it after all this time in space? And you've more energy than any of us."

Myri said nothing. Bruno was good at making remarks there was nothing to say to.

"What's it about, this story of yours?" he pursued. "At least you can tell us that."

"I have told you. It's about normal life. Life on Earth before there were any space stations, lots of different people doing dif-ferent things, not this—"

"That's normal life, is it, different people doing different things? I can't wait to hear what the things are. Who's the hero, Myri? Our dear Clovis?"

Myri put her hand on Clovis's shoulder. "No more, please, Bruno. Let's go back to your point about the routine. I couldn't understand why you left out the most important part, the part that keeps us busiest of all."

"Ah, the strange happenings." Bruno dipped his head in a characteristic gesture, half laugh, half nervous tremor. "And the hours we spend discussing them. Oh yes. How could I have failed to mention all that?"

"If you've got any sense you'll go on not mentioning it," Clovis snapped. "We're all fed up with the whole business."

"You may be, but I'm not. I want to discuss it. So does Myri, don't you, Mryi?"

"I do think perhaps it's time we made another attempt to find a pattern," Myri said. This was a case of Bruno not being pleasant but being right.

"Oh, not again." Clovis bounded up and went over to the drinks table. "Ah, hallo, Lia," he said to the tall, thin, blonde woman who had just entered with a tray of cold dishes. "Let me get you a drink. Bruno and Myri are getting philosophical—looking for patterns. What do you think? I'll tell you what I think. I think we're doing enough already. I think patterns are Base's job."

"We can make it ours, too," Bruno said. "You agree, Lia?"

"Of course," Lia said in the deep voice that seemed to Myri to carry so much more firmness and individuality in its tone than any of its owner's words or actions.

"Very well. You can stay out of this if you like, Clovis. We start from the fact that what we see and hear need not be illusions, although they may be."

"At least that they're illusions that any human being might have, they're not special to us, as we know from Base's reports of what happens to other stations."

"Correct, Myri. In any event, illusions or not, they are being directed at us by an intelligence and for a purpose."

"We don't know that," Myri objected. "They may be natural phenomena, or the by-product of some intelligent activity not directed at us."

"Correct again, but let us reserve these less probable possibilities until later. Now, as a sample, consider the last week's strange happenings. I'll fetch the log so that there can be no dispute."

"I wish you'd stop it," Clovis said when Bruno had gone out to the apparatus room. "It's a waste of time."

"Time's the only thing we're not short of."

"I'm not short of anything," he said, touching her thigh. "Come with me for a little while."

"Later."

"Lia always goes with Bruno when he asks her."

"Oh yes, but that's my choice," Lia said. "She doesn't want to now. Wait until she wants to."

"I don't like waiting."

"Waiting can make it better."

"Here we are," Bruno said briskly, returning. "Right. . . . Monday. *Within a few seconds the sphere became encased in a thick brownish damp substance that tests revealed to be both impermeable and infinitely thick. No action by the staff suggested itself. After three hours and eleven minutes the substance disappeared.* It's the *infintely thick* thing that's interesting. That must have been an illusion, or something would have happened to all the other stations at the same time, not to speak of the stars and planets. A total or partial illusion, then. Agreed?"

"Go on."

"Tuesday. *Metallic object of size comparable to that of the sphere approaching on collision course at 500 kilometres per second. No countermeasures available. Object appeared instantaneously at 35 million kilometres'* distance and disappeared instanteneously at 1500 kilometres. What about that?"

"We've had ones like that before," Lia put in. "Only this was the longest time it's taken to approach and the nearest it's come before disappearing."

"Incomprehensible or illusion," Myri suggested.

"Yes, I think that's the best we can do at the moment. Wednesday: a very trivial one, not worth discussing. *A being apparently constructed entirely of bone approached the main port and made beckoning motions.* Whoever's doing this must be running out of ideas. Thursday. *All bodies external to the sphere vanished to all instruments simultaneously, reappearing to all instruments simultaneously two hours later.* That's not a new one either, I seem to remember. Illusion? Good. Friday. *Beings resembling terrestrial reptiles covered the sphere, fighting ceaselessly and eating portions of one another. Loud rustling and slithering sounds.* The sounds at least must have been an illusion, with no air out there, and I never heard of a reptile that didn't breathe. The same sort of thing applies to yesterday's performance. *Human screams of pain and extreme astonishment approaching and receding. No visual or other accompaniment.*" He paused and looked round at them. "Well? Any uniformities suggest themselves?"

"No," Clovis said, helping himself to salad, for they sat now at the lunch table. "And I defy any human brain to devise any. The whole thing's arbitrary."

"On the contrary, the very next happening—today's when it comes—might reveal an unmistakable pattern."

"The one to concentrate on," Myri said, "is the approaching object. Why did it vanish before striking the sphere?"

Bruno stared at her. "It had to, if it was an illusion."

"Not at all. Why couldn't we have had an illusion of the sphere being struck? And supposing it wasn't an illusion?"

"Next time there's an object, perhaps it will strike," Lia said.

Clovis laughed. "That's a good one. What would happen if it did, I wonder? And it wasn't an illusion?"

They all looked at Bruno for an answer. After a moment or two, he said: "I presume the sphere would shatter and we'd all be thrown into space. I simply can't imagine what that would be like. We should be. . . Never to see one another again, or anybody or anything else, to be nothing more than a senseless lump floating in space for ever. The chances of—"

"It would be worth something to be rid of your conversation," Clovis said, amiable again now that Bruno was discomfited. "Let's be practical for a change. How long will it take you to run off your analyses this afternoon? There's a lot of stuff to go out to Base and I shan't be able to give you a hand."

"An hour, perhaps, after I've run the final tests."

"Why run tests at all? She was lined up perfectly when we finished this morning."

"Fortunately."

"Fortunately indeed. One more variable and we might have found it impossible."

"Yes," Bruno said abstractedly. Then he got to his feet so abruptly that the other three started. "But we didn't, did we? There wasn't one more variable, was there? It didn't quite happen, you see, the thing we couldn't handle."

Nobody spoke.

"Excuse me, I must be by myself."

"If Bruno keeps this up," Clovis said to the two women, "Base will send up a relief sooner than we think."

Myri tried to drive the thought of Bruno's strange behaviour out of her head when, half an hour later, she sat down to work on her story. The expression on his face as he left the table had been one she could not name. Excitement? Dislike? Surprise? That was the nearest—a kind of persistent surprise. Well, he was certain, being Bruno, to set about explaining it at dinner. She wished he were more pleasant, because he did think well.

Finally expelling the image of Bruno's face, she began rereading the page of manuscript she had been working on when the screams had interrupted her the previous afternoon. It was part of a difficult scene, one in which a woman met by chance a man who had been having her ten years earlier, with the complication that she was at the time in the company of the man who was currently having her. The scene was an eating alcove in a large city.

"Go away," Volsci said, "or I'll hit you."

Norbu smiled in a not-pleasant way. "What good would that do? Irmy likes me better than she likes you. You are more pleasant, no doubt, but she likes me better. She remembers me having her ten years ago more clearly than she remembers you having her last night. I am good at thinking, which is better than any amount of being pleasant."

"She's having her meal with me," Volsci said, pointing to the cold food and drinks in front of them. "Aren't you, Irmy?"

"Yes, Irmy," Norbu said. "You must choose. If you can't let both of us have you, you must say which of us you like better."

Irmy looked from one man to the other. There was so much difference between them that she could hardly begin to choose: The one more pleasant, the other better at thinking, the one slim, the other plump. She decided being pleasant was better. It was more important and more significant—better in every way that made a real difference. She said: "I'll have Volsci."

Norbu looked surprised and sorry. "I think you're wrong."

"You might as well go now," Volsci said. "Ila will be waiting."

"Yes," Norbu said. He looked extremely sorry now.

Irmy felt quite sorry too. "Goodbye, Norbu," she said.

Myri smiled to herself. It was good, even better than she had remembered—there was no point in being modest inside one's own mind. She must be a real writer in spite of Bruno's scoffing, or how could she have invented these characters, who were so utterly unlike anybody she knew, and then put them into a situation that was so completely outside her experience? The only thing she was not sure about was whether she might not have overplayed the part about feeling or dwelt on it at too great length. Perhaps *extemely sorry* was a little heavy; she replaced it by *sorrier than before.* Excellent: now there was just the right touch of restraint in the middle of all the feeling. She decided she could finish off the scene in a few lines.

"Probably see you at some cocktail hour," Volsci said, she wrote, then looked up with a frown as the buzzer sounded at her door. She crossed her tiny wedge-shaped room—its rear wall was part of the outer wall of the sphere, but it had no port—threw the lock and found Bruno on the threshold. He was breathing fast, as if he had been hurrying or lifting a heavy weight, and she saw with distaste that there were drops of sweat on his thick skin. He pushed past her and sat down on her bed, his mouth open.

"What is it?" she asked, displeased. The afternoon was a private time unless some other arrangement were made at lunch.

"I don't know what it is. I think I must be ill."

"Ill? But you can't be. Only people on Earth get ill. Nobody on a station is ever ill: Base told us that. Illness is caused by—"

"I don't think I believe some of the things that Base says."

"But who can we believe if we don't believe Base?"

Bruno evidently did not hear her question. He said: "I had to come to you—Lia's no good for this. Please let me stay with you, I've got so much to say."

"It's no use, Bruno. Clovis is the one who has me. I thought you understood that I didn't—"

"That's not what I mean," he said impatiently. "Where I need you is in thinking. Though that's connected with the other, the having. I don't expect you to see that. I've only just begun to see it myself."

Myri could make nothing of this last part. "Thinking?" Thinking about what?"

He bit his lip and shut his eyes for a moment. "Listen to this," he said. "It was the analyser that set my mind going. Almost every other day it breaks down. And the computer, the counters, the repellers, the scanners and the rest of them—they're always breaking down too, and so are their power supplies. But not the purifier or the fluid-reconstitutor or the fruit and vegetable growers or the heaters or the main power source. Why not?"

"Well, they're less complicated. How can a fruit grower go wrong? A chemical tank and a water tank is all there is to it. You ask Lia about that."

"All right. Try answering this, then. The strange happenings. If they're illusions, why are they always outside the sphere? Why are there never any inside?"

"Perhaps there are," Myri said.

"Don't. I don't want that. I shouldn't like that. I want everything in here to be real. Are you real? I must believe you are."

"Of course I'm real." She was now thoroughly puzzled.

"And it makes a difference, doesn't it? It's very important that you and everything else should be real, everything in the sphere. But tell me: whatever's arranging these happenings must be pretty powerful if it can fool our instruments and our senses so completely and consistently, and yet it can't do anything—anything we recognise as strange, that is—inside this punny little steel skin. Why not?"

"Presumably it has its limitations. We should be pleased."

"Yes. All right, next point. You remember the time I tried to sit up in the lounge after midnight and stay awake?"

"That was silly. Nobody can stay awake after midnight. Standing Orders were quite clear on that point."

"Yes, they were, weren't they?" Bruno seemed to be trying to grin. "Do you remember my telling you how I couldn't account for being in my own bed as usual when the music woke us—you remember the big music? And—this is what I'm really after—do you remember how we all agreed at breakfast that life in space must have conditioned us in such a way that falling asleep at a fixed time had become an automatic mechanism? You remember that?"

"Naturally I do."

"Right. Two questions, then. Does that strike you as a likely explanation? That sort of complete self-conditioning in all four of us after . . . just a number of months?"

"Not when you put it like that."

"But we all agreed on it, didn't we? Without hesitation."

Myri, leaning against a side wall, fidgeted. He was being not pleasant in a new way, one that made her want to stop him talking even while he was thinking at his best. "What's your other question, Bruno?" Her voice sounded unusual to her.

"Ah, you're feeling it too, are you?"

"I don't know what you mean."

"I think you will in a minute. Try my other question. The night of the music was a long time ago, soon after we arrived here, but you remember it clearly. So do I. And yet when I try to remember what I was doing only a couple of months earlier, on Earth, finishing up my life there, getting ready for this, it's just a vague blur. Nothing stands out."

"It's all so remote."

"Maybe. But I remember the trip clearly enough, don't you?"

Myri caught her breath. I feel surprised, she told herself. Or something like that. I feel the way Bruno looked when he left the lunch table. She said nothing.

"You're feeling it now all right, aren't you?" He was watching her closely with his narrow eyes. "Let me try to describe it. A surprise that goes on and on. Puzzlement. Symptoms of physical exertion or strain. And above all a . . . a sort of discomfort, only in the mind. Like having a sharp object pressed against a tender part of your body, except that this is in your mind."

"What are you talking about?"

"A difficulty of vocabulary."

The loudspeaker above the door clicked on and Clovis's voice said: "Attention. Strange happening. Assemble in the lounge at once. Strange happening."

Myri and Bruno stopped staring at each other and hurried out along the narrow corridor. Clovis and Lia were already in the lounge, looking out of the port.

Apparently only a few feet beyond the steelhard glass, and illuminated from some invisible source, were two floating figures. The detail was excellent, and the four inside the sphere could distinguish without difficulty every fold in the naked skin of the two caricatures of humanity presented, it seemed, for their thorough inspection, a presumption given added weight by the slow rotation of the pair that enabled their every portion to be scrutinised. Except for a scrubby growth at the base of the skull, they were hairless. The limbs were foreshortened, lacking the normal narrowing at the joints, and the bellies protuberant. One had male characteristics, the other female, yet in neither case were these complete. From each open, wet, quivering toothless mouth there came a loud, clearly audible yelling, higher in pitch than any those in the sphere could have produced, and of an unfamiliar emotional range.

"Well, I wonder how long this will last," Clovis said.

"Is it worth trying the repellers on them?" Lia asked. "What does the radar say? Does it see them?"

"I'll go and have a look."

Bruno turned his back on the port. "I don't like them."

"Why not?" Myri saw he was sweating again.

"They remind me of something."

"What?"

"I'm trying to think."

But although Bruno went on trying to think for the rest of that day, with such obvious seriousness that even Clovis did his best to help with suggestions, he was no nearer a solution when they parted, as was their habit, at five minutes to midnight. And when, several times in the next couple of days, Myri mentioned the afternoon of the caricatures to him, he showed little interest.

"Bruno, you are extraordinary," she said one evening. "What

happened to those odd feelings of yours you were so eager to describe to me just before Clovis called us into the lounge?"

He shrugged his narrow shoulders in the almost girlish way he had. "Oh, I don't know what could have got into me," he said. "I expect I was just angry with the confounded analyser and the way it kept breaking down. It's been much better recently."

"And all that thinking you used to do."

"That was a complete waste of time."

"Surely not."

"Yes, I agree with Clovis, let Base do all the thinking."

Myri was disappointed. To hear Bruno resigning the task of thought seemed like the end of something. This feeling was powerfully underlined for her when, a little later, the announcement came over the loudspeaker in the lounge. Without any preamble at all, other than the usual click on, a strange voice said: "Your attention, please. This is Base calling over your intercom."

They all looked up in great surprise, especially Clovis, who said quickly to Bruno: "Is that possible?"

"Oh yes, they've been experimenting," Bruno replied as quickly.

"It is perhaps ironical," the voice went on, "that the first transmission we have been able to make to you by the present means is also the last you will receive by any. For some time the maintenance of space stations has been uneconomic, and the decision has just been taken to discontinue them altogether. You will therefore make no further reports of any kind, or rather you may of course continue to do on the understanding that nobody will be listening. In many cases it has fortunately been found possible to arrange for the collection of station staffs and their return to Earth: in others, those involving a journey to the remoter parts of the galaxy, a prohibitive expenditure of time and effort would be entailed. I am sorry to have to tell you that your own station is one of these. Accordingly, you will never be relieved. All of us here are confident that you will respond to this new situation with dignity and resource.

"Before we sever communication for the last time, I have one more point to make. It involves a revelation which may prove so unwelcome that only with the greatest reluctance can I bring myself to utter it. My colleagues, however, insisted that those in your predicament deserve, in your own interest, to hear the whole truth about it. I must tell you, then, that contrary to your earlier information we have had no reports from any other station whose content resembles in the slightest degree your accounts of the strange happenings you claim to have witnessed. The deception was considered necessary so that your morale might be maintained, but the time for deceptions is over. You are unique, and in the variety of mankind that is no small distinction. Be proud of it. Goodbye for ever."

They sat without speaking until five minutes to midnight. Try as she would, Myri found it impossible to conceive their future, and the next morning she had no more success. That was as long as any of them had leisure to come to terms with their permanent isolation, for by midday a quite new phase of strange happenings had begun. Myri and Lia were preparing lunch in the kitchen when Myri, opening the cupboard where the dishes were kept, was confronted by a flattish, reddish creature with many legs and a pair of unequally sized pincers. She gave a gasp, almost a shriek, of astonishment.

"What is it?" Lia said, hurrying over, and then in a high voice: "Is it alive?"

"It's moving. Call the men."

Until the others came, Myri simply stared. She found her lower lip shaking in a curious way. *Inside* now, she kept thinking. Not just outside. *Inside.*

"Let's have a look," Clovis said. "I see. Pass me a knife or something." He rapped at the creature, making a dry, bony sound. "Well, it works for tactile and aural, as well as visual, anyway. A thorough illusion. If it is one."

"It must be," Bruno said. "Don't you recognise it?"

"There is something familiar about it, I suppose."

"You suppose? You mean you don't know a crab when you see one?"

"Oh, of course," Clovis looked slightly sheepish. "I remember now. A terrestrial animal, isn't it? Lives in the water. And so it must be an illusion. Crabs don't cross space as far as I know, and even if they could they'd have a tough time carving their way through the skin of the sphere."

His sensible manner and tone helped Myri to get over her astonishment, and it was she who suggested that the crab be disposed of down the waste chute. At lunch, she said: "It was a remarkably specific illusion, don't you think? I wonder how it was projected."

"No point in wondering about that," Bruno told her.

"How can we ever know? And what use would the knowledge be to us if we did know?"

"Knowing the turth has its own value."

"I don't understand you."

Lia came in with the coffee just then. "The crab's back," she said. "Or there's another one there, I can't tell."

More crabs, or simulacra thereof, appeared at intervals for the rest of the day, eleven of them in all. It seemed, as Clovis put it, that the illusion-producing technique had its limitations, inasmuch as none of them saw a crab actually materialise: the new arrival would be "discovered" under a bed or behind a bank of apparatus. On the other hand, the depth of illusion produced was very great, as they all agreed when Myri, putting the eighth crab down the chute, was nipped in the finger, suffered pain and exuded a few drops of blood.

"Another new departure," Clovis said. "An illusory physical process brought about on the actual person of one of us. They're improving."

Next morning there were the insects. The main apparatus room was found to be infested with what, again on Bruno's prompting, they recognised as cockroaches. By lunch-time there were moths and flying beetles in all the main rooms, and a number of large flies became noticeable towards the evening. The whole of their attention became concentrated upon avoiding these creatures as far as possible. The day passed without Clovis asking Myri to go with him. This had never happened before.

The following afternoon a fresh problem was raised by Lia's announcement that the garden now contained no fruits or vege-

tables—none, at any rate, that were accessible to her senses. In this
the other three concurred. Clovis put the feelings of all of them
when he said: "If this is an illusion, it's as efficient as the reality,
because fruits and vegetables you can never find are the same as
no fruits and vegetables."

The evening meal used up all the food they had. Soon after
two o'clock in the morning Myri was aroused by Clovis's voice
saying over the loudspeaker: "Attention, everyone. Strange happening. Assemble in the lounge immediately."

She was still on her way when she became aware of a new
quality in the background of silence she had grown used to. It
was a deeper silence, as if some sound at the very threshold of
audibility had ceased. There were unfamiliar vibrations under-
foot.

Clovis was standing by the port, gazing through it with interest. "Look at this, Myri," he said.

At a distance impossible to gauge, an oblong of light had
become visible, a degree or so in breadth and perhaps two and a
half times as high. The light was of comparable quality to that
illuminating the inside of the sphere. Now and then it flickered.

"What is it?" Myri asked.

"I don't know, it's only just appeared." The floor beneath
them shuddered violently. "That was what woke me, one of those
tremors. Ah, here you are, Bruno. What do you make of it?"

Bruno's large eyes widened further, but he said nothing. A
moment later Lia arrived and joined the silent group by the port.
Another vibration shook the sphere. Some vessel in the kitchen
fell to the floor and smashed. Then Myri said: "I can see what
looks like a flight of steps leading down from the lower edge of
the light. Three or four of them, perhaps more."

She had barely finished speaking when a shadow appeared
before them, cast by the rectangle of light on to a surface none of
them could identify. The shadow seemed to them of a stupefying
vastness, but it was beyond question that of a man. A moment
later the man came into view, outlined by the light, and descended the steps. Another moment or two and he was evidently
a few feet from the port, looking in on them, their own lights

bright on the upper half of him. He was a well-built man wearing a grey uniform jacket and a metal helmet. An object recognisable as a gun of some sort was slung over his shoulder. While he watched them, two other figures, similarly accoutred, came down the steps and joined him. There was a brief interval, then he moved out of view to their right, doing so with the demeanour of one walking on a level surface.

None of the four inside spoke or moved, not even at the sound of heavy bolts being drawn in the section of outer wall directly in front of them, not even when that entire section swung away from them like a door opening outwards and the three men stepped through into the sphere. Two of them had unslung the guns from their shoulders.

Myri remembered an occasion, weeks ago, when she had risen from a stooping position in the kitchen and struck her head violently on the bottom edge of a cupboard door Lia had happened to leave open. The feeling Myri now experienced was similar, except that she had no particular physical sensations. Another memory, a much fainter one, passed across the far background of her mind: somebody had once tried to explain to her the likeness between a certain mental state and the bodily sensation of discomfort, and she had not understood. The memory faded sharply.

The man they had first seen said: "All roll up your sleeves."

Clovis looked at him with less curiosity than he had been showing when Myri first joined him at the port, a few minutes earlier. "You're an illusion," he said.

"No I'm not. Roll up your sleeves, all of you."

He watched them closely while they obeyed, becoming impatient at the slowness with which they moved. The other man whose gun was unslung, a younger man, said: "Don't be hard on them, Allen. We've no idea what they've been through."

"I'm not taking any chances," Allen said. "Not after that crowd in the trees. Now this is for your own good," he went on, addressing the four. "Keep quite still. All right, Douglas."

The third man came forward, holding what Myri knew to be a hypodermic syringe. He took her firmly by her bare arm and gave her an injection. At once her feelings altered, in the sense that, although there was still discomfort in her mind, neither this nor anything else seemed to matter.

After a time she heard the young man say: "You can roll your sleeves down now. You can be quite sure that nothing bad will happen to you."

"Come with us," Allen said.

Myri and the others followed the three men out of the sphere, across a gritty floor that might have been concrete and up the steps, a distance of perhaps thirty feet. They entered a corridor with artificial lighting and then a room into which the sun was streaming. There were twenty or thirty people in the room, some of them wearing the grey uniform. Now and then the walls shook as the sphere had done, but to the accompaniment of distant explosions. A faint shouting could also be heard from time to time.

Allen's voice said loudly: "Let's try and get a bit of order going. Douglas, they'll be wanting you to deal with the people in the tank. They've been conditioned to believe they're congenitally aquatic, so you'd better give them a shot that'll knock them out straight away. Holmes is draining the tank now. Off you go. Now you, James, you watch this lot while I find out some more about them. I wish those psycho chaps would turn up—we're just working in the dark." His voice moved further away. "Sergeant —get these five out of here."

"Where to, sir?"

"I don't mind where—just out of here. And watch them."

"They've all been given shots, sir."

"I know, but look at them, they're not human any more. And it's no use talking to them, they've been deprived of language. That's how they got the way they are. Now get them out right away."

Myri looked slowly at the young man who stood near them: James. "Where are we?" she asked.

James hesitated. "I was ordered to tell you nothing," he said. "You're supposed to wait for the psychological team to get to you and treat you."

"Please."

"All right. This much can't hurt you, I suppose. You four and a number of other groups have been the subject of various experiments. This building is part of Special Welfare Research Station No. 4. Or rather it was. The government that set it up no longer exists. It has been removed by the revolutionary army of which I'm a member. We had to shoot our way in here and there's fighting still going on."

"Then we weren't in space at all."

"No."

"Why did they make us believe we were?"

"We don't know yet."

"And how did they do it?"

"Some new form of deep-level hypnosis, it seems, probably renewed at regular intervals. Plus various apparatus for producing illusions. We're still working on that. Now, I think that's enough questions for the moment. The best thing you can do is sit down and rest."

"Thank you. What's hypnosis?"

"Oh, of course they'd have removed knowledge of that. It'll all be explained to you later."

"James, come and have a look at this, will you?" Allen's voice called. "I can't make much of it."

Myri followed James a little way. Among the clamour of voices, some speaking languages unfamiliar to her, others speaking none, she heard James ask: "Is this the right file? Fear Elimination?"

"Must be," Allen answered. "Here's the last entry. *Removal of Bruno V and substitution of Bruno VI accomplished, together with memory-adjustment of other three subjects. Memo to Preparation Centre: avoid repetition of Bruno V personality-type with strong curiosity-drives.* Started catching on to the set-up, eh? Wonder what they did with him."

"There's that psycho hospital across the way they're still investigating; perhaps he's in there."

"With Brunos I to IV, no doubt. Never mind that for the moment. Now. *Procedures: penultimate phase. Removal of all*

*ultimate confidence: serverance of communication, total denial
of prospective change, inculcation of "uniqueness" syndrome, environment shown to be violable, unkowable crisis in prospect
(food deprivation).* I can understand that last bit. They don't
look starved, though."

"Perhaps they've only just started them on it."

"We'll get them fed in a minute. Well, all this still beats me,
James. *Reactions. Little change. Responses poor. Accelerating im-
poverishment of emotional life and its vocabulary: compare portion of novel written by Myri VII with contributions of predeces-
sors. Prognosis: further affective deterioration: catatonic apathy:
failure of experiment.* That's a comfort, anyway. But what has all
this got to do with fear elimination?"

They stopped talking suddenly and Myri followed the direction of their gaze. A door had been opened and the man called
Douglas was supervising the entry of a number of others, each
supporting or carrying a human form wrapped in a blanket.

"This must be the lot from the tank," Allen or James said.

Myri watched while those in the blankets were made as comfortable as possible on benches or on the floor. One of them,
however, remained totally wrapped in his blanket and was paid
no attention.

"He's had it, has he?"

"Shock, I'm afraid." Douglas's voice was unsteady. "There
was nothing we could do. Perhaps we shouldn't have—"

Myri stooped and turned back the edge of the blanket. What
she saw was much stranger than anything she had experienced in
the sphere. "What's the matter with him?" she asked James.

"Matter with him? You can die of shock, you know."

"I can do what?"

Myri, staring at James, was aware that his face had become
distorted by a mixture of expressions. One of them was understanding: all the others were painful to look at. They were render-
ings of what she herself was feeling. Her vision darkened and she
ran from the room, back the way they had come, down the steps,
across the floor, back into the sphere.

James was unfamiliar with the arrangement of the rooms there and did not reach her until she had picked up the manuscript of the novel, hugged it to her chest with crossed arms and fallen on to her bed, her knees drawn up as far as they would go, her head lowered as it had been before her birth, an event of which she knew nothing.

She was still in the same position when, days later, somebody sat heavily down beside her. "Myri. You must know who this is. Open your eyes, Myri. Come out of there."

After he had said this, in the same gentle voice, some hundreds of times, she did open her eyes a little. She was in a long, high room, and near her was a fat man with a pale skin. He reminded her of something to do with space and thinking. She screwed her eyes shut.

"Myri. I know you remember me. Open your eyes again."

She kept them shut while he went on talking.

"Open your eyes. Straighten your body."

"Straighten your body, Myri. I love you." She did not move. Slowly her feet crept down the bed and her head lifted.

Sold to Satan

by Mark Twain

It was at this time that I concluded to sell my soul to Satan. Steel was away down, so was St. Paul; it was the same with all the desirable stocks, in fact, and so, if I did not turn out to be away down myself, now was my time to raise a stake and make my fortune. Without further consideration I sent word to the local agent, Mr. Blank, with description and present condition of the property, and an interview with Satan was promptly arranged, on a basis of 2 1/2 per cent, this commission payable only in case a trade should be consummated.

I sat in the dark, waiting and thinking. How still it was! Then came the deep voice of a far-off bell proclaiming midnight—Boom-m-m! Boom-m-m! Boom-m-m!—and I rose to receive my guest, and braced myself for the thunder crash and the brimstone stench which should announce his arrival. But there was no crash, no stench. Through the closed door, and noiseless, came the modern Satan, just as we see him on the stage—tall, slender, graceful, in tights and trunks, a short cape mantling his shoulders, a rapier at his side, a single drooping feather in his jaunty cap, and on his intellectual face the well-known and high-bred Mephistophelian smile.

But he was not a fire coal; he was not red, no! On the contrary. He was a softly glowing, richly smoldering torch, column, statue of pallid light, faintly tinted with a spiritual green, and out from him a lunar splendor flowed such as one sees glinting from the crinkled waves of tropic seas when the moon rides high in cloudless skies.

He made his customary stage obeisance, resting his left hand upon his sword hilt and removing his cap with his right and making that handsome sweep with it which we know so well; then we sat down. Ah, he was an incandescent glory, a nebular dream, and so much improved by his change of color. He must have seen the admiration in my illuminated face, but he took no notice of it, being long ago used to it in faces of other Christians with whom he had had trade relations.

... A half hour of hot toddy and weather chat, mixed with occasional tentative feelers on my part and rejoinders of, "Well, I could hardly pay *that* for it, you know," on his, had much modified my shyness and put me so much at my ease that I was emboldened to feed my curiosity a little. So I chanced the remark that he was surprisingly different from the traditions, and I wished I knew what it was he was made of. He was not offended, but answered with frank simplicity:

"Radium!"

"That accounts for it!" I exclaimed. "It is the loveliest effulgence I have ever seen. The hard and heartless glare of the electric doesn't compare with it. I suppose Your Majesty weighs about—about—"

"I stand six feet one; fleshed and blooded I would weigh two hundred and fifteen; but radium, like other metals, is heavy. I weigh nine hundred-odd"

I gazed hungrily upon him, saying to myself:

"What riches! what a mine! Nine hundred pounds at, say, $3,500,000 a pound, would be—would be—" Then a treacherous thought burst into my mind!

He laughed a good hearty laugh, and said:

"I perceive your thought; and what a handsomely original idea it is!—to kidnap Satan, and stock him, and incorporate him, and water the stock up to ten billions—just three times its actual value—and blanket the world with it!" My blush had turned the moonlight to a crimson mist, such as veils and spectralizes the domes and towers of Florence at sunset and makes the spectator drunk with joy to see, and he pitied me, and dropped his tone of irony, and assumed a grave and reflective one which had a pleasanter sound for me, and under its kindly influence my pains were presently healed, and I thanked him for his courtesy. Then he said:

"One good turn deserves another, and I will pay you a compliment. Do you know I have been trading with your poor pathetic race for ages, and you are the first person who has ever been intelligent enough to divine the large commercial value of my make-up."

I purred to myself and looked as modest as I could.

"Yes, you are the first," he continued. "All through the Middle dle Ages I used to buy Christian souls at fancy rates, building bridges and cathedrals in a single night in return, and getting swindled out of my Christian nearly every time that I dealt with a priest—as history will concede—but making it up on the lay square-dealer now and then, as *I* admit; but none of those people ever guessed where the *real* big money lay. You are the first."

I refilled his glass and gave him another Cavour. But he was experienced, by this time. He inspected the cigar pensively awhile; then:

"What do you pay for these?" he asked.

"Two cents—but they come cheaper when you take a barrel."

He went on inspecting; also mumbling comments, apparently to himself:

"Black—rough-skinned—rumpled, irregular, wrinkled, barky, with crispy curled-up places on it—burnt-leather aspect, like the shoes of the damned that sit in pairs before the room doors at home of a Sunday morning." He sighed at thought of his home, and was silent a moment; then he said, gently, "Tell me about this projectile."

"It is the discovery of a great Italian statesman," I said. "Cavour. One day he lit his cigar, then laid it down and went on writing and forgot it. It lay in a pool of ink and got soaked. By and by he noticed it and laid it on the stove to dry. When it was dry he lit it and at once noticed that it didn't taste the same as it did before. And so—"

"Did he say what it tasted like before?"

"No, I think not. But he called the government chemist and told him to find out the source of that new taste, and report. The chemist applied the tests, and reported that the source was the presence of sulphate of iron, touched up and spiritualized with vinegar—the combination out of which one makes ink. Cavour told him to introduce the brand in the interest of the finances. So, ever since then this brand passes through the ink factory, with the great result that both the ink and the cigar suffer a sea change into something new and strange. This is history, Sire, not a work of the imagination."

So then he took up his present again, and touched it to the forefinger of his other hand for an instant, which made it break into flame and fragrance—but he changed his mind at that point and laid the torpedo down, saying courteously:

"With permission I will save it for Voltaire."

I was greatly pleased and flattered to be connected in even this little way with that great man and be mentioned to him, as no doubt would be the case, so I hastened to fetch a bundle of fifty for distribution among others of the renowed and lamented—Goethe, and Homer, and Socrates, and Confucius, and so on—but Satan said he had nothing against those. Then he dropped back into reminiscences of the old times once more, and presently said:

"They knew nothing about radium, and it would have had no value for them if they had known about it. In twenty million years it has had no value for your race until the revolutionizing steam-and-machinery age was born—which was only a few years before you were born yourself. It was a stunning little century, for sure, that nineteenth! But it's a poor thing compared to what the twentieth is going to be."

By request, he explained why he thought so.

"Because power was so costly, then, and everything goes by power—the steamship, the locomotive, and everything else. Coal, you see! You have to have it; no steam and no electricity without it; and it's such a waste—for you burn it up, and it's gone! But radium—that's another matter! With my nine hundred pounds you could light the world, and heat it, and run all its ships and machines and railways a hundred million years, and not use up five pounds of it in the whole time! And then—"

"Quick—my soul is yours, dear Ancestor; take it—we'll start a company!"

But he asked my age, which is sixty-eight then politely sidetracked the proposition, probably not wishing to take advantage of himself. Then he went on talking admiringly of radium, and how with its own natural and inherent heat it could go on melting its own weight of ice twenty-four times in twenty-four hours, and keep it up forever without losing bulk or weight; and how a pound of it, if exposed in this room, would blast the place like a breath from hell, and burn me to a crisp in a quarter of a minute —and was going on like that, but I interrupted and said:

"But *you* are here, Majesty—nine hundred pounds—and the temperature is balmy and pleasant. I don't understand."

"Well," he said, hesitatingly, "it is a secret, but I may as well reveal it, for these prying and impertinent chemists are going to find it out sometime or other, anyway. Perhaps you have read what Madame Curie says about radium; how she goes searching among its splendid secrets and seizes upon one after another of them and italicizes its specialty; how she says 'the compounds of radium are *spontaneously luminous*'—require no coal in the production of light, you see; how she says, 'a glass vessel containing radium *spontaneously charges itself with electricity*'—no coal or water power required to generate it, you see; how she says 'radium possesses the remarkable property of *liberating heat spontaneously and continuously*'—no coal required to fire-up on the world's machinery, you see. She ransacks the pitch-blende for its radioactive substances, and captures three and labels them; one, which is embodied with bismuth, she names polonium; one,

which is embodied with barium, she names radium; the name given
to the third was actinium. Now listen; she says *'the question now
was to separate the polonium from the bismuth* ... this is the
task that has occupied us for years and has been a most difficult
one.' For years, you see—for *years*. That is their way, those
plagues, those scientists—peg, peg, peg—dig, dig, dig—plod, plod,
plod. I wish I could catch a cargo of them for my place; it would
be an economy. Yes, for years, you see. They never give up.
Patience, hope, faith, perseverance; it is the way of all the breed.
Columbus and the rest. In radium this lady has added a new
world to the planet's possessions, and matched—Columbus—and
his peer. She has set herself the task of divorcing polonium and
bismuth; when she succeeds she will have done—what, should you
say?"

"Pray name it, Majesty."

"It's another new world added—a gigantic one. I will explain;
for you would never divine the size of it, and she herself does not
suspect it."

"Do, Majesty, I beg of you."

"Polonium, freed from bismuth and made independent, is the
one and only power that can control radium, restrain its destructive forces, tame them, reduce them to obedience, and make them
do useful and profitable work for your race. Examine my skin.
What do you think of it?"

"It is delicate, silky, transparent, thin as a gelatine film—
exquisite, beautiful, Majesty!"

"It is made of polonium. All the rest of me is radium. If I
should strip off my skin the world would vanish away in a flash
of flame and a puff of smoke, and the remnants of the extinguished moon would sift down through space a mere snow-shower of
gray ashes!"

I made no comment, I only trembled.

"You understand, now," he continued. "I burn, I suffer within, my pains are measureless and eternal, but my skin protects
you and the globe from harm. Heat is power, energy, but is only
useful to man when he can control it and graduate its application
to his needs. You cannot do that with radium, now; it will not be

prodigiously useful to you until polonium shall put the slave whip in your hand. I can release from my body the radium force in any measure I please, great or small; at my will I can set in motion the works of a lady's watch or destroy a world. You saw me light that unholy cigar with my finger?"

I remembered it.

"Try to imagine how minute was the fraction of energy released to do that small thing! You are aware that everything is made up of restless and revolving molecules?—everything— furniture, rocks, water, iron, horses, men—everything that exists."

"Yes."

"Molecules of scores of different sizes and weights, but none of them big enough to be seen by help of any microscope?"

"Yes."

"And that each molecule is made up of thousands of separate and never-resting little particles called atoms?"

"Yes."

"And that up to recent times the smallest atom known to science was the hydrogen atom, which was a thousand times smaller than the atom that went to the building of any other molecule?"

"Yes."

"Well, the radium atom from the positive pole is 5,000 times smaller than *that* atom! This unspeakably minute atom is called an *electron*. Now then, out of my long affection for you and for you lineage, I will reveal to you a secret—a secret known to no scientist as yet—the secret of the firefly's light and the glow-worm's; it is produced by a single electron imprisoned in a polonium atom."

"Sire, it is a wonderful thing, and the scientific world would be grateful to know this secret, which has baffled and defeated all its searchings for more than two centuries. To think!—a single electron, 5,000 times smaller than the invisible hydrogen atom, to produce that explosion of vivid light which makes the summer night so beautiful!"

"And consider," said Satan; "it is the only instance in all nature where radium exists in a pure state unencumbered by fettering alliances; where polonium enjoys the like emancipation; and where the pair are enabled to labor together in a gracious and beneficent and effective partnership. Suppose the protecting polonium envelope were removed; the radium spark would flash but once and the firefly would be consumed to vapor! Do you value this old iron letterpress?"

"No, Majesty, for it is not mine."

"Then I will destroy it and let you see. I lit the ostensible cigar with the heat energy of a single electron, the equipment of a single lightning bug. I will turn on twenty thousand electrons now."

He touched the massive thing and it exploded with a cannon crash, leaving nothing but vacancy where it had stood. For three minutes the air was a dense pink fog of sparks, through which Satan loomed dim and vague, then the place cleared and his soft rich moonlight pervaded it again. He said:

"You see? The radium in 20,000 lightning bugs would run a racing-mobile forever. There's no waste, no diminution of it." Then he remarked in a quite casual way, "We use nothing but radium at home."

I was astonished. And interested, too, for I have friends there, and relatives. I had always believed—in accordance with my early teachings—that the fuel was soft coal and brimstone. He noticed the thought, and answered it.

"Soft coal and brimstone is the tradition, yes, but it is an error. We could use it; at least we could make out with it after a fashion, but it has several defects: it is not cleanly, it ordinarily makes but a temperate fire, and it would be exceedingly difficult, if even possible, to heat it up to standard, Sundays; and as for the supply, all the worlds and systems could not furnish enough to keep us going halfway through eternity. Without radium there could be no hell; certainly not a satsifactory one."

"Why?"

"Because if we hadn't radium we should have to dress the souls in some other material; then, of course, they would burn up and get out of trouble. They would not last an hour. You know that?"

"Why—yes, now that you mention it. But I supposed they were dressed in their natural flesh; they look so in the pictures—in the Sistine Chapel and in the illustrated books, you know."

"Yes, our damned look as they looked in the world, but it isn't flesh; flesh could not survive any longer than that copying press survived—it would explode and turn to a fog of sparks, and the result desired in sending it there would be defeated. Believe me, radium is the only wear."

"I see it now," I said, with prophetic discomfort, "I know that you are right, Majesty."

"I am. I speak from experience. You shall see, when you get there."

He said this as if he thought I was eaten up with curiosity, but it was because he did not know me. He sat reflecting a minute, then he said:

"I will make your fortune."

It cheered me up and I felt better. I thanked him and was all eagerness and attention.

"Do you know," he continued, "where they find the bones of the extinct moa, in New Zealand? All in a pile—thousands and thousands of them banked together in a mass twenty feet deep. And do you know where they find the tusks of the extinct mastodon of the Pleistocene? Banked together in acres off the mouth of the Lena—an ivory mine which has furnished freight for Chinese caravans for five hundred years. Do you know the phosphate beds of our South? They are miles in extent, a limitless mass and jumble of bones of vast animals whose like exists no longer in the earth—a cemetery, a mighty cemetery, that is what it is. All over the earth there are such cemeteries. Whence came the instinct that made those families of creatures go to a chosen and particular spot to die when sickness came upon them and they perceived that their end was near? It is a mystery; not even science has been able to uncover the secret of it. But there stands the fact. Listen, then. For a million years there has been a firefly cemetery."

Hopefully, appealingly, I opened my mouth—he motioned me to close it, and went on:

"It is in a scooped-out bowl half as big as this room on the top of a snow summit of the Cordileras. That bowl is level full—of what? Pure firefly radium and the glow and heat of hell! For countless ages myriads of fireflies have daily flown thither and died in that bowl and been burned to vapor in an instant, each fly leaving as its contribution its only indestructible particle, its single electron of pure radium. There is energy enough there to light the whole world, heat the whole world's machinery, supply the whole world's transportation power from now till the end of eternity. The massed riches of the planet could not furnish its value in money. You are mine, it is yours; when Madame Curie isolates polonium, clothe yourself in a skin of it and go and take possession!"

Then he vanished and left me in the dark when I was just in the act of thanking him. I can find the bowl by the light it will cast upon the sky; I can get the polonium presently, when that illustrious lady in France isolates it from the bismuth. Stock is for sale. Apply to Mark Twain.

The End of the Party

by Graham Greene

Peter Morton woke with a start to face the first light. Through the window he could see a bare bough dropping across a frame of silver. Rain tapped against the glass. It was January the fifth.

He looked across a table, on which a night-light had guttered into a pool of water, at the other bed. Francis Morton was still asleep, and Peter lay down again with his eyes on his brother. It amused him to imagine that it was himself whom he watched, the same hair, the same eyes, the same lips and line of cheek. But the thought soon palled, and the mind went back to the fact which lent the day importance. It was the fifth of January. He could hardly believe that a year had passed since Mrs. Henne-Falcon had given her last children's party.

Francis turned suddenly upon his back and threw an arm across his face, blocking his mouth. Peter's heart began to beat fast, not with pleasure now but with uneasiness. He sat up and called across the table, "Wake up." Francis's shoulders shook and he waved a clenched fist in the air, but his eyes remained closed. To Peter Morton the whole room seemed suddenly to darken, and he had the impression of a great bird swooping. He cried again,

76

"Wake up," and once more there was silver light and the touch of rain on the windows. Francis rubbed his eyes. "Did you call out?" he asked.

"You are having a bad dream," Peter said with confidence. Already experience had taught him how far their minds reflected each other. But he was the elder, by a matter of minutes, and that brief extra interval of light, while his brother still struggled in pain and darkness, had given him self-reliance and an instinct of protection towards the other who was afraid of so many things.

"I dreamed that I was dead," Francis said.

"What was it like?" Peter asked with curiosity.

"I can't remember," Francis said, and his eyes turned with relief to the silver of day, as he allowed the fragmentary memories to fade.

"You dreamed of a big bird."

"Did I?" Francis accepted his brother's knowledge without question, and for a little the two lay silent in bed facing each other, the same green eyes, the same nose tilting at the tip, the same firm lips parted, and the same premature modelling of the chin. The fifth of January, Peter thought again, his mind drifting idly from the image of cakes to the prizes which might be won. Egg-and-spoon races, spearing apples in basins of water, blind-man's-buff.

"I don't want to go," Francis said suddenly. "I suppose Joyce will be there. . . .Mabel Warren." Hateful to him, the thought of a party shared with those two. They were older than he. Joyce was eleven and Mabel Warren thirteen. Their long pigtails swung superciliously to a masculine stride. Their sex humiliated him, as they watched him fumble with his egg, from under lowered scornful lids. And last year. . .he turned his face away from Peter, his cheeks scarlet.

"What's the matter?" Peter asked.

"Oh, nothing. I don't think I'm well. I've got a cold. I oughtn't to go to the party."

Peter was puzzled. "But, Francis, is it a bad cold?"

"It will be a bad cold if I go to the party. Perhaps I shall die."

"Then you mustn't go," Peter said with decision, prepared to

solve all difficulites with one plain sentence, and Francis let his
nerves relax in a delicious relief, ready to leave everything to
Peter. But though he was grateful he did not turn his face towards
his brother. His cheeks still bore the badge of a shameful memory, of the game of hide-and-seek last year in the darkened house,
and of how he had screamed when Mabel Warren put her hand
suddenly upon his arm. He had not heard her coming. Girls were
like that. Their shoes never squeaked. No boards whined under
their tread. They slunk like cats on padded claws. When the nurse
came in with hot water Francis lay tranquil, leaving everything to
Peter. Peter said, "Nurse, Francis has got a cold."

The tall starched woman laid the towels across the cans and
said, without turning, "The washing won't be back till tomorrow.
You must lend him some of your handkerchiefs."

"But, Nurse," Peter asked, "hadn't he better stay in bed?"

"We'll take him for a good walk this morning," the nurse said.
"Wind'll blow away the germs. Get up now, both of you," and
she closed the door behind her.

"I'm sorry," Peter said, and then, worried at the sight of a face
creased again by misery and foreboding, "Why don't you just stay
in bed? I'll tell mother you felt too ill to get up." But such a
rebellion against destiny was not in Francis's power. Besides, if he
stayed in bed they would come up and tap his chest and put a
thermometer in his mouth and look at his tongue, and they
would discover that he was malingering. It was true that he felt
ill, a sick empty sensation in his stomach and a rapidly beating
heart, but he knew that the cause was only fear, fear of the party,
fear of being made to hide by himself in the dark, uncompanioned
by Peter and with no night-light to make a blessed breach.

"No, I'll get up," he said, and then with sudden desperation,
"But I won't go to Mrs. Henne-Falcon's party. I swear on the
Bible I won't". Now surely all would be well, he thought. God
would not allow him to break so solemn an oath. He would show
him a way. There was all the morning before him and all the
afternoon until four o'clock. No need to worry now when the
grass was still crisp with the early frost. Anything might happen.
He might cut himself or break his leg or really catch a bad cold.
God would manage somehow.

He has such confidence in God that when at breakfast his
mother said, "I hear you have a cold, Francis," he made light of
it. "We should have heard more about it," his mother said with
irony, "if there was not a party this evening," and Francis smiled
uneasily, amazed and daunted by her ignorance of him. His happiness would have lasted longer if, out for a walk that morning, he
had not met Joyce. He was alone with his nurse, for Peter had
leave to finish a rabbit-hutch in the woodshed. If Peter had been
there he would have cared less; the nurse was Peter's nurse also,
but now it was as though she were employed only for his sake,
because he could not be trusted to go for a walk alone. Joyce was
only two years older and she was by herself.

She came striding towards them, pigtails flapping. She glanced
scornfully at Francis and spoke with ostentation to the nurse.
"Hello, Nurse. Are you bringing Francis to the party this evening?
Mabel and I are coming." And she was off again down the street
in the direction of Mabel Warren's home, consciously alone and
self-sufficient in the long empty road. "Such a nice girl," the
nurse said. But Francis was silent, feeling again the jump-jump of
his heart, realizing how soon the hour of the party would arrive.
God had nothing for him, and the minutes flew.

They flew too quickly to plan any evasion, or even to prepare
his heart for the coming ordeal. Panic nearly overcame him when,
all unready, he found himself standing on the door-step, with
coat-collar turned up against a cold wind, and the nurse's electric
torch making a short luminous trail through the darkness. Behind
him were the lights of the hall and the sound of a servant laying
the table for dinner, which his mother and father would eat
alone. He was nearly overcome by a desire to run back into the
house and call out to his mother that he would not go to the
party, that he dared not go. They could not make him go. He
could almost hear himself saying those final words, breaking
down for ever, as he knew instinctively, the barrier of ignorance
that saved his mind from his parents' knowledge. "I'm afraid of
going. I won't go. I daren't go. They'll make me hide in the dark
and I'm afraid of the dark. I'll scream and scream and scream."
He could see the expression of amazement on his mother's face,
and then the cold confidence of a grown-up's retort. "Don't be

silly. You must go. We've accepted Mrs. Henne-Falcon's invitation."

But they couldn't make him go; hesitating on the door-step while the nurse's feet crunched across the frost-covered grass to the gate, he knew that. He would answer, "You can say I'm ill. I won't go. I'm afraid of the dark." And his mother, "Don't be silly. You know there's nothing to be afraid of in the dark." But he knew the falsity of that reasoning; he knew how they taught also that there was nothing to fear in death, and how fearfully they avoided the idea of it. But they couldn't make him go to the party. "I'll scream. I'll scream."

"Francis, come along." He heard the nurse's voice across the dimly phosphorescent lawn and saw the small yellow circle of her torch wheel from tree to shrub and back to tree again. "I'm coming," he called with despair, leaving the lighted doorway of the house; he couldn't bring himself to lay bare his last secrets and end reserve between his mother and himself, for there was still in the last resort a further appeal possible to Mrs. Henne-Falcon. He comforted himself with that, as he advanced steadily across the hall, very small, towards her enormous bulk. His heart beat unevenly, but he had control now over his voice, as he said with meticulous accent, "Good evening, Mrs. Henne-Falcon. It was very good of you to ask me to your party." With his strained face lifted towards the curve of her breasts, and his polite set speech, he was like an old withered man. For Francis mixed very little with other children. As a twin he was in many ways an only child. To address Peter was to speak to his own image in a mirror, an image a little altered by a flaw in the glass, so as to throw back less a likeness of what he was than of what he wished to be, what he would be without his unreasoning fear of darkness, footsteps of strangers, the flight of bats in duskfilled gardens.

"Sweet child," said Mrs. Henne-Falcon absent-mindedly, before, with a wave of her arms, as though the children were a flock of chickens, she whirled them into her set programme of entertainments: egg-and-spoon races, three-legged races, the spearing of apples, games which held for Francis nothing worse than humiliation. And in the frequent intervals when nothing was required of him and he could stand alone in corners as far removed as possible from Mabel Warren's scornful gaze, he was able to plan how he might avoid the approaching terror of the dark. He knew there was nothing to fear until after tea, and not until he was sitting down in a pool of yellow radiance cast by the ten candles on Colin Henne-Falcon's birthday cake did he become fully conscious of the imminence of what he feared. Through the confusion of his brain, now assailed suddenly by a dozen contradictory plans, he heard Joyce's high voice down the table. "After tea we are going to play hide-and-seek in the dark."

"Oh, no," Peter said, watching Francis's troubled face with pity and an imperfect understanding, "don't let's. We play that every year."

"But it's in the programme," cried Mabel Warren. "I saw it myself. I looked over Mrs. Henne-Falcon's shoulder. Five o'clock, tea. A quarter to six to half-past, hide-and-seek in the dark. It's all written down in the programme."

Peter did not argue, for if hide-and-seek had been inserted in Mrs. Henne-Falcon's programme, nothing which he could say could avert it. He asked for another piece of birthday cake and sipped his tea slowly. Perhaps it might be possible to delay the game for a quarter of an hour, allow Francis at least a few extra minutes to form a plan, but even in that Peter failed, for children were already leaving the table in twos and threes. It was his third failure, and again, the reflection of an image in another's mind, he saw a great bird darken his brother's face with its wings. But he upbraided himself silently for his folly, and finished his cake encouraged by the memory of that adult refrain, "There's nothing to fear in the dark." The last to leave the table, the brothers came together to the hall to meet the mustering and impatient eyes of Mrs. Henne-Falcon.

"And now," she said, "we will play hide-and-seek in the dark."

Peter watched his brother and saw, as he had expected, the lips tighten. Francis, he knew, had feared this moment from the beginning of the party, had tried to meet it with courage and had abandoned the attempt. He must have prayed desperately for cunning to evade the game, which was now welcomed with cries of excitement by all the other children. "Oh, do let's." "We must pick sides." "Is any of the house out of bounds?" "Where shall home be?"

"I think," said Franics Morton, approaching Mrs. Henne-Falcon, his eyes focused unwaveringly on her exuberant breasts, "it will be no use my playing. My nurse will be calling for me very soon."

"Oh, but your nurse can wait, Francis," said Mrs. Henne-Falcon absent-mindedly, while she clapped her hands together to summon to her side a few children who were already straying up the wide staircase to upper floors. "Your mother will never mind."

That had been the limit of Francis's cunning. He had refused to believe that so well prepared an excuse could fail. All that he could say now, still in the precise tone which other children hated, thinking it a symbol of conceit, was, "I think I had better not play." He stood motionless, retaining, though afraid, unmoved features. But the knowledge of his terror, or the reflection of the terror itself, reached his brother's brain. For the moment, Peter Morton could have cried aloud with the fear of bright lights going out, leaving him alone in an island of dark surrounded by the gentle lapping of strange footsteps. Then he remembered that the fear was not his own, but his brother's. He said impulsively to Mrs. Henne-Falcon, "Please. I don't think Francis should play. The dark makes him jump so." They were the wrong words. Six children began to sing, "Cowardy, cowardy custard," turning torturing faces with the vacancy of wide sunflowers towards Francis Morton.

Without looking at his brother, Francis said, "Of course I will play. I am not afraid. I only thought. . ." But he was already forgotten by his human tormentors and was able in loneliness to contemplate the approach of the spiritual, the more unbounded, torture. The children scrambled round Mrs. Henne-Falcon, their shrill voices pecking at her with questions and suggestions. "Yes,

anywhere in the house. We will turn out all the lights. Yes, you
can hide in the cupboards. You must stay hidden as long as you
can. There will be no home."

Peter, too, stood apart, ashamed of the clumsy manner in
which he had tried to help his brother. Now he could feel, creeping in at the corners of his brain, all Francis's resentment of his
championing. Several children ran upstairs, and the lights on the
top floor went out. Then darkness came down like the wings of a
bat and settled on the landing. Others began to put out the lights
at the edge of the hall, till the children were all gathered in the
central radiance of the chandelier, while the bats squatted round
on hooded wings and waited for that, too, to be extinguished.

"You and Francis are on the hiding side," a tall girl said, and
then the light was gone, and the carpet wavered under his feet
with the sibilance of footfalls, like small cold draughts, creeping
away into corners.

"Where's Francis?" he wondered. "If I join him he'll be less
frightened of all these sounds." "These sounds" were the casing
of silence. The squeak of a loose board, the cautious closing of a
cupboard door, the whine of a finger drawn along polished wood.

Peter stood in the centre of the dark deserted floor, not listening but waiting for the idea of his brother's whereabouts to enter
his brain. But Francis crouched with fingers on his ears, eyes
uselessly closed, mind numbed against impressions, and only a
sense of strain could cross the gap of dark. Then a voice called
"Coming," and as though his brother's self-possession had been
shattered by the sudden cry, Peter Morton jumped with his fear.
But it was not his own fear. What in his brother was a burning
panic, admitting no ideas except those which added to the flame,
was in him an altruistic emotion that left the reason unimpaired.
"Where, if I were Francis, should I hide?" Such, roughly, was his
thought. And because he was, if not Francis himself, at least a
mirror to him, the answer was immediate. "Between the oak
bookcase on the left of the study door and the leather settee."
Peter Morton was unsurprised by the swiftness of the response.
Between the twins there could be no jargon of telepathy. They
had been together in the womb, and they could not be parted.

Peter Morton tiptoed towards Francis's hiding place. Occasionally a board rattled, and because he feared to be caught by one of the soft questers through the dark, he bent and untied his laces. A tag struck the floor and the metallic sound set a host of cautious feet moving in his direction. But by that time he was in his stockings and would have laughed inwardly at the pursuit had not the noise of someone stumbling on his abandoned shoes made his heart trip in the reflection of another's surprise. No more boards revealed Peter Morton's progress. On stockinged feet he moved silently and unerringly towards his object. Instinct told him that he was near the wall, and, extending a hand, he laid the fingers across his brother's face.

Francis did not cry out, but the leap of his own heart revealed to Peter a proportion of Francis's terror. "It's all right," he whispered, feeling down the squatting figure until he captured a clenched hand. "It's only me. I'll stay with you." And grasping the other tightly, he listened to the cascade of whispers his utterance had caused to fall. A hand touched the bookcase close to Peter's head and he was aware of how Francis's fear continued in spite of his presence. It was less intense, more bearable, he hoped, but it remained. He knew that it was his brother's fear and not his own that he experienced. The dark to him was only an absence of light; the groping hand that of a familiar child. Patiently he waited to be found.

He did not speak again, for between Francis and himself touch was the most intimate communion. By way of joined hands thought could flow more swiftly than lips could shape themselves round words. He could experience the whole progress of his brother's emotion, from the leap of panic at the unexpected contact to the steady pulse of fear, which now went on and on with the regularity of a heart-beat. Peter Morton thought with intensity, "I am here. You needn't be afraid. The lights will go on again soon. That rustle, that movement is nothing to fear. Only Joyce, only Mabel Warren." He bombarded the drooping form with thoughts of safety, but he was conscious that the fear continued. "They are beginning to whisper together. They are tired of looking for us. The lights will go on soon. We shall have won.

Don't be afraid. That was only someone on the stairs. I believe it's Mrs. Henne-Falcon. Listen. They are feeling for the lights." Feet moving on a carpet, hands brushing a wall, a curtain pulled apart, a clicking handle, the opening of a cupboard door. In the case above their heads a loose book shifted under a touch. "Only Joyce, only Mabel Warren, only Mrs. Henne-Falcon," a crescendo of reasuring thought before the chandelier burst, like a fruit tree, into bloom.

The voices of the children rose shrilly into the radiance. "Where's Peter?" "Have you looked upstairs?" "Where's Francis?" but they were silenced again by Mrs. Henne-Falcon's scream. But she was not the first to notice Francis Morton's stillness, where he had collapsed against the wall at the touch of his brother's hand. Peter continued to hold the clenched fingers in an arid and puzzled grief. It was not merely that his brother was dead. His brain, too young to realize the full paradox, yet wondered with an obscure self-pity why it was that the pulse of his brother's fear went on and on, when Francis was now where he had been always told there was no more terror and no more darkness.

The Circular Ruins

by Jorge Luis Borges

Translated by James E. Irby
from *Fictions* and *Labyrinths*

And if he left off dreaming about you . . .
—*Through the Looking Glass, VI*

No one saw him disembark in the unanimous night, no one saw
the bamboo canoe sinking into the sacred mud, but within a few
days no one was unaware that the silent man came from the
South and that his home was one of the infinite villages upstream,
on the violent mountainside, where the Zend tongue is not con-
taminated with Greek and where leprosy is infrequent. The truth
is that the obscure man kissed the mud, came up the bank without pushing aside (probably without feeling) the brambles which
dilacerated his flesh, and dragged himself, nauseous and blood-
stained, to the circular enclosure crowned by a stone tiger or
horse, which once was the color of fire and now was that of
ashes. This circle was a temple, long ago devoured by fire, which
the malarial jungle had profaned and whose god no longer received the homage of men. The stranger stretched out beneath
the pedestal. He was awakened by the sun high above. He evi-
denced without astonishment that his wounds had closed; he shut
his pale eyes and slept, not out of bodily weakness but out of
determination of will. He knew that this temple was the place
required by his invincible purpose; he knew that, downstream,
the incessant trees had not managed to choke the ruins of another

propitious temple, whose gods were also burned and dead; he knew that his immediate obligation was to sleep. Towards midnight he was awakened by the disconsolate cry of a bird. Prints of bare feet, some figs and a jug told him that men of the region had respectfully spied upon his sleep and were solicitous of his favor or feared his magic. He felt the chill of fear and sought out a burial niche in the dilapidated wall and covered himself with some unknown leaves.

The purpose which guided him was not impossible, though it was supernatural. He wanted to dream a man: he wanted to dream him with minute integrity and insert him into reality. This magical project had exhausted the entire content of his soul; if someone had asked him his own name or any trait of his previous life, he would not have been able to answer. The uninhabited and broken temple suited him, for it was a minimum of visible world; the nearness of the peasants also suited him, for they would see that his frugal necessities were supplied. The rice and fruit of their tribute were sufficent sustenance for his body, consecrated to the sole task of sleeping and dreaming.

At first, his dreams were chaotic; somewhat later, they were of a dialectical nature. The stranger dreamt that he was in the center of a circular amphitheater which in some way was the burned temple: clouds of silent students filled the gradins; the faces of the last ones hung many centuries away and at a cosmic height, but were entirely clear and precise. The man was lecturing to them on anatomy, cosmography, magic; the countenances listened with eagerness and strove to respond with understanding, as if they divined the importance of the examination which would redeem one of them from his state of vain appearance and interpolate him into the world of reality. The man, both in dreams and awake, considered his phantoms' replies, was not deceived by impostors, divined a growing intelligence in certain perplexities. He sought a soul which would merit participation in the universe.

After nine or ten nights, he comprehended with some bitterness that he could expect nothing of those students who passively accepted his doctrines, but that he could of those who, at times, would venture a reasonable contradiction. The former, though worthy of love and affection, could not rise to the state of individuals; the latter pre-existed somewhat more. One afternoon (now his afternoons too were tributaries of sleep, now he remained awake only for a couple of hours at dawn) he dismissed the vast illusory college forever and kept one single student. He was a silent boy, sallow, sometimes obstinate, with sharp features which reproduced those of the dreamer. He was not long disconcerted by his companions' sudden elimination; his progress, after a few special lessons, astounded his teacher. Nevertheless, catastrophe ensued. The man emerged from sleep one day as if from a viscous desert, looked at the vain light of afternoon, which at first he confused with that of dawn, and understood that he had not really dreamt. All that night and all day, the intolerable lucidity of insomnia weighed upon him. He tried to explore the jungle, to exhaust himself; amidst the hemlocks, he was scarcely able to manage a few snatches of feeble sleep, fleetingly mottled with with some rudimentary visions which were useless. He tried to convoke the college and had scarcely uttered a few brief words of exhortation, when it became deformed and was extinguished. In his almost perpetual sleeplessness, his old eyes burned with tears of anger.

He comprehended that the effort to mold the incoherent and vertiginous matter dreams are made of was the most arduous task a man could undertake, though he might penetrate all the enigmas of the upper and lower orders: much more arduous than weaving a rope of sand or coining the faceless wind. He comprehended that an initial failure was inevitable. He swore he would forget the enormous hallucination which had misled him at first, and he sought another method. Before putting it into effect, he dedicated a month to replenishing the powers his delirium had wasted. He abandoned any premeditation of dreaming and, almost at once, was able to sleep for a considerable part of the day. The few times he dreamt during this period, he did not take notice of the dreams. To take up his task again, he waited until the moon's disk was perfect. Then, in the afternoon, he purified himself in the waters of the river, worshiped the planetary gods, uttered the lawful syllables of a powerful name and slept. Almost immediately, he dreamt of a beating heart.

He dreamt it as active, warm, secret, the size of a closed fist, of garnet color in the penumbra of a human body as yet without face or sex; with minute love he dreamt it, for fourteen lucid nights. Each night he perceived it with greater clarity. He did not touch it, but limited himself to witnessing it, observing it, perhaps correcting it with his eyes. He perceived it, lived it, from many distances and many angles. On the fourteenth night he touched the pulmonary artery with his finger, and then the whole heart, inside and out. The examination satisfied him. Deliberately, he did not dream for a night; then he took the heart again, invoked the name of a planet and set about to envision another of the principal organs. Within a year he reached the skeleton, the eyelids. The innumerable hair was perhaps the most difficult task. He dreamt a complete man, a youth, but this youth could not rise nor did he speak nor could he open his eyes. Night after night, the man dreamt him as asleep.

In the Gnostic cosmogonies, the demiurgi knead and mold a red Adam who cannot stand alone; as unskillful and crude and elementary as this Adam of dust was the Adam of dreams fabricated by the magician's nights of effort. One afternoon, the man almost destroyed his work but then repented. (It would have been better for him had he destroyed it.) Once he had completed his supplications to the numina of the earth and the river, he threw himself down at the feet of the effigy which was perhaps a tiger and perhaps a horse, and implored its unknown succor. That twilight, he dreamt of the statue. He dreamt of it as a living, tremulous thing: it was not an atrocious mongrel of tiger and horse, but both these vehement creatures at once and also a bull, a rose, a tempest. This multiple god revealed to him that its earthly name was Fire, that in the circular temple (and in others of its kind) people had rendered it sacrifices and cult and that it would magically give life to the sleeping phantom, in such a way that all creatures except Fire itself and the dreamer would believe him to be a man of flesh and blood. The man was ordered by the divinity to instruct his creature in its rites, and send him to the other broken temple whose pyramids survived downstream, so that in this deserted edifice a voice might give glory to the god. In the dreamer's dream, the dreamed one awoke.

The magician carried out these orders. He devoted a peroid of time (which finally comprised two years) to revealing the arcana of the universe and of the fire cult to his dream child. Inwardly, it pained him to be separated from the boy. Under the pretext of pedagogical necessity, each day he prolonged the hours he dedicated to his dreams. He also redid the right shoulder, which was perhaps deficient. At times, he was troubled by the impression that all this had happened before. . . . In general, his days were happy; when he closed his eyes, he would think: *Now I shall be with my son.* Or, less often: *The child I have engendered awaits me and will not exist if I do not go to him.*

Gradually, he accustomed the boy to reality. Once he ordered him to place a banner on a distant peak. The following day, the banner flickered from the mountain top. He tried other analogous experiments, each more daring than the last. He understood with certain bitterness that his son was ready—and perhaps impatient—to be born. That night he kissed him for the first time and sent him to the other temple whose debris showed white downstream, through many leagues of inextricable jungle and swamp. But first (so that he would never know he was a phantom, so that he would be thought a man like others) he instilled into him a complete oblivion of his years of apprenticeship.

The man's victory and peace were dimmed by weariness. At dawn and at twilight, he would prostrate himself before the stone figure, imagining perhaps that his unreal child was practicing the same rites, in other circular ruins, downstream; at night, he would not dream, or would dream only as all men do. He perceived the sounds and forms of the universe with a certain colorlessness: his absent son was being nurtured with these diminutions of his soul. His life's purpose was complete; the man persited in a kin of ecstasy. After a time, which some narrators of his story prefer to compute in years and others in lustra, he was awakened one midnight by two boatmen; he could not see their faces, but they told him of a magic man in a temple of the North who could walk upon fire and not be burned. The magician suddenly remembered the words of the god. He recalled that, of all the creatures of the world, fire was the only one that knew his son was a phantom. This recollection, at first soothing, finally tormented him. He feared his son might meditate on his abnormal privilege and discover in some way that his condition was that of a mere image. Not to be a man, to be the projection of another man's dream, what a feeling of humiliation, of vertigo! All fathers are interested in the children they have procreated (they have permitted to exist) in mere confusion or pleasure; it was natural that the magician should fear for the future of that son, created in thought, limb by limb and feature by feature, in a thousand and one secret nights.

The end of his meditations was sudden, though it was foretold in certain signs. First (after a long drought) a far-away cloud on a hill, light and rapid as a bird; then, toward the south, the sky which had the rose color of the leopard's mouth; them the smoke which corroded the metallic nights; finally, the panicky flight of the animals. For what was happening had happened many centuries ago. The ruins of the fire god's sanctuary were destroyed by fire. In a birdless dawn the magician saw the concentric blaze close round the walls. For a moment, he thought of taking refuge in the river, but then he knew that death was coming to crown his old age and absolve him of his labors. He walked into the shreds of flame. But they did not bite into his flesh, they caressed him and engulfed him without heat or combustion. With relief, with humiliation, with terror, he understood that he too was a mere appearance, dreamt by another.

The Shout

by Robert Graves

When we arrived with our bags at the Asylum cricket ground, the chief medical officer, whom I had met at the house where I was staying, came up to shake hands. I told him that I was only scoring for the Lampton team today (I had broken a finger the week before, keeping wicket on a bumpy pitch). He said: 'Oh, then you'll have an interesting companion.'

'The other scoresman?' I asked.

'Crossley is the most intelligent man in the asylum,' answered the doctor, 'a wide reader, a first-class chess-player, and so on. He seems to have travelled all over the word. He's been sent here for delusions. His most serious delusion is that he a murderer, and his story is that he killed two men and a woman at Sydney, Australia. The other delusion, which is more humorous, is that his soul is split in pieces—whatever that means. He edits our monthly magazine, he stage manages our Christmas theatricals, and he gave a most original conjuring performance the other day. You'll like him.'

He introduced me. Crossley, a big man of forty or fifty, had a queer, not unpleasant, face. But I felt a little uncomfortable, sitting next to him in the scoring box, his black-whiskered hands so close to mine. I had no fear of physical violence, only the sense of being in the presence of a man of unusual force, even perhaps, it somehow came to me, of occult powers.

It was hot in the scoring box in spite of the wide window. 'Thunderstorm weather,' said Crossley, who spoke in what country people call a 'college voice,' though I could not identify the college. 'Thunderstorm weather makes us patients behave even more irregularly than usual.'

I asked whether any patients were playing.

'Two of them, this first wicket partnership. The tall one, B. C. Brown, played for Hants three years ago, and the other is a good club player. Pat Slingsby usually turns out for us too—the Australian fast bowler, you know—but we are dropping him to-day. In weather like this he is apt to bowl at the batsman's head. He is not insane in the usual sense, merely magnificently ill-tempered. The doctors can do nothing with him. He wants shooting, really.' Crossley began talking about the doctor. 'A good-hearted fellow and, for a mental-hospital physician, technically well advanced. He actually studies morbid pyschology and is fairly well-read, up to about the day before yesterday. I have a good deal of fun with him. He reads neither German nor French, so I keep a stage or two ahead in psychological fashions; he has to wait for the English translations. I invent significant dreams for him to interpret; I find he likes me to put in snakes and apple pies, so I usually do. He is convinced that my mental trouble is due to the good old "antipaternal fixation"—I wish it were as simple as that.'

Then Crossley asked me whether I could score and listen to a story at the same time. I said that I could. It was slow cricket.

'My story is true,' he said, 'every word of it. Or, when I say that my story is "true," I mean at least that I am telling it in a new way. It is always the same story, but I sometimes vary the climax and even recast the characters. Variation keeps it fresh and therefore true. If I were always to use the same formula, it would soon drag and become false. I am interested in keeping it alive, and it is a true story, every word of it. I know the people in it personally. They are Lampton people.'

We decided that I should keep score of the runs and extras and that he should keep the bowling analysis, and at the fall of every wicket we should copy from each other. This made story-telling possible.

Richard awoke one morning saying to Rachel: 'But what an unusual dream.'

'Tell me, my dear,' she said, 'and hurry, because I want to tell you mine.'

'I was having a conversation,' he said, 'with a person (or persons, because he changed his appearance so often) of great intelligence, and I can clearly remember the argument. Yet this is the first time I have ever been able to remember any argument that came to me in sleep. Usually my dreams are so different from waking that I can only describe them if I say: "It is as though I were living and thinking as a tree, or a bell, or middle C, or a five-pound note; as though I had never been human." Life there is sometimes rich for me and sometimes poor, but I repeat, in every case so different, that if I were to say: "I had a conversation," or "I was in love," or "I heard music," or "I was angry," it would be as far from the fact as if I tried to explain a problem of philosophy, as Rabelais's Panurge did to Thaumanst, merely by grimacing with my eyes and lips."

'It is much the same with me,' she said. 'I think that when I am asleep I become, perhaps, a stone with all the natural appetites and convictions of a stone. "Senseless as a stone" is a proverb, but there may be more sense in a stone, more sensiblility, more sensitivity, more sentiment, more sensibleness, than in many men and women. And no less sensuality,' she added thoughtfully.

It was Sunday morning, so that they could lie in bed, their arms about each other, without troubling about the time; and they were childless, so breakfast could wait. He told her that in his dream he was walking in the sand hills with this person or persons, who said to him: 'These sand hills are a part neither of the sea before us nor of the grass links behind us, and are not related to the mountains beyond the links. They are of themselves. A man walking on the sand hills soon knows this by the tang in the air, and if he were to refrain from eating and drinking, from sleeping and speaking, from thinking and desiring, he could continue among them for ever without change. There is no life and no death in the sand hills. Anything might happen in the sand hills.'

Rachel said that this was nonsense, and asked: 'But what was the argument? Hurry up!'

He said it was about the whereabouts of the soul, but that now she had put it out of his head by hurrying him. All that he remembered was that the man was first a Japanese, then an Italian, and finally a kangaroo.

In return she eagerly told her dream, gabbling over the words. 'I was walking in the sand hills; there were rabbits there, too; how does that tally with what he said of life and death? I saw the man and you walking arm in arm towards me, and I ran from you both and I noticed that he had a black silk handkerchief; he ran after me and my shoe buckle came off and I could not wait to pick it up. I left it lying, and he stooped and put it into his pocket.'

'How do you know that it was the same man?' he asked.

'Because,' she said, laughing, 'he had a black face and wore a blue coat like that picture of Captain Cook. And because it was in the sand hills.'

He said, kissing her neck: 'We not only live together and talk together and sleep together, but it seems we now even dream together.'

So they laughed.

Then he got up and brought her breakfast.

At about half past eleven, she said: 'Go out now for a walk, my dear, and bring home something for me to think about: and be back in time for dinner at one o'clock.'

It was a hot morning in the middle of May, and he went out through the wood and struck the coast road, which after half a mile led into Lampton.

('Do you know Lampton well?' asked Crossley. 'No,' I said, 'I am only here for the holidays, staying with friends.')

He went a hundred yards along the coast road, but then turned off and went across the links: thinking of Rachel and watching the blue butterflies and looking at the heath roses and thyme, and thinking of her again, and how strange it was that they could be so near to each other; and then taking a pinch of gorse flower and smelling it, and considering the smell and thinking, 'If she should die, what would become of me?' and taking a slate from the low wall and skimming it across the pond and thinking, 'I am a clumsy fellow to be her husband'; and walking towards the sand hills, and then edging away again, perhaps half in fear of meeting the person of their dream, and at last making a half circle towards the old church beyond Lampton, at the foot of the mountain.

The morning service was over and the people were out by the cromlechs behind the church, walking in twos and threes, as the custom was, on the smooth turf. The squire was talking in a loud voice about King Charles, the Martyr: 'A great man, a very great man, but betrayed by those he loved best,' and the doctor was arguing about organ music with the rector. There was a group of children playing ball. 'Throw it here, Elsie. No, to me, Elsie, Elsie, Elsie.' Then the rector appeared and pocketed the ball and said that it was Sunday; they should have remembered. When he was gone they made faces after him.

Presently a stranger came up and asked permission to sit down beside Richard; they began to talk. The stranger had been to the church service and wished to discuss the sermon. The text had been the immortality of the soul: the last of a series of sermons that had begun at Easter. He said that he could not grant the preacher's premiss that *the soul is continually resident in the body.* Why should this be so? What duty did the soul perform in the daily routine task of the body? The soul was neither the brain, nor the lungs, nor the stomach, nor the heart, nor the mind, nor the imagination. Surely it was a thing apart? Was it not indeed less likely to be resident in the body than outside the body? He had no proof one way or the other, but he would say: Birth and death are so odd a mystery that the principle of life may well lie outside the body which is the visible evidence of living. 'We cannot,' he said, 'even tell to a nicety what are the moments of birth and death. Why, in Japan, where I have travelled, they reckon a man to be already one year old when he is born; and lately in Italy a dead man—but come and walk on the sand hills and let me tell you my conclusions. I find it easier to talk when I am walking.'

Richard was frightened to hear this, and to see the man wipe his forehead with a black silk handkerchief. He stuttered out something. At this moment the children, who had crept up behind the cromlech, suddenly, at an agreed signal, shouted loud in the ears of the two men; and stood laughing. The stranger was startled into anger; he opened his mouth as if he were about to curse them, and bared his teeth to the gums. Three of the children screamed and ran off. But the one whom they called Elsie fell down in her fright and lay sobbing. The doctor, who was near, tried to comfort her. 'He has a face like a devil,' they heard the child say.

The stranger smiled good-naturedly: 'And a devil I was not so very long ago. That was in Northern Australia, where I lived with the black fellows for twenty years. "Devil" is the nearest English word for the position that they gave me in their tribe; and they also gave me an eighteenth-century British naval uniform to wear as my ceremonial dress. Come and walk with me in the sand hills and let me tell you the whole story. I have a passion for walking in the sand hills: that is why I came to this town . . . My name is Charles.'

Richard said: 'Thank you, but I must hurry home to my dinner.'

'Nonsense,' said Charles, 'dinner can wait. Or, if you wish, I can come to dinner with you. By the way, I have had nothing to eat since Friday. I am without money.'

Richard felt uneasy. He was afraid of Charles, and did not wish to bring him home to dinner because of the dream and the sand hills and the handkerchief: yet on the other hand the man was intelligent and quiet and decently dressed and had eaten nothing since Friday; if Rachel knew that he had refused him a meal, she would renew her taunts. When Rachel was out of sorts, her favourite complaint was that he was overcareful about money; though when she was at peace with him, she owned that he was the most generous man she knew, and that she did not mean what she said; when she was angry with him again, out came the taunt of stinginess: 'Tenpence-halfpenny,' she would say, 'tenpence-halfpenny and threepence of that in stamps'; his ears would burn and he would want to hit her. So he said now: 'By all means come along to dinner, but that little girl is still sobbing for fear of you. You ought to do something about it.'

Charles beckoned her to him and said a single soft word; it was an Australian magic word, he afterwards told Richard, meaning *Milk:* immediately Elsie was comforted and came to sit on Charles' knee and played with the buttons of his waistcoat for awhile until Charles sent her away.

'You have strange powers, Mr. Charles,' Richard said.

Charles, answered: 'I am fond of children, but the shout startled me; I am pleased that I did not do what, for a moment, I was tempted to do.'

'What was that?' asked Richard.

'I might have shouted myself,' said Charles.

'Why,' said Richard, 'they would have liked that better. It would have been a great game for them. They probably expected it of you.'

'If I had shouted,' said Charles, 'my shout would have either killed them outright or sent them mad. Probably it would have killed them, for they were standing close.'

Richard smiled a little foolishly. He did not know whether or not he was expected to laugh, for Charles spoke so gravely and carefully. So he said: 'Indeed, what sort of shout would that be? Let me hear you shout.'

'It is not only children who would be hurt by my shout,' Charles said. 'Men can be sent raving mad by it; the strongest, even, would be flung to the ground. It is a magic shout that I learned from the chief devil of the Northern Territory. I took eighteen years to perfect it, and yet I have used it, in all, no more than five times.'

Richard was so confused in his mind with the dream and the

handkerchief and the word spoken to Elsie that he did not know
what to say, so he muttered: 'I'll give you fifty pounds now to
clear the cromlechs with a shout.'

'I see that you do not believe me,' Charles said. 'Perhaps you
have never before heard of the terror shout?'

Richard considered and said: 'Well, I have read of the hero
shout which the ancient Irish warriors used, that would drive
armies backwards; and did not Hector, the Trojan, have a terrible
shout? And there were sudden shouts in the woods of Greece.
They were ascribed to the god Pan and would infect men with a
madness of fear; from this legend indeed the word "panic" has
come into the English language. And I remember another shout in
the *Mabinogion,* in the story of Lludd and Llevelys. It was a
shriek that was heard on every May Eve and went through all
hearts and so scared them that the men lost their hue and their
strength and the women their children, and the youths and
maidens their senses, and the animals and trees, the earth and the
waters were left barren. But it was caused by a dragon.'

'It must have been a British magician of the dragon clan,' said
Charles. 'I belonged to the Kangaroos. Yes, that tallies. The effect
is not exactly given, but near enough.'

They reached the house at one o'clock, and Rachel was at the
door, the dinner ready. 'Rachel,' said Richard, 'here is Mr. Charles
to dinner; Mr. Charles is a great traveller.'

Rachel passed her hand over her eyes as if to dispel a cloud,
but it may have been the sudden sunlight. Charels took her hand
and kissed it, which surprised her. Rachel was graceful, small,
with eyes unusually blue for the blackness of her hair, delicate in
her movements, and with a voice rather low-pitched; she had a
freakish sense of humour.

('You would like Rachel,' said Crossley, 'she visits me here
sometimes.')

Of Charles it would be difficult to say one thing or another:
he was of middle age, and tall; his hair grey; his face never still for
a moment; his eyes large and bright, sometimes yellow, sometimes brown, sometimes grey; his voice changed its tone and
accent with the subject; his hands were brown and hairy at the

back, his nails well cared for. Of Richard it is enough to say that he was a musician, not a strong man but a lucky one. Luck was his strength.

After dinner Charles and Richard washed the dishes together, and Richard suddenly asked Charles if he would let him hear the shout: for he thought that he could not have peace of mind until he had heard it. So horrible a thing was, surely, worse to think about than to hear: for now he believed in the shout.

Charles stopped washing up; mop in hand. 'As you wish,' said he, 'but I have warned you what a shout it is. And if I shout it must be in a lonely palce where nobody else can hear; and I shall not shout in the second degree, the degree which kills certainly, but in the first, which terrifies only, and when you want me to stop put your hands to yours ears.'

'Agreed,' said Richard.

'I have never yet shouted to satisfy an idle curiosity,' said Charles, 'but only when in danger of my life from enemies, black or white, and once when I was alone in the desert without food or drink. Then I was forced to shout, for food.'

Richard thought: 'Well, at least I am a lucky man, and my luck will be good enough even for this.'

'I am not afraid,' he told Charles.

'We will walk out on the sand hills tomorrow early,' Charles said, 'when nobody is stirring; and I will shout. You say you are not afraid.'

But Richard was very much afraid, and what made his fear worse was that somehow he could not talk to Rachel and tell her of it: he knew that if he told her she would either forbid him to go or she would come with him. If she forbade him to go, the fear of the shout and the sense of cowardice would hang over him ever afterwards; but if she came with him, either the shout would be nothing and she would have a new taunt for his credulity and Charles would laugh with her, or if it were something, she might well be driven mad. So he said nothing.

Charles was invited to sleep at the cottage for the night, and they stayed up late talking.

Rachel told Richard when they were in bed that she liked

Charles and that he certainly was a man who had seen many things, though a fool and a big baby. Then Rachel talked a great deal of nonsense, for she had had two glasses of wine, which she seldom drank, and she said: 'Oh, my dearest, I forgot to tell you. When I put on my buckled shoes this morning while you were away I found a buckle missing. I must have noticed that it was lost before I went to sleep last night and yet not fixed the loss firmly in my mind, so that it came out as a discovery in my dream; but I have a feeling, in fact I am certain, that Mr. Charles has that buckle in his pocket; and I am sure that he is the man whom we met in our dream. But I don't care, not I.'

Richard grew more and more afraid, and he dared not tell of the black silk handkerchief, or of Charles' invitations to him to walk in the sand hills. And what was worse, Charles had used only a white handkerchief while he was in the house, so that he could not be sure whether he had seen it after all. Turning his head away, he said lamely: 'Well, Charles knows a lot of things. I am going for a walk with him early tomorrow if you don't mind; an early walk is what I need.'

'Oh, I'll come too,' she said.

Richard could not think how to refuse her; he knew that he had made a mistake in telling her of the walk. But he said: 'Charles will be very glad. At six o'clock then.'

At six o'clock he got up, but Rachel after the wine was too sleepy to come with them. She kissed him goodbye and off he went with Charles.

Richard had had a bad night. In his dreams nothing was in human terms, but confused and fearful, and he had felt himself more distant from Rachel than he had ever felt since their marriage, and the fear of the shout was gnawing at him. He was also hungry and cold. There was a stiff wind blowing towards the sea from the mountains and a few splashes of rain. Charles spoke hardly a word, but chewed a stalk of grass and walked fast.

Richard felt giddy, and said to Charles: 'Wait a moment, I have a stitch in my side.' So they stopped, and Richard asked, gasping: 'What sort of shout is it? Is it loud, or shrill? How is it produced? How can it madden a man?'

Charles was silent, so Richard went on with a foolish smile: 'Sound, though, is a curious thing. I remember once, when I was at Cambridge, that a King's College man had his turn of reading the evening lesson. He had not spoken ten words before there was a groaning and ringing and creaking, and pieces of wood and dust fell from the roof; for his voice was exactly attuned to that of the building, so that he had to stop, else the roof might have fallen; as you can break a wine glass by playing its note on a violin.'

Charels consented to answer: 'My shout is not a matter of tone or vibration but something not to be explained. It is a shout of pure evil, and there is no fixed place for it on the scale. It may take any note. It is pure terror, and if it were not for a certain intention of mine, which I need not tell you, I would not shout for you.'

Richard has a great gift of fear, and this new account of the shout disturbed him more and more; he wished himself at home in bed, and Charles two continents away. But he was fascinated. They were crossing the links now and going through the bent grass that pricked through his stockings and soaked them.

Now they were on the bare sand hills. From the highest of them Charles looked about him; he could see the beach stretched out for two miles and more. There was no one in sight. Then Richard saw Charles take something out of his pocket and begin carelessly to juggle with it as he stood, tossing it from finger tip to finger tip and spinning it up with finger and thumb to catch it on the back of his hand. It was Rachel's buckle.

Richard's breath came in gasps, his heart beat violently and he nearly vomited. He was shivering with cold, and yet sweating. Soon they came to an open place among the sand hills near the sea. There was a raised bank with sea holly growing on it and a little sickly grass; stones were strewn all around, brought there, it seemed, by the sea years before. Though the place was behind the first rampart of sand hills, there was a gap in the line through which a high tide might have broken, and the winds that continually swept through the gap kept them uncovered of sand. Richard had his hands in his trouser pockets for warmth and was nervously twisting a soft piece of wax around his right forefinger—a candle end that was in his pocket from the night before when he had gone downstairs to lock the door.

'Are you ready?' asked Charles.

Richard nodded.

A gull dipped over the crest of the hand hills and rose again screaming when it saw them. 'Stand by the sea holly,' said Richard, with a dry mouth, 'and I'll be here among the stones, not too near. When I raise my hand, shout! When I put my fingers to my ears, stop at once.'

So Charles walked twenty steps towards the holly. Richard saw his broad back and the black silk handkerchief sticking from his pocket. He rememberd the dream, and the shoe buckle and Elsie's fear. His resolution broke: he hurriedly pulled the piece of wax in two, and sealed his ears. Charles did not see him.

He turned, and Richard gave the signal with his hand.

Charles leaned forward oddly, his chin thrust out, his teeth bared, and never before had Richard seen such a look of fear on a man's face. He had not been prepared for that. Charles' face, that was usually soft and changing, uncertain as a cloud, now hardened to a rough stone mask, dead white at first, and then flushing outwards from the cheek bones red and redder, and at last as black, as if he were about to choke. His mouth then slowly opened to the full, and Richard fell on his face, his hands to his ears, in a faint.

When he came to himself he was lying alone among the stones. He sat up, wondering numbly whether he had been there long. He felt very weak and sick, with a chill on his heart that was worse than the chill of his body. He could not think. He put his hand down to lift himself up and it rested on a stone, a larger one than most of the others. He picked it up and felt its surface, absently. His mind wandered. He began to think about shoemaking, a trade of which he had known nothing, but now every trick was familiar to him. 'I must be a shoemaker,' he said aloud.

Then he corrected himself: 'No, I am a musician. Am I going mad?' He threw the stone from him; it struck against another and bounced off.

He asked himself: 'Now why did I say that I was a shoemaker?

It seemed a moment ago that I knew all there was to be known about shoemaking and now I know nothing at all about it. I must get home to Rachel. Why did I ever come out?'

Then he saw Charles on a sand hill a hundred yards away, gazing out to sea. He remembered his fear and made sure that the wax was in his ears: he stumbled to his feet. He saw a flurry on the sand and there was a rabbit lying on its side, twitching in a convulsion. As Richard moved towards it, the flurry ended: the rabbit was dead. Richard crept behind a sand hill out of Charles' sight and then struck homeward, running awkwardly in the soft sand. He had gone twenty paces before he came upon the gull. It was standing stupidly on the sand and did not rise at his approach, but fell over dead.

How Richard reached home he did not know, but there he was opening the back door and crawling upstairs on his hands and knees. He unsealed his ears.

Rachel was sitting up in bed, pale and trembling. 'Thank God you're back,' she said; 'I have had a nightmare, the worst of all my life. It was frightful. I was in my dream, in the deepest dream of all, like the one of which I told you. I was like a stone, and I was aware of you near me; you were you, quite plain, though I was a stone, and you were in great fear and I could do nothing to help you, and you were waiting for something and the terrible thing did not happen to you, but it happened to me. I can't tell you what it was, but it was as though all my nerves cried out in pain at once, and I was pierced through and through with a beam of some intense evil light and twisted inside out. I woke up and my heart was beating so fast that I had to gasp for breath. Do you think I had a heart attack and my heart missed a beat? They say it feels like that. Where have you been, dearest? Where is Mr. Charles?'

Richard sat on the bed and held her hand. 'I have had a bad experience too,' he said. 'I was out with Charles by the sea and as he went ahead to climb on the highest sand hill I felt very faint and fell down among a patch of stones, and when I came to myself I was in a desperate sweat of fear and had to hurry home. So I came back running alone. It happened perhaps half an hour ago,' he said.

He did not tell her more. He asked, could he come back to bed and would she get breakfast; That was a thing she had not done all the years they were married.

'I am as ill as you,' said she. It was understood between them always that when Rachel was ill, Richard must be well.

'You are not,' said he, and fainted again.

She helped him to bed ungraciously and dressed herself and went slowly downstairs. A smell of coffee and bacon rose to meet her and there was Charles, who had lit the fire, putting two breakfasts on a tray. She was so relieved at not having to get breakfast and so confused by her experience that she thanked him and called him a darling, and he kissed her hand gravely and pressed it. He had made the breakfast exactly to her liking: the coffee was strong and eggs fried on both sides.

Rachel fell in love with Charles. She had often fallen in love with men before and since her marriage, but it was her habit to tell Richard when this happened, as he agreed to tell her when it happened to him: so that the suffocation of passion was given a vent and there was no jealousy, for she used to say (and he had the liberty of saying): 'Yes, I am in *love* with so-and-so, but I only *love* you.'

That was as far as it had ever gone. But this was different. Somehow, she did not know why, she could not own to being in love with Charles: for she no longer loved Richard. She hated him for being ill, and said that he was lazy, and a sham. So about noon he got up, but went groaning around the bedroom until she sent him back to bed to groan.

Charles helped her with the housework, doing all the cooking, but he did not go up to see Richard, since he had not been asked to do so. Rachel was ashamed, and aplologized to Charles for Richard's rudeness in running away from him. But Charles said mildly that he took it as no insult; he had felt queer himself that morning; it was as though something evil was astir in the air as they reached the sand hills. She told him that she too had had the same queer feeling.

Later she found all Lampton talking of it. The doctor maintained that it was an earth tremor, but the country people said that it had been the Devil passing by. He had come to fetch the black soul of Solomon Jones, the gamekeeper, found dead that morning in his cottage by the sand hills.

When Richard could go downstairs and walk about a little without groaning, Rachel sent him to the cobbler's to get a new buckle for her shoe. She came with him to the bottom of the garden. The path ran beside a steep bank. Richard looked ill and groaned slightly as he walked, so Rachel, half in anger, half in fun, pushed him down the bank, where he fell sprawling among the nettles and old iron. Then she ran back into the house laughing loudly.

Richard sighed, tried to share the joke against himself with Rachel—but she had gone—heaved himself up, picked the shoes from among the nettles, and after awhile walked slowly up the bank, out of the gate, and down the lane in the unaccustomed glare of the sun.

When he reached the cobbler's he sat down heavily. The cobbler was glad to talk to him. 'You are looking bad,' said the cobbler.

Richard said: 'Yes, on Friday morning I had a bit of a turn; I am only now recovering from it.'

'Good God,' burst out the cobbler, 'if you had a bit of a turn, what did I not have? It was as if someone handled me raw, without my skin. It was as if someone seized my very soul and juggled with it, as you might juggle with a stone, and hurled me away. I shall never forget last Friday morning.'

A strange notion came to Richard that it was the cobbler's soul which he had handled in the form of a stone. 'It may be,' he thought, 'that the souls of every man and woman and child in Lampton are lying there.' But he said nothing about this, asked for a buckle, and went home.

Rachel was ready with a kiss and a joke; he might have kept silent, for his silence always made Rachel ashamed. 'But,' he thought, 'why make her ashamed? From shame she goes to self-justification and picks a quarrel over something else and it's ten times worse. I'll be cheerful and accept the joke.'

He was unhappy. And Charles was established in the house: gentle-voiced, hard-working, and continually taking Richard's part against Rachel's scoffing. This was galling, because Rachel did not resent it.

('The next part of the story,' said Crossley, 'is the comic relief, an account of how Richard went again to the sand hills, to the heap of stones, and identified the souls of the doctor and rector—the doctor's because it was shaped like a whiskey bottle and the rector's because it was as black as original sin—and how he proved to himself that the notion was not fanciful. But I will skip that and come to the point where Rachel two days later suddenly became affectionate and loved Richard she said, more than ever before.')

The reason was that Charles had gone away, nobody knows where, and had relaxed the buckle magic for the time, because he was confident that he could renew it on his return. So in a day or two Richard was well again and everything was as it had been, until one afternoon the door opened, and there stood Charles.

He entered without a word of greeting and hung his hat upon a peg. He sat down by the fire and asked: 'When is supper ready?'

Richard looked at Rachel, his eyebrows raised, but Rachel seemed fascinated by the man.

She answered: 'Eight o'clock,' in her low voice, and stooping down, drew off Charles' muddy boots and found him a pair of Richard's slippers.

Charles said: 'Good. It is now seven o'clock. In another hour, supper. At nine o'clock the boy will bring the evening paper. At ten o'clock, Rachel, you and I sleep together.'

Richard thought that Charles must have gone suddenly mad. But Rachel answered quietly: 'Why, of course, my dear.' Then she turned viciously to Richard: 'And you run away, little man!' she said, and slapped his cheek with all her strength.

Richard stood puzzled, nursing his cheek. Since he could not believe that Rachel and Charles had both gone mad together, he must be mad himself. At all events, Rachel knew her mind, and they had a secret compact that if either of them ever wished to break the marriage promise, the other should not stand in the way. They had made this compact because they wished to feel themselves bound by love rather than by ceremony. So he said as calmly as he could: 'Very well, Rachel. I shall leave you two together.'

Charles flung a boot at him, saying: 'If you put your nose inside the door between now and breakfast time, I'll shout the ears off your head.'

Richard went out this time not afraid, but cold inside and quite clear-headed. He went through the gate, down the lane, and across the links. It wanted three hours yet until sunset. He joked with the boys playing stump cricket on the school field. He skipped stones. He thought of Rachel and tears started to his eyes. Then he sang to comfort himself. 'Oh, I'm certainly mad,' he said, 'and what in the world has happened to my luck?'

At last he came to the stones. 'Now,' he said, 'I shall find my soul in this heap and I shall crack it into a hundred pieces with this hammer'—he had picked up the hammer in the coal shed as he came out.

Then he began looking for his soul. Now, one may recognize the soul of another man or woman, but one can never recognize one's own. Richard could not find his. But by chance he came upon Rachel's soul and recognized it (a slim green stone with glints of quartz in it) because she was estranged from him at the time. Against it lay another stone, an ugly misshapen flint of a mottled brown. He swore: 'I'll destroy this. It must be the soul of Charles.'

He kissed the soul of Rachel; it was like kissing her lips. Then he took the soul of Charles and poised his hammer. 'I'll knock you into fifty fragments!'

He paused. Richard had scruples. He knew that Rachel loved Charles better than himself, and he was bound to respect the compact. A third stone (his own, it must be) was lying the other side of Charles' stone; it was of smooth grey granite, about the size of a cricket ball. He said to himself: 'I will break my own soul in pieces and that will be the end of me.' The world grew black, his eyes ceased to focus, and he all but fainted. But he recovered himself, and with a great cry brought down the coal hammer crack, and crack again, on the grey stone.

It split in four pieces, exuding a smell like gunpowder: and when Richard found that he was still alive and whole, he began to laugh and laugh. Oh, he was mad, quite mad! He flung the hammer away, lay down exhausted, and fell asleep.

He awoke as the sun was just setting. He went home in confusion, thinking: 'This is a very bad dream and Rachel will help me out of it.'

When he came to the edge of the town he found a group of men talking excitedly under a lamppost. One said: 'About eight o'clock it happened, didn't it?' The other said: 'Yes.' A third said: 'Ay, mad as a hatter. "Touch me," he says, "and I'll shout. I'll shout you mad." And the inspector says: "Now, Crossley, put your hands up, we've got you cornered at last." "One last chance," says he. "Go and leave me or I'll shout you stiff and dead." '

Richard has stopped to listen. 'And what happened to Crossley then?' he said. 'And what did the woman say?'

' "For Christ's sake," she said to the inspector, "go away or he'll kill you." '

'And did he shout?'

'He didn't shout. He screwed up his face for a moment and drew in his breath. A'mighty, I've never seen such a ghastly looking face in my life. I had to take three or four brandies afterwards. And the inspector he drops the revolver and it goes off; but nobody hit. Then suddenly a change comes over this man Crossley. He claps his hands to his side and again to his heart, and his face goes smooth and dead again. Then he begins to laugh and dance and cut capers. And the woman stares and can't believe her eyes and the police lead him off. If he was mad before, he was just harmless dotty now; and they had no trouble with him. He's been taken off in the ambulance to the Royal West County Asylum.'

So Richard went home to Rachel and told her everything and she told him everything, though there was not much to tell. She had not fallen in love with Charles, she said; she was only teasing Richard and she had never said anything or heard Charles say anything in the least like what he told her; it was part of his dream. She loved him always and only him, for all his faults;

which she went through—his stinginess, his talkativeness, his untidiness. Charles and she had eaten a quiet supper, and she did think it had been bad of Richard to rush off without a word of explanation and stay away for three hours like that. Charles might have murdered her. He did start pulling her about a bit, in fun, wanting her to dance with him, and then the knock came on the door, and the inspector shouted: 'Walter Charles Crossley, in the name of the King, I arrest you for the murder of George Grant, Harry Grant, and Ada Coleman at Sydney, Australia.' Then Charles had gone absolutely mad. He had pulled out a shoe buckle and said to it: 'Hold her for me.' And then he had told the police to go away or he'd shout them dead. After that he made a dreadful face at them and went to pieces altogether. 'He was rather a nice man; I liked his face so much and feel so sorry for him.'

'Did you like that story?' asked Crossley.

'Yes,' said I, busy scoring, 'a Milesian tale of the best. Lucius Apuleius, I congratulate you.'

Crossley turned to me with a troubled face and hands clenched trembling. 'Every word of it is true,' he said. 'Crossley's soul was cracked in four pieces and I'm a madman. Oh, I don't blame Richard and Rachel. They are a pleasant, loving pair of fools and I've never wished them harm; they often visit me here. In any case, now that my soul lies broken in pieces, my powers are gone. Only one thing remains to me,' he said, 'and that is the shout.'

I had been so busy scoring and listening to the story at the same time that I had not noticed the immense bank of black cloud that swam up until it spread across the sun and darkened the whole sky. Warm drops of rain fell: a flash of lightning dazzled us and with it came a smashing clap of thunder.

In a moment all was confusion. Down came a drenching rain, the cricketers dashed for cover, the lunatics began to scream bellow, and fight. One tall young man, the same B. C. Brown who had once played for Hants, pulled all his clothes off and ran

about stark naked. Outside the scoring box an old man with a
beard began to pray to the thunder: 'Bah! Bah! Bah!'

Crossley's eyes twitched proudly. 'Yes,' said he, pointing to
the sky, 'that's the sort of shout it is; that's the effect it has; but I
can do better than that.' Then his face fell suddenly and became
childishly unhappy and anxious. 'Oh dear God,' he said, 'he'll
shout at me again, Crossley will. He'll freeze my marrow.'

The rain was rattling on the tin roof so that I could hardly
hear him. Another flash, another clap of thunder even louder
than the first. 'But that's only the second degree,' he shouted in
my ear; 'it's the first that kills.'

'Oh,' he said. 'Don't you understand?' He smiled foolishly.
'I'm Richard now, and Crossley will kill me.'

The naked man was running about brandishing a cricket stump
in either hand and screaming: an ugly sight. 'Bah! Bah! Bah!'
prayed the old man, the rain spouting down his back from his
uptilted hat.

'Nonsense,' said I, 'be a man, remember you're Crossley.
You're a match for a dozen Richards. You played a game and
lost, because Richard had the luck; but you still have the shout.'

I was feeling rather mad myself. Then the Asylum doctor
rushed into the scoring box, his flannels streaming wet, still
wearing pads and batting gloves, his glasses gone; he had heard
our voices raised, and tore Crossley's hands from mine. 'To your
dormitory at once, Crossley!' he ordered.

'I'll not go,' said Crossley, proud again, 'you miserable Snake
and Apple Pie Man!'

The doctor seized him by his coat and tried to hustle him out.

Crossley flung him off, his eyes blazing with madness. 'Get
out,' he said, 'and leave me alone here or I'll shout. Do you hear?
I'll shout. I'll kill the whole damn lot of you. I'll shout the
Asylum down. I'll wither the grass. I'll shout.' His face was
distorted in terror. A red spot appeared on either cheek bone and
spread over his face.

I put my fingers to my ears and ran out of the scoring box. I
had run perhaps twenty yards, when an indescribable pang of fire
spun me about and left me dazed and numbed. I escaped death

somehow; I suppose that I am lucky, like the Richard of the story. But the lightning struck Crossley and the doctor dead.

Crossley's body was found rigid, the doctor's was crouched in a corner, his hands to his ears. Nobody could understand this because death had been instantaneous, and the doctor was not a man to stop his ears against thunder.

It makes a rather unsatisfactory end to the story to say that Rachel and Richard were the friends with whom I was staying—Crossley had described them most accurately—but that when I told them that a man called Charles Crossley had been struck at the same time as their friend the doctor, they seemed to take Crossley's death casually by comparison with his. Richard looked blank; Rachel said: 'Crossley? I think that was the man who called himself the Australian Illusionist and gave that wonderful conjuring show the other day. He had practically no apparatus but a black silk handkerchief. I liked his face so much. Oh, and Richard didn't like it at all.'

'No, I couldn't stand the way he looked at you all the time,' Richard said.

The Door

by E. B. White

Everything (he kept saying) is something it isn't. And everybody is always somewhere else. Maybe it was the city, being in the city, that made him feel how queer everything was and that it was something else. Maybe (he kept thinking) it was the names of the things. The names were tex and frequently koid. Or they were flex and oid or they were duroid (sani) or flexsan (duro), but everything was glass (but not quite glass) and the thing that you touched (the surface, washable, crease-resistant) was rubber, only it wasn't quite rubber and you didn't quite touch it but almost. The wall, which was glass but thrutex, turned out on being approached not to be a wall, it was something else, it was an opening or doorway—and the doorway (through which he saw himself approaching) turned out to be something else, it was a wall. And what he had eaten not having agreed with him.

He was in a washable house, but he wasn't sure. Now about those rats, he kept saying to himself. He meant the rats that the Professor had driven crazy by forcing them to deal with problems which were beyond the scope of rats, the insoluble problems. He meant the rats that had been trained to jump at the square card with the circle in the middle, and the card (because it was

113

something it wasn't) would give way and let the rat into a place where the food was, but then one day it would be a trick played on the rat, and the card would be changed, and the rat would jump but the card wouldn't give way and it was an impossible situation (for a rat) and the rat would go insane and into its eyes would come the unspeakably bright imploring look of the frustrated, and after the convulsions were over and the frantic racing around, then the passive stage would set in and the willingness to let anything be done to it, even if it was something else.

He didn't know which door (or wall) or opening in the house to jump at, to get through, because one was an opening that wasn't a door (it was a void, or koid) and the other was a wall that wasn't an opening, it was a sanitary cupboard of the same color. He caught a glimpse of his eyes staring into his eyes, in the thrutex, and in them was the expression he had seen in the picture of the rats—weary after convulsions and the frantic racing around, when they were willing and did not mind having anything done to them. More and more (he kept saying) I am confronted by a problem which is incapable of solution (for this time even if he chose the right door, there would be no food behind it) and that is what madness is, and things seeming different from what they are. He heard, in the house where he was, in the city to which he had gone (as toward a door which might, or might not, give way), a noise—not a loud noise but more of a low prefabricated humming. It came from a place in the base of the wall (or stat) where the flue carrying the filterable air was, and not far from the Minipiano, which was made of the same material nailbrushes are made of, and which was under the stairs. "This, too, has been tested," she said, pointing, but not at it, "and found viable." It wasn't a loud noise, he kept thinking, sorry that he had seen his eyes, even though it was through his own eyes that he had seen them.

First will come the convulsions (he said), then the exhaustion, then the willingness to let anything be done. "And you better believe it *will* be."

All his life he had been confronted by situations which were incapable of being solved, and there was a deliberateness behind all this, behind this changing of the card (or door), because they would always wait till you had learned to jump at the certain card (or door)—the one with the circle—and then they would change it on you. There have been so many doors changed on me, he said, in the last twenty years, but it is now becoming clear that it is an impossible situation, and the question is whether to jump again, even though they ruffle you in the rump with a blast of air—to make you jump. He wished he wasn't standing by the Minipiano. First they would teach you the prayers and the Psalms, and that would be the right door (the one with the circle), and the long sweet words with the holy sound, and that would be the one to jump at to get where the food was. Then one day you jumped and it didn't give way, so that all you got was the bump on the nose, and the first bewilderment, the first young bewilderment.

I don't know whether to tell her about the door they substituted or not, he said, the one with the equation on it and the picture of the amoeba reproducing itself by division. Or the one with the photostatic copy of the check for thirty-two dollars and fifty cents. But the jumping was so long ago, although the bump is . . . how those old wounds hurt! Being crazy this way wouldn't be so bad if only, if only. If only when you put your foot forward to take a step, the ground wouldn't come up to meet your foot the way it does. And the same way in the street (only I may never get back to the street unless I jump at the right door), the curb coming up to meet your foot, anticipating ever so delicately the weight of the body, which is somewhere else. "We could take your name," she said, "and send it to you." And it wouldn't be so bad if only you could read a sentence all the way through without jumping (your eye) to something else on the same page; and then (he kept thinking) there was that man out in Jersey, the one who started to chop his trees down, one by one, the man who began talking about how he would take his house to pieces, brick by brick, because he faced a problem incapable of solution, probably, so he began to hack at the trees in the yard, began to pluck with trembling fingers at the bricks in the house. Even if a house is not washable, it is worth taking down. It is not till later that the exhaustion sets in.

But it is inevitable that they will keep changing the doors on you, he said, because that is what they are for; and the thing is to get used to it and not let it unsettle the mind. But that would mean not jumping, and you can't. Nobody can not jump. There will be no not-jumping. Among rats, perhaps, but among people never. Everybody has to keep jumping at a door (the one with the circle on it) because that is the way everybody is, specially some people. You wouldn't want me, standing here, to tell you, would you, about my friend the poet (deceased) who said, "My heart has followed all my days something I cannot name"? (It had the circle on it.) And like many poets, although few so beloved, he is gone. It killed him, the jumping. First, of course, there were the preliminary bouts, the convulsions, and the calm and the willingness.

I remember the door with the picture of the girl on it (only it was spring), her arms outstretched in loveliness, her dress (it was the one with the circle on it) uncaught, beginning the slow, clear, blinding cascade—and I guess we would all like to try that door again, for it seemed like the way and for a while it was the way, the door would open and you would go through winged and exalted (like any rat) and the food would be there, the way the Professor had it arranged, everything O.K., and you had chosen the right door for the world was young. The time they changed that door on me, my nose bled for a hundred hours—how do you like that, Madam? Or would you prefer to show me further through this so strange house, or you could take my name and send it to me, for although my heart has followed all my days something I cannot name, I am tired of the jumping and I do not know which way to go, Madam, and I am not even sure that I am not tried beyond the endurance of man (rat, if you will) and have taken leave of sanity. What are you following these days, old friend, after your recovery from the last bump? What is the name, or is it something you cannot name? The rats have a name for it by this time, perhaps, but I don't know what they call it. I call it plexikoid and it comes in sheets, something like insulating board, unattainable and ugli-proof.

And there was the man out in Jersey, because I keep thinking about his terrible necessity and the passion and trouble he had gone to all those years in the indescribable abundance of a householder's detail, building the estate and the planting of the trees and in spring the lawn-dressing and in fall the bulbs for the spring burgeoning, and the watering of the grass on the long light evenings in summer and the gravel for the driveway (all had to be thought out, planned) and the decorative borders, probably, the perennials and the bug spray, and the building of the house from plans of the architect, first the sills, then the studs, then the full corn in the ear, the floors laid on the floor timbers, smoothed, and then the carpets upon the smooth floors and the curtains and the rods therefor. And then, almost without warning, he would be jumping at the same old door and it wouldn't give: they had changed it on him, making life no longer supportable under the elms in the elm shade, under the maples in the maple shade.

"Here you have the maximum of openness in a small room."

It was impossible to say (maybe it was the city) what made him feel the way he did, and I am not the only one either, he kept thinking—ask any doctor if I am. The doctors, they know how many there are, they even know where the trouble is only they don't like to tell you about the prefrontal lobe because that means making a hole in your skull and removing the work of centuries. It took so long coming, this lobe, so many, many years. (Is is something you read in the paper, perhaps?) And now, the strain being so great, the door having been changed by the Professor once too often . . . but it only means a whiff of ether, a few deft strokes, and the higher animal becomes a little easier in his mind and more like the lower one. From now on, you see, that's the way it will be, the ones with the small prefrontal lobes will win because the other ones are hurt too much by this incessant bumping. They can stand just so much, eh, Doctor? (And what is that, pray, that you have in your hand?) Still, you never can tell, eh, Madam?

He crossed (carefully) the room, the thick carpet under him

softly, and went toward the door carefully, which was glass and he could see himself in it, and which, at his approach, opened to allow him to pass through; and beyond he half expected to find one of the old doors that he had known, perhaps the one with the circle, the one with the girl her arms outstretched in loveliness and beauty before him. But he saw instead a moving stairway, and descended in light (he kept thinking) to the street below and to the other people. As he stepped off, the ground came up slightly, to meet his foot.

The Machine Stops

by E. M. Forster

Part I

THE AIRSHIP

Imagine, if you can, a small room hexagonal in shape like the cell of a bee. It is lighted neither by window nor by lamp, yet it is filled with a soft radiance. There are no apertures for ventilation, yet the air is fresh. There are no musical instruments, and yet, at the moment that my meditation opens, this room is throbbing with melodious sounds. An armchair is in the center, by its side a reading desk—that is all the furniture. And in the armchair there sits a swaddled lump of flesh—a woman, about five feet high, with a face as white as a fungus. It is to her that the little room belongs.

An electric bell rang.

The woman touched a switch and the music was silent.

"I suppose I must see who it is," she thought, and set her chair in motion. The chair, like the music, was worked by machinery, and it rolled her to the other side of the room, where the bell still rang importunately.

"Who is it?" she called. Her voice was irritable, for she had been interrupted often since the music began. She knew several thousand people; in certain directions human intercourse had advanced enormously.

But when she listened into the receiver, her white face wrinkled into smiles, and she said:

"Very well. Let us talk, I will isolate myself. I do not expect anything important will happen for the next five minutes—for I can give you fully five minutes, Kuno. Then I must deliver my lecture on 'Music during the Australian Period.' "

She touched the isolation knob, so that no one else could speak to her. Then she touched the lighting apparatus, and the little room was plunged into darkness.

"Be quick!" she called, her irritation returning. "Be quick, Kuno; here I am in the dark wasting my time."

But it was fully fifteen seconds before the round plate that she held in her hands began to glow. A faint blue light shot across it, darkening to purple, and presently she could see the image of her son, who lived on the other side of the earth, and he could see her.

"Kuno, how slow you are."

He smiled gravely.

"I really believe you enjoy dawdling."

"I have called you before, Mother, but you were always busy or isolated. I have something particular to say."

"What is it, dearest boy? Be quick. Why could you not send it by pneumatic post?"

"Because I prefer saying such a thing. I want—"

"Well?"

"I want you to come and see me."

Vashti watched his face in the blue plate.

"But I can see you!" she exclaimed. "What more do you want?"

"I want to see you not through the Machine," said Kuno. "I want to speak to you not through the wearisome Machine."

"Oh, hush!" said his mother, vaguely shocked. "You mustn't say anything against the Machine."

"Why not?"

"One mustn't."

"You talk as if a god had made the Machine," cried the other. "I believe that you pray to it when you are unhappy. Men made it, do not forget that. Great men, but men. The Machine is much, but it is not everything. I see something like you in this plate, but I do not see you. I hear something like you through this telephone, but I do not hear you. That is why I want you to come. Come and stop with me. Pay me a visit, so that we can meet face to face, and talk about the hopes that are in my mind."

She replied that she could scarcely spare the time for a visit.

"The airship barely takes two days to fly between me and you."

"I dislike airships."

"Why?"

"I dislike seeing the horrible brown earth, and the sea, and the stars when it is dark. I get no ideas in an airship."

"I do not get them anywhere else."

"What kind of ideas can the air give you?"

He paused for an instant.

"Do you not know four big stars that form an oblong, and three stars close together in the middle of the oblong, and hanging from these stars, three other stars?"

"No, I do not. I dislike the stars. But did they give you an idea? How interesting; tell me."

"I had an idea that they were like a man."

"I do not understand."

"The four big stars are the man's shoulders and his knees. The three stars in the middle are like the belts that men wore once, and the three stars hanging are like a sword."

"A sword?"

"Men carried swords about with them, to kill animals and other men."

"It does not strike me as a very good idea, but it is certainly original. When did it come to you first?"

"In the airship—" He broke off, and she fancied that he looked sad. She could not be sure, for the Machine did not transmit *nuances* of expression. It gave only a general idea of people—an idea that was good enough for all practical purposes,

Vashti thought. The imponderable bloom, declared by a discredited philosophy to be the actual essence of intercourse, was rightly ignored by the Machine, just as the imponderable bloom of the grape was ignored by the manufacturers of artificial fruit. Something "good enough" had long since been accepted by our race.

"The truth is," he continued, "that I want to see these stars again. They are curious stars. I want to see them not from the airship, but from the surface of the earth, as our ancestors did, thousands of years ago. I want to visit the surface of the earth."

She was shocked again.

"Mother, you must come, if only to explain to me what is the harm of visiting the surface of the earth."

"No harm," she replied, controlling herself. "But no advantage. The surface of the earth is only dust and mud; no life remains on it, and you would need a respirator, or the cold of the outer air would kill you. One dies immediately in the outer air."

"I know; of course I shall take all precautions."

"And besides—"

"Well?"

She considered, and chose her words with care. Her son had a queer temper, and she wished to dissuade him from the expedition.

"It is contrary to the spirit of the age," she asserted.

"Do you mean by that, contrary to the Machine?"

"In a sense, but—"

His image in the blue plate faded.

"Kuno!"

He had isolated himself.

For a moment Vashit felt lonely.

Then she generated the light, and the sight of her room, flooded with radiance and studded with electric buttons, revived her. There were buttons and switches everywhere—buttons to call for food, for music, for clothing. There was the hot-bath button, by pressure of which a basin of (imitation) marble rose out of the floor, filled to the brim with a warm deodorized liquid. There was the cold-bath button. There was the button that produced literature. And there were of course the buttons by which she communicated with her friends. The room, though it contained nothing, was in touch with all that she cared for in the world.

Vashit's next move was to turn off the isolation switch, and all the accumulations of the last three minutes burst upon her. The room was filled with the noise of bells, and speaking tubes. What was the new food like? Could she recommend it? Had she had any ideas lately? Might one tell her one's own ideas? Would she made an engagement to visit the public nurseries at an early date?—say this day month.

To most of these questions she replied with irritation—a growing quality in that accelerated age. She said that the new food was horrible. That she could not visit the public nurseries through press of engagements. That she had no ideas of her own but had just been told one—that four stars and three in the middle were like a man: she doubted there was much in it. Then she switched off her correspondents, for it was time to deliver her lecture on Australian music.

The clumsy system of public gatherings had been long since abandoned; neither Vashti nor her audience stirred from their rooms. Seated in her armchair she spoke, while they in their armchairs heard her, fairly well, and saw her, fairly well. She opened with a humorous account of music in the pre-Mongolian epoch, and went on to describe the great outburst of song that followed the Chinese conquest. Remote and primeval as were the methods of I-San-So and the Brisbane school, she yet felt (she said) that study of them might repay the musician of today: they had freshness; they had, above all, ideas.

Her lecture, which lasted ten minutes, was well received, and at its conclusion she and many of her audience listened to a lecture on the sea; there were ideas to be got from the sea; the speaker had donned a respirator and visited it lately. Then she fed, talked to many friends, had a bath, talked again, and summoned her bed.

The bed was not to her liking. It was too large, and she had a feeling for a small bed. Complaint was useless, for beds were of the same dimension all over the world, and to have had an alternative size would have involved vast alterations in the Machine. Vashti isolated herself—it was necessary, for neither day nor night existed under the ground—and reviewed all that had happened since she had summoned the bed last. Ideas? Scarcely any. Events—was Kuno's invitation an event?

By her side, on the little reading desk, was a survival from the ages of liter—one book. This was the Book of the Machine. In it were instructions against every possible contingency. If she was hot or cold or dyspeptic or at a loss for a word, she went to the book, and it told her which button to press. The Central Committee published it. In accordance with a growing habit, it was richly bound.

Sitting up in the bed, she took it reverently in her hands. She glanced round the glowing room as if someone might be watching her. Then, half ashamed, half joyful, she murmured "O Machine! O Machine!" and raised the volume to her lips. Thrice she kissed it, thrice inclined her head, thrice she felt the delirium of acquiescence. Her ritual performed, she turned to page 1367, which gave the times of the departure of the airships from the island in the Southern Hemisphere, under whose soil she lived, to the island in the Northern Hemisphere, whereunder lived her son.

She thought, "I have not the time."

She made the room dark and slept; she woke and made the room light; she ate and exchanged ideas with her friends, and listened to music and attended lectures; she made the room dark and slept. Above her, beneath her, and around her, the Machine hummed eternally; she did not notice the noise, for she had been born with it in her ears. The earth, carrying her, hummed as it sped through silence, turning her now to the invisible sun, now to the invisible stars. She awoke and made the room light.

"Kuno!"

"I will not talk to you," he answered, "until you come."

"Have you been on the surface of the earth since we spoke last?"

His image faded.

Again she consulted the book. She became very nervous and lay back in her chair palpitating. Think of her as without teeth or hair. Presently she directed the chair to the wall, and pressed an unfamiliar button. The wall swung apart slowly. Through the opening she saw a tunnel that curved slightly, so that its goal was not visible. Should she go to see her son, here was the beginning of the journey.

Of course, she knew all about the communication system. There was nothing mysterious in it. She would summon a car and it would fly with her down the tunnel until it reached the lift that communicated with the airship station: the system had been in use for many, many years, long before the universal establishment of the Machine. And of course she had studied the civilization that had immediately preceded her own—the civilization that had mistaken the functions of the system, and had used it for bringing people to things, instead of for bringing things to people. Those funny old days, when men went for change of air instead of changing the air in their rooms! And yet—she was frightened of the tunnel: she had not seen it since her last child was born. It curved—but not quite as she remembered; it was brilliant—but not quite as brilliant as a lecturer had suggested. Vashti was seized with the terrors of direct experience. She shrank back into the room, and the wall closed up again.

"Kuno," she said, "I cannot come to see you. I am not well."

Immediately an enormous apparatus fell onto her out of the ceiling, a thermometer was automatically inserted between her lips, a stethoscope was automatically laid upon her heart. She lay powerless. Cool pads soothed her forehead. Kuno had telegraphed to her doctor.

So the human passions still blundered up and down in the Machine. Vashti drank the medicine that the doctor projected into her mouth, and the machinery retired into the ceiling. The voice of Kuno was heard asking how she felt.

"Better." Then, with irritation: "But why do you not come to me instead?"

"Because I cannot leave this place."

"Why?"

"Because, any moment, something tremendous may happen."

"Have you been on the surface of the earth yet?"

"Not yet."

"Then what is it?"

"I will not tell you through the machine."

She resumed her life.

But she thought of Kuno as a baby, his birth, his removal to the public nurseries, her one visit to him there, his visits to her—visits which stopped when the Machine had assigned him a room on the other side of the earth. "Parents, duties of," said the book of the Machine, "cease at the moment of birth. P. 422327483." True, but there was something special about Kuno—indeed there had been something special about all her children—and, after all, she must brave the journey if he desired it. And "something tremendous might happen." What did that mean? The nonsense of a youthful man, no doubt, but she must go. Again she pressed the unfamiliar button, again the wall swung back, and she saw the tunnel that curved out of sight. Clasping the Book, she rose, tottered onto the platform, and summoned the car. Her room closed behind her: the journey to the Northern Hemisphere had begun.

Of course, it was perfectly easy. The car approached and in it she found armchairs exactly like her own. When she signaled, it stopped, and she tottered into the lift, One other passenger was in the lift, the first fellow creature she had seen face to face for months. Few traveled in these days, for, thanks to the advance of science, the earth was exactly alike all over. Rapid intercourse, from which the previous civilization had hoped so much, had ended by defeating itself. What was the good of going to Peking when it was just like Shrewsbury? Why return to Shrewsbury when it would be just like Peking? Men seldom moved their bodies; all unrest was concentrated in the soul.

The airship service was a relic from the former age. It was kept up because it was easier to keep it up than to stop it or to diminish it, but it now far exceeded the wants of the population. Vessel after vessel would rise from the vomitories of Rye or of Christchurch (I use the antique names), would sail into the crowded sky, and would draw up at the wharves of the south—empty. So nicely adjusted was the system, so independent of meteorology, that the sky, whether calm or cloudy, resembled a vast kaleidoscope whereon the same patterns periodically recurred. The ship on which Vashti sailed started now at sunset, now at dawn. But always, as it passed above Rheims, it would neighbor the ship that served between Helsingfors and the Brazils, and, every third time it surmounted the Alps, the fleet of Palermo would cross its track behind. Night and day, wind and storm, tide and earthquake impeded man no longer. He had harnessed Leviathan. All the old literature, with its praise of Nature and its fear of Nature, rang false as the prattle of a child.

Yet as Vashti saw the vast flank of the ship, stained with exposure to the outer air, her horror of direct experience returned. It was not quite like the airship in the cinematophote. For one thing it smelled—not strongly or unpleasantly, but it did smell, and with her eyes shut she should have known that a new thing was close to her. Then she had to walk to it from the lift, had to submit to glances from the other passengers. The man in front dropped his Book—no great matter, but it disquieted them all. In the rooms, if the Book was dropped, the floor raised it mechanically, but the gangway to the airship was not so prepared, and the sacred volume lay motionless. They stopped—the thing was unforeseen—and the man, instead of picking up his property, felt the muscles of his arm to see how they had failed him. Then someone actually said with direct utterance: "We shall be late"—and they trooped on board, Vashti treading on the pages as she did so.

Inside, her anxiety increased. The arrangements were old-fashioned and rough. There was even a female attendant, to whom she would have to announce her wants during the voyage. Of course, a revolving platform ran the length of the boat, but she was expected to walk from it to her cabin. Some cabins were better than others, and she did not get the best. She thought the attendant had been unfair, and spasms of rage shook her. The glass valves had closed; she could not go back. She saw, at the end of the vestibule, the lift in which she had ascended going quietly up and down, empty. Beneath those corridors of shining tiles were rooms, tier below tier, reaching far into the earth, and in each room there sat a human being, eating, or sleeping, or producing ideas. And buried deep in the hive was her own room. Vashti was afraid.

"O Machine! O Machine!" she murmured, and caressed her Book, and was comforted.

Then the sides of the vestibule seemed to melt together, as do the passages that we see in dreams; the lift vanished, the Book that had been dropped slid to the left and vanished, polished tiles rushed by like a stream of water, there was a slight jar, and the airship, issuing from its tunnel, soared above the waters of a tropical ocean.

It was night. For a moment she saw the coast of Sumatra edged by the phosphorescence of waves, and crowned by lighthouses, still sending forth their disregarded beams. These also vanished, and only the stars distracted her. They were not motionless, but swayed to and fro above her head, thronging out of one skylight into another, as if the universe and not the airship was careening. And, as often happens on clear nights, they seemed now to be in perspective, now on a plane; now piled tier beyond tier into the infinite heavens, now concealing infinity, a roof limiting for ever the visions of men. In either case they seemed intolerable. "Are we to travel in the dark?" called the passengers angrily, and the attendant, who had been careless, generated the light and pulled down the blinds of pliable metal. When the airships had been built, the desire to look direct at things still lingered in the world. Hence the extraordinary number of skylights and windows, and the proportionate discomfort to those who were civilized and refined. Even in Vashti's cabin one star peeped throgh a flaw in the blind, and after a few hours' uneasy slumber, she was disturbed by an unfamiliar glow, which was the dawn.

Quick as the ship had sped westward, the earth had rolled eastward quicker still, and had dragged back Vashti and her companions toward the sun. Science could prolong the night, but only for a little, and those high hopes of neutralizing the earth's diurnal revolution had passed, together with hopes that were possibly higher. To "keep pace with the sun," or even to outstrip it, had been the aim of the civilization preceding this. Racing airplanes had been built for the purpose, capable of enormous speed, and steered by the greatest intellects of the epoch. Round the globe went eastward quicker still, horrible accidents occurred, and the Committee of the Machine, at the time rising into prominence, declared the pursuit illegal, unmechanical, and punishable by Homelessness.

Of Homelessness more will be said later.

Doubtless the Committee was right. Yet the attempt to "defeat the sun" aroused the last common interest that our race experienced about the heavenly bodies, or indeed about anything. It was the last time that men were compacted by thinking of a power outside the world. The sun had conquered, yet it was the end of his spiritual dominion. Dawn, midday, twilight, the zodiacal path, touched neither men's lives nor their hearts, and science retreated into the ground, to concentrate herself upon problems that she was certain of solving.

So when Vashti found her cabin invaded by a rosy finger of light, she was annoyed and tried to adjust the blind. But the blind flew up altogether, and she saw through the skylight small pink clouds, swaying against a background of blue, and as the sun crept higher, its radiance entered direct, brimming down the wall, like a golden sea. It rose and fell with the airship's motion, just as waves rise and fall, but it advanced steadily, as the tide advances. Unless she was careful, it would strike her face. A spasm of horror shook her, and she rang for the attendant. The attendant too was horrified, but she could do nothing; it was not her place to mend the blind. She could only suggest that the lady should change her cabin, which she accordingly prepared to do.

People were almost exactly alike all over the world, but the attendant of the airship, perhaps owing to her exceptional duties, had grown a little out of the common. She had often to address passengers with direct speech, and this had given her a certain roughness and originality of manner. When Vashti swerved away from the sunbeams with a cry, she behaved barbarically—she put out her hand to steady her.

"How dare you!" exclaimed the passenger. "You forget yourself!"

The woman was confused, and apologized for not having let

her fall. People never touched one another. The custom had become obsolete, owing to the Machine.

"Where are we now?" asked Vashti haughtily.

"We are over Asia," said the attendant, anxious to be polite.

"Asia?"

"You must excuse my common way of speaking. I have got into the habit of calling places over which I pass by their unmechanical names."

"Oh, I remember Asia. The Mongols came from it."

"Beneath us, in the open air, stood a city that was once called Simla."

"Have you ever heard of the Mongols and of the Brisbane school?"

"No."

"Brisbane also stood in the open air."

"Those mountains to the right—let me show you them." She pushed back a metal blind. The main chain of the Himalayas was revealed. "They were once called the Roof of the World, those mountains."

"What a foolish name!"

"You must remember that, before the dawn of civilization, they seemed to be an impenetrable wall that touched the stars. It was supposed that no one but the gods could exist above their summits. How we have advanced, thanks to the Machine!"

"How we have advanced, thanks to the Machine!" said Vashti.

"How we have advanced, thanks to the Machine!" echoed the passenger who had dropped his Book the night before and who was standing in the passage.

"And that white stuff in the cracks?—what is it?"

"I have forgotten its name."

"Cover the window, please. These mountains give me no ideas."

The northern aspect of the Himalayas was in deep shadow: on the Indian slope the sun had just prevailed. The forest had been destroyed during the literature epoch for the purpose of making newspaper pulp, but the snows were awakening to their morning glory, and clouds still hung on the breasts of Kinchinjunga. In the plain were seen the ruins of cities, with diminished rivers creeping by their walls, and by the sides of these were sometimes the signs of vomitories, marking the cities of today. Over the whole prospect airships rushed, crossing and intercrossing with incredible aplomb, and rising nonchalantly when they desired to escape the perturbations of the lower atmosphere and to traverse the Roof of the World.

"We have indeed advanced, thanks to the Machine," repeated the attendant, and hid the Himalayas behind a metal blind.

The day dragged wearily forward. The passengers sat each in his cabin, avoiding one another with an almost physical repulsion and longing to be once more under the surface of the earth. There were eight or ten of them, mostly young males, sent out from the public nurseries to inhabit the rooms of those who had died in various parts of the earth. The man who had dropped his Book was on the homeward journey. He had been sent to Sumatra for the purpose of propagating the race. Vashti alone was traveling by her private will.

At midday she took a second glance at the earth. The airship was crossing another range of mountains, but she could see little, owing to clouds. Masses of black rock hovered below her and merged indistinctly into gray. Their shapes were fantastic; one of them resembled a prostrate man.

"No ideas here," murmured Vashti, and hid the Caucasus behind a metal blind.

In the evening she looked again. They were crossing a golden sea, in which lay many small islands and one peninsual.

She repeated, "No ideas here," and hid Greece behind a metal blind.

PART II

THE MENDING APPARATUS

By a vestibule, by a lift, by a tubular railway, by a platform, by a sliding door—by reversing all the steps of her departure did Vashti arrive at her son's room, which exactly resembled her own. She might well declare that the visit was superfluous. The buttons, the knobs, the reading desk with the Book, the temperature, the atmosphere, the illumination—all were exactly the same. And if Kuno himself, flesh of her flesh, stood close beside her at last, what profit was there in that? She was too well bred to shake him by the hand.

Averting her eyes, she spoke as follows:

"Here I am. I have had the most terrible journey and greatly retarded the development of my soul. It is not worth it, Kuno; it is not worth it. My time is too precious. The sunlight almost touched me, and I have met with the rudest people. I can stop only a few minutes. Say what you want to say, and then I must return."

"I have been threatened with Homelessness," said Kuno.

She looked at him now.

"I have been threatened with Homelessness, and I could not tell you such a thing through the Machine."

Homelessness means death. The victim is exposed to the air, which kills him.

"I have been outside since I spoke to you last. The tremendous thing had happened, and they have discovered me."

"But why shouldn't you go outside?" she exclaimed. "It is perfectly legal, perfectly mechanical, to visit the surface of the earth. I have lately been to a lecture on the sea; there is no objections to that; one simply summons a respirator and gets an Egression permit. It is not the kind of thing that spiritually minded people do, and I begged you not to do it, but there is no legal objection to it."

"I did not get an Egression permit."

"Then how did you get out?"

"I found out a way of my own."

The phrase conveyed no meaning to her, and he had to repeat it.

"A way of your own?" she whispered. "But that would be wrong."

"Why?"

The question shocked her beyond measure.

"You are beginning to worship the Machine," he said coldly. "You think it irreligious of me to have found out a way of my own. It was just what the Committee thought, when they threatened me with Homelessness."

At this she grew angry. "I worship nothing!" she cried. "I am most advanced. I don't think you irreligious, for there is no such thing as religion left. All the fear and the superstition that existed once have been destroyed by the Machine. I meant only that to find out a way of your own was—Besides there is no new way out."

"So it is always supposed."

"Except through the vomitories, for which one must have an Egression permit, it is impossible to get out. The Book says so."

"Well, the Book's wrong, for I have been out on my feet."

For Kuno was possessed of a certain physical strength.

By these days it was a demerit to be muscular. Each infant was examined at birth, and all who promised undue strength were destroyed. Humanitarians may protest, but it would have been no true kindness to let an athlete live; he would never have been happy in that state of life to which the Machine had called him; he would have yearned for trees to climb, rivers to bathe in, meadows and hills against which he might measure his body. Man must be adapted to his surroundings, must he not? In the dawn of the world our weakly must be exposed on Mount Taygetus; in its twilight our strong will suffer euthanasia, that the Machine may progress, that the Machine may progress, that the Machine may progress eternally.

"You know that we have lost the sense of space. We say space is 'annihilated,' but we have annihilated not space but the sense thereof. We have lost a part of ourselves. I determined to recover it, and I began by walking up and down the platform of the railway outside my room. Up and down, until I was tired, and so did recapture the meaning of 'Near' and 'Far.' 'Near' is a place to which I can get quickly *on my feet,* not a place to which the train or the airship will take me quickly. 'Far' is a place to which I cannot get quickly on my feet; the vomitory is 'far,' though I could be there in thirty-eight seconds by summoning the train. Man is the measure. That was my first lesson. Man's feet are the measure for distance, his hands are the measure for ownership, his body is the measure for all that is lovable and desirable and strong. Then I went further: it was then that I called to you for the first time, and you would not come.

"This city, as you know, is built deep beneath the surface of the earth, with only the vomitories protruding. Having paced the platform outside my own room, I took the lift to the next platform and paced that also, and so with each in turn, until I came to the topmost, above which begins the earth. All the platforms were exactly alike, and all that I gained by visiting them was to develop my sense of space and my muscles. I think I should have been content with this—it is not a little thing—but as I walked and brooded, it occurred to me that our cities had been built in the days when men still breathed the outer air, and that there had been ventilation shafts for the workmen. I could think of nothing but these ventilation shafts. Had they been destroyed by all the foodtubes and medicine tubes and music tubes that the Machine has evolved lately? Or did traces of them remian? One thing was certain. If I came upon them anywhere, it would be in the railway tunnels of the topmost story. Everywhere else, all space was accounted for.

"I am telling my story quickly, but don't think that I was not a coward or that your answers never depressed me. It is not the proper thing, it is not mechanical, it is not decent to walk along a railway tunnel. I did not fear that I might tread upon a live rail and be killed. I feared something far more intangible—doing what was not contemplated by the Machine. Then I said to myself, 'Man is the measure,' and I went, and after many visits I found an opening.

"The tunnels, of course, were lighted. Everything is light, artificial light; darkness is the exception. So when I saw a black gap in the tiles, I knew that it was an exception, and rejoiced. I put in my arm—I could put in no more at first—and waved it round and round in ecstasy. I loosened another tile, and put in my head, and shouted into the darkness: 'I am coming, I shall do it yet,' and my voice reverberated down endless passages. I seemed to hear the spirits of those dead workmen who had returned each evening to the starlight and to their wives, and all the generations who had lived in the open air called back to me, 'You will do it yet, you are coming.' "

He paused, and, absurd as he was, his last words moved her. For Kuno had lately asked to be a father, and his request had been refused by the Committee. His was not a type that the Machine desired to hand on.

"Then a train passed. It brushed by me, but I thrust my head and arms into the hole. I had done enough for one day, so I crawled back to the platform, went down in the lift, and summoned my bed. Ah, what dreams! And again I called you, and again you refused."

She shook her head and said:

"Don't. Don't talk of these terrible things. You make me miserable. You are throwing civilization away."

"But I had got back the sense of space, and a man cannot rest then. I determined to get in at the hole and climb the shaft. And so I exercised my arms. Day after day I went through ridiculous movements, until my flesh ached, and I could hang by my hands and hold the pillow of my bed outstretched for many minutes. Then I summoned a respirator, and started.

"It was easy at first. The mortar had somehow rotted, and I soon pushed some more tiles in, and clambered after them into the darkness, and the spirits of the dead comforted me. I don't know what I mean by that. I just say what I felt. I felt, for the first time, that a protest had been lodged against corruption, and that even as the dead were comforting me, so I was comforting the unborn. I felt that humanity existed, and that it existed without clothes. How can I possibly explain this? It was naked, humanity seemed naked, and all these tubes and buttons and machineries neither came into the world with us, nor will they follow us out, nor do they matter supremely while we are here. Had I been strong, I would have torn off every garment I had, and gone out into the outer air unswaddled. But this is not for me, nor perhaps for my generation. I climbed with my respirator and my hygienic clothes and my dietetic tabloids! Better thus than not at all.

"There was a ladder, made of some primeval metal. The light from the railway fell upon its lowest rungs, and I saw that it led straight upward out of the rubble at the bottom of the shaft. Perhaps our ancestors ran up and down it a dozen times daily, in their building. As I climbed, the rough edges cut through my gloves so that my hands bled. The light helped me for a little, and then came darkness and, worse still, silence which pierced my ears like a sword. The Machine hums! Did you know that? Its hum penetrates our blood, and may even guide our thoughts. Who knows! I was getting beyond its power. Then I thought: 'This silence means that I am doing wrong.' But I heard voices in the silence, and again they strengthened me." He laughed. "I had need of them. The next moment I cracked my head against something."

She sighed.

"I had reached one of those pneumatic stoppers that defend us from the outer air. You may have noticed them on the airship. Pitch dark, my feet on the rungs of an invisible ladder, my hands cut; I cannot explain how I lived through this part, but the voices still comforted me, and I felt for fastenings. The stopper, I suppose, was about eight feet across. I passed my hand over it as far as I could reach. It was perfectly smooth. I felt it almost to the center. Not quite to the center, for my arm was too short. Then the voice said: 'Jump. It is worth it. There may be a handle in the center, and you may catch hold of it and so come to us your own way. And if there is no handle, so that you may fall and are dashed to pieces—it is still worth it: you will still come to us your own way.' So I jumped. There was a handle, and—"

He paused. Tears gathered in his mother's eyes. She knew that he was fated. If he did not die today he would die tomorrow. There was not room for such a person in the world. And with her pity disgust mingled. She was ashamed at having borne such a son, she who had always been so respectable and so full of ideas. Was he really the little boy to whom she had taught the use of his stops and buttons, and to whom she had given his first lessons in the Book? The very hair that disfigured his lip showed that he was reverting to some savage type. On atavism the Machine can have no mercy.

"There was a handle, and I did catch it. I hung tranced over the darkness and heard the hum of these workings as the last whisper in a dying dream. All the things I had cared about and all the people I had spoken to through tubes appeared infinitely little. Meanwhile the handle revolved. My weight had set something in motion and I spun slowly, and then—

"I cannot describe it. I was lying with my face to the sunshine. Blood poured from my nose and ears and I heard a tremendous roaring. The stopper, with me clinging to it, had simply been blown out of the earth, and the air that we make down here was escaping through the vent into the air above. It burst up like a fountain. I crawled back to it—for the upper air hurts—and, as it were, I took great sips from the edge. My respirator had flown goodness knows where, my clothes were torn. I just lay with my lips close to the hole, and I sipped until the bleeding stopped. You can imagine nothing so curious. This hollow in the grass—I will speak of it in a minute—the sun shining into it, not brilliantly but through marbled clouds—the peace, the nonchalance, the sense of space, and, brushing my cheek, the roaring fountain of our artificial air! Soon I spied my respirator, bobbing up and down in the current high above my head, and higher still were many airships. But no one ever looks out of airships, and in any case they could not have picked me up. There I was, stranded. The sun shone a little way down the shaft, and revealed the topmost rung of the ladder, but it was hopeless trying to reach it. I should either have been tossed up again by the escape, or else have fallen in, and died. I could only lie on the grass, sipping and sipping, and from time to time glancing around me.

"I knew that I was in Wessex, for I had taken care to go to a lecture on the subject before starting. Wessex lies above the room in which we are talking now. It was once an important state. Its kings held all the southern coast from the Andredswald to Cornwall, while the Wansdyke protected them on the north, running over the high ground. The lecturer was concerned only with the rise of Wessex, so I do not know how long it remained an international power, nor would the knowledge have assisted me. To tell the truth, I could do nothing but laugh during this part. There was I, with a pneumatic stopper by my side and a respirator bobbing over my head, imprisoned, all three of us, in a grass-grown hollow that was edged with fern."

Then he grew grave again.

"Lucky for me that it was a hollow. For the air began to fall back into it and to fill it as water fills a bowl. I could crawl about. Presently I stood. I breathed a mixture, in which the air that hurts predominated whenever I tried to climb the sides. This was not so bad. I had not lost my tabloids and remained ridiculously cheerful, and as for the Machine, I forgot about it altogether. My one aim now was to get to the top, where the ferns were, and to view whatever objects lay beyond.

"I rushed the slope. The new air was still too bitter for me and I came rolling back, after a momentary vision of something gray. The sun grew very feeble, and I remembered that he was in Scorpio—I had been to a lecture on that too. If the sun is in Scorpio and you are in Wessex, it means that you must be as quick as you can or it will get too dark. (This is the first bit of useful information I have ever got from a lecture, and I expect it will be the last.) It made me try frantically to breathe the new air, and to advance as far as I dared out of my pond. The hollow filled so slowly. At times I thought that the fountain played with less vigor. My respirator semed to dance nearer the earth; the roar was decreasing."

He broke off.

"I don't think this is interesting you. The rest will interest you even less. There are no ideas in it, and I wish that I had not troubled you to come. We are too different, Mother."

She told him to continue.

"It was evening before I climbed the bank. The sun had very nearly slipped out of the sky by this time, and I could not get a good view. You, who have just crossed the Roof of the World, will not want to hear an account of the little hills that I saw—low colorless hills. But to me they were living and the turf that covered them was skin, under which their muscles rippled, and I felt that those hills had called with incalculable force to men in the past, and that men had loved them. Now they sleep—perhaps for ever. They commune with humanity in dreams. Happy the man, happy the woman, who awakes the hills of Wessex. For though they sleep, they will never die."

His voice rose passionately.

"Cannot you see, cannot all you lecturers see, that it is we that are dying, and that down here the only thing that really lives is the Machine? We created the Machine, to do our will, but we cannot make it do our will now. It has robbed us of the sense of space and of the sense of touch; it has blurred every human relation and narrowed down love to a carnal act, it has paralyzed our bodies and our wills, and now it compels us to worship it. The Machine develops—but not on our lines. The Machine proceeds—but not to our goal. We exist only as the blood corpuscles that course through its arteries, and if it could work without us, it would let us die. Oh, I have no remedy—or, at least, only one—to tell men again and again that I have seen the hills of Wessex as Aelfrid saw them when he overthrew the Danes.

"So the sun set. I forgot to mention that a belt of mist lay between my hill and other hills, and that it was the color of pearl."

He broke off for the second time.

"Go on," said his mother wearily.

He shook his head.

"Go on. Nothing that you say can distress me now. I am hardened."

"I had meant to tell you the rest, but I cannot: I know that I cannot: good-bye."

Vashti stood irresolute. All her nerves were tingling with his blasphemies. But she was also inquisitive.

"This is unfair," she complained. "You have called me across the world to hear your story, and hear it I will. Tell me—as briefly as possible, for this is a disastrous waste of time—tell me how you returned to civilization."

"Oh—that!" he said, starting. "You would like to hear about civilization. Certainly. Had I got to where my respirator fell down?"

"No—but I understand everything now. You put on your respirator, and managed to walk along the surface of the earth to a vomitory, and there your conduct was reported to the Central Committee."

"By no means."

He passed his hand over his forehead, as if dispelling some strong impression. Then, resuming his narrative, he warmed to it again.

"My respirator fell about sunset. I had mentioned that the fountain seemed feebler, had I not?"

"Yes."

"About sunset, it let the respirator fall. As I said, I had entirely forgotten about the Machine, and I paid no great attention at the time, being occupied with other things. I had my pool of air, into which I could dip when the outer keenness became intolerable, and which would possibly remain for days, provided that no wind sprang up to disperse it. Not until it was too late did I realize what the stoppage of the escape implied. You see—the gap in the tunnel had been mended; the Mending Apparatus; the Mending Apparatus, was after me.

"One other warning I had, but I neglected it. The sky at night was clearer than it had been in the day, and the moon, which was about half the sky behind the sun, shone into the dell at moments quite brightly. I was in my usual place—on the boundary between the two atmospheres—when I thought I saw something dark move across the bottom of the dell, and vanish into the shaft. In my folly, I ran down. I bent over and listened, and I thought I heard a faint scraping noise in the depths.

"At this—but it was too late—I took alarm. I determined to put on my respirator and to walk right out of the dell. But my respirator had gone. I knew exactly where it had fallen—between the stopper and the aperture—and I could even feel the mark that it had made in the turf. It had gone, and I realized that something evil was at work, and I had better escape to the other air, and, if I must die, die running toward the cloud that had been the color of a pearl. I never started. Out of the shaft—it is too horrible. A worm, a long white worm, had crawled out of the shaft and was gliding over the moonlit grass.

"I screamed. I did everything that I should not have done; I stamped upon the creature instead of flying from it, and it at once curled round the ankle. Then we fought. The worm let me run all over the dell, but edged up my leg as I ran. 'Help!' I cried. (That part is too awful. It belongs to the part that you will never know.) 'Help!' I cried. (Why cannot we suffer in silence?) 'Help!' I cried. Then my feet were wound together. I fell, I was dragged away from the dear ferns and the living hills, and past the great metal stopper (I can tell you this part), and I thought it might save me again if I caught hold of the handle. It also was enwrapped, it also. Oh, the whole dell was full of the things. They were searching it in all directions; they were denuding it, and the white snouts of others peeped out of the hole, ready if needed. Everything that could be moved they brought—brushwood, bundles of fern, everything, and down we all went intertwined into hell. The last things that I saw, ere the stopper closed after us, were certain stars, and I felt that a man of my sort lived in the sky. For I did fight, I fought till the very end, and it was only my head hitting against the ladder that quieted me. I woke up in this room. The worms had vanished; I was surrounded by artificial air, artifical light, artifical peace, and my friends were calling to me down speaking-tubes to know whether I had come across any new ideas lately."

Here his story ended. Discussion of it was impossible, and Vashti turned to go.

"It will end in Homelessness," she said quietly.

"I wish it would," retorted Kuno.

"The Machine has been most merciful."

"I prefer the mercy of God."

"By that superstitious phrase, do you mean that you could live in the outer air?"

"Yes."

"Have you ever seen, round the vomitories, the bones of those who were extruded after the Great Rebellion?"

"Yes."

"They were left where they perished for our edification. A few crawled away, but they perished, too—who can doubt it? And so with the Homeless of our own day. The surface of the earth supports life no longer."

"Indeed."

"Ferns and a little grass may survive, but all higher forms have perished. Has any airship detected them?"

"No."

"Has any lecturer dealt with them?"

"No."

"Then why this obstinacy?"

"Becasue I have seen them," he exploded.

"Seen *what*?"

"Because I have seen her in the twilight—because she came to my help when I called—because she, too, was entangled by the worms, and, luckier than I, was killed by one of them piercing her throat."

He was mad. Vashti departed, nor, in the troubles that followed, did she ever see his face again.

PART III

THE HOMELESS

During the years that followed Kuno's escapade, two important developments took place in the Machine. On the surface they were revolutionary, but in either case men's minds had been prepared beforehand, and they did but express tendencies that were latent already.

The first of these was the abolition of respirators.

Advanced thinkers, like Vashti, had always held it foolish to visit the surface of the earth. Airships might be necessary, but what was the good of going out for mere curiosity and crawling along for a mile or two in a terrestrial motor? The habit was vulgar and perhaps faintly improper: it was unproductive of ideas, and had no connection with the habits that really mattered. So respirators were abolished, and with them, of course, the terrestrial motors, and except for a few lecturers, who complained that they were debarred access to their subject matter, the development was accepted quietly. Those who still wanted to know what the earth was like had after all only to listen to some gramophone or to look into some cinematophote. And even the lecturers acquiesced when they found that a lecture on the sea was none the less stimulating when compiled out of other lectures that had already been delivered on the same subject. "Beware of first-hand ideas!" exclaimed one of the most advanced of them. "Firsthand ideas do not really exist. They are but the physical impressions produced by love and fear, and on this gross foundation who could erect a philosophy? Let your ideas be secondhand, and if possible tenthhand, for then they will be far removed from that disturbing element—direct observation. Do not learn anything about this subject of mine—the French Revolution. Learn instead what I think that Enich-armon thought Urizen thought Gutch thought Ho-Yung thought Chi-Bo-Sing thought Lafcadio Hearn thought Carlyle thought Mirabeau said about the French Revolution. Through the medium of these ten great minds the blood that was shed at Paris and the windows that were broken at Versailles will be clarifed to an idea which you may employ most profitably in your daily lives. But be sure that the intermediates are many and varied, for in history one authority exists to counteract another. Urizen must counteract the skepticism of Ho-Young and Enicharmon, I must myself counteract the impetuosity of Gutch. You who listen to me are in a better position to judge about the French Revolution than I am. Your descendants will be even in a better position than you, for they will learn what you think. I think, and yet another intermediate will be added to the chain. And in time"—his voice rose—"there will come a generation that has got beyond facts, beyond impressions, a generation absolutely colorless, a generation

seraphically free
From taint of personality,

which will see the French Revolution not as it happened, nor as they would like it to have happened, but as it would have happened had it taken place in the days of the Machine."

Tremendous applause greeted this lecture, which did but voice a feeling already latent in the minds of men—a feeling that terrestrial facts must be ignored, and that the abolition of respirators was a positive gain. It was even suggested that airships should be abolished too. This was not done, because airships had somehow worked themselves into the Machine's system. But year by year they were used less, and mentioned less by thoughtful men.

The second great development was the reestablishment of religion.

This, too, had been voiced in the celebrated lecture. No one could mistake the reverent tone in which the peroration had concluded, and it awakened a responsive echo in the heart of each. Those who had long worshiped silently now began to talk. They described the strange feeling of peace that came over them when they handled the Book of the Machine, the pleasure that it was to repeat certain numerals out of it, however little meaning those numerals conveyed to the outward ear, the ecstasy of touching a button however unimportant, or of ringing an electric bell however superfluously.

"The Machine," they exclaimed, "feeds us and clothes us and houses us; through it we speak to one another, through it we see one another, in it we have our being. The Machine is the friend of ideas and the enemy of superstition: the Machine is omnipotent, eternal; blessed is the Machine." And before long this allocution was printed on the first page of the Book, and in subsequent editions the ritual swelled into a complicated system of praise and prayer. The word "religion" was sedulously avoided, and in theory the Machine was still the creation and the implement of man. But in practice all, save a few retrogrades, worshiped it as divine. Nor was it worshiped in unity. One believer would be chiefly impressed by the blue optic plates, through which he saw other believers; another by the Mending Apparatus, which sinful Kuno had compared to worms; another by the lifts, another by the Book. And each would pray to this or to that, and ask it to intercede for him with the Machine as a whole. Persecution—that also was present. It did not break out, for reasons that will be set forward shortly. But it was latent, and all who did not accept the minimum known as "undenominational Mechanism" lived in danger of Homelessness, which means death, as we know.

To attribute these two great developments to the Central Committee is to take a very narrow view of civilization. The Central Committee announced the developments, it is true, but they were no more the cause of them than were the kings of the imperialistic period the cause of war. Rather did they yield to some invincible pressure, which came no one knew whither, and which, when gratified, was succeeded by some new pressure equally invincible. To such a state of affairs it is convenient to give the name of progress. No one confessed the Machine was out of hand. Year by year it was served with increased efficiency and decreased intelligence. The better a man knew his own duties upon it, the less he understood the duties of his neighbor, and in all the world there was not one who understood the monster as a whole. Those master brains had perished. They had left full directions, it is true, and their successors had each of them mastered a portion of those directions. But Humanity, in its desire for comfort, had overreached itself. It had exploited the riches of nature too far. Quietly and complacently, it was sinking into decadence, and progress had come to mean the progress of the Machine.

As for Vashti, her life went peacefully forward until the final disaster. She made her room dark and slept; she awoke and made the room light. She lectured and attended lectures. She exchanged ideas with her innumerable friends and believed she was growing more spiritual. At times a friend was granted Euthanasia, and left his or her room for the homelessness that is beyond all human conception. Vashti did not much mind. After an unsuccessful lecture, she would sometimes ask for Euthanasis herself. But the death rate was not permitted to exceed the birth rate, and the Machine had hitherto refused it to her.

The troubles began quietly, long before she was conscious of them.

One day she was astonished at receiving a message from her

son. They never communicated, having nothing in common, and she had only heard indirectly that he was still alive, and had been transferred from the Northern Hemisphere, where he had behaved so mischievously, to the Southern—indeed, to a room not far from her own.

"Does he want me to visit him?" she thought. "Never again, never. And I have not the time."

No, it was madness of another kind.

He refused to visualize his face upon the blue plate, and speaking out of the darkness with solemnity said:

"The Machine stops."

"What do you say?"

"The Machine is stopping, I know it; I know the sign."

She burst into a peal of laughter. He heard her and was angry, and they spoke no more.

"Can you imagine anything more absurd?" she cried to a friend. "A man who was my son believes that the Machine is stopping. It would be impious if it was not mad."

"The Machine is stopping?" her friend replied. "What does that mean? The phrase conveys nothing to me."

"Nor to me."

"He does not refer, I suppose, to the trouble there has been lately with the music?"

"Oh, no, of course not. Let us talk about music."

"Have you complained to the authorities?"

"Yes, and they say it wants mending, and referred me to the Committee of the Mending Apparatus. I complained of those curious gasping sighs that disfigure the symphonies of the Brisbane school. They sound like someone in pain. The Committee of the Mending Apparatus say that it shall be remedied shortly."

Obscurely worried, she resumed her life. For one thing, the defect in the music irritated her. For another thing, she could not forget Kuno's speech. If he had known that the music was out of repair—he could not know it, for he detested music—if he had known that it was wrong, "the Machine stops" was exactly the venomous sort of remark he would have made. Of course, he had made it at a venture, but the coincidence annoyed her, and she spoke with some petulance to the Committee of the Mending Apparatus.

They replied, as before, that the defect would be set right shortly.

"Shortly! At once!" she retorted. "Why should I be worried by imperfect music? Things are always put right at once. If you do not mend it at once, I shall complain to the Central Committee."

"No personal complaints are received by the Central Committee," the Committee of the Mending Apparatus replied.

"Through whom am I to make my complaint, then?"

"Through us."

"I complain then."

"Your complaint shall be forwarded in its turn."

"Have others complained?"

This question was unmechanical, and the Committee of the Mending Apparatus refused to anwer it.

"It is too bad!" she exclaimed to another of her friends. "There never was such an unfortunate woman as myself. I can never be sure of my music now. It gets worse and worse each time I summon it."

"I too have my troubles," the friend replied. "Sometimes my ideas are interrupted by a slight jarring noise."

"What is it?"

"I do not know whether it is inside my head or inside the wall."

"Complain in either case."

"I have complained, and my complaint will be forwarded in its turn to the Central Committee."

Time passed, and they resented the defects no longer. The defects had not been remedied, but the human tissues in that latter day had become so subservient that they readily adapted themselves to every caprice of the Machine. The sigh at the crisis of the Brisbane symphony no longer irritated Vashti; she accepted it as part of the melody. The jarring noise, whether in the head or in the wall, was no longer resented by her friend. And so with the moldy artificial fruit, so with the bath water that began to stink, so with the defective rhymes that the poetry machine had taken to emitting. All were bitterly complained of at first, and then acquiesced in and forgotten. Things went from bad to worse unchallenged.

It was otherwise with the failure of the sleeping apparatus. That was a more serious stoppage. There came a day when over the whole world—in Sumatra, in Wessex, in the innumerable cities of Courland and Brazil—the beds, when summoned by their tired owners, failed to appear. It may seem a ludicrous matter, but from it we may date the collapse of humanity. The Committee responsible for the failure was assailed by complaints, whom it referred, as usual, to the Committee of the Mending Apparatus, who in its turn assured them that their complaints would be forwarded to the Central Committee. But the discontent grew, for mankind was not yet sufficiently adaptable to do without sleeping.

"Someone is meddling with the Machine—" they began.

"Someone is trying to make himself king, to reintroduce the personal element."

"Punish that man with Homelessness."

"To the rescue! Avenge the Machine! Avenge the Machine!"

"War! Kill the man!"

But the Committee of the Mending Apparatus now came forward, and allayed the panic with well-chosen words. It confessed that the Mending Apparatus was itself in need of repair.

The effect of this frank confession was admirable.

"Of course," said a famous lecturer—he of the French Revolution, who gilded each new decay with splendor—"of course we shall not press our complaints now. The Mending Apparatus has treated us so well in the past that we all sympathize with it, and will wait patiently for its recovery. In its own good time it will resume its duties. Meanwhile let us do without our beds, our tabloids, our other little wants. Such, I feel sure, would be the wish of the Machine."

Thousands of miles away his audience applauded. The Machine still linked them. Under the seas, beneath the roots of the mountains, ran the wires through which they saw and heard, the enormous eyes and ears that were their heritage, and the hum of many workings clothed their thoughts in one garment of subserviency. Only the old and sick remained ungrateful, for it was rumored that Euthanasia, too, was out of order, and that pain had reappeared among men.

It became difficult to read. A blight entered the atmosphere and dulled its luminosity. At times Vashti could scarcely see across her room. The air, too, was foul. Loud were the complaints, impotent the remedies, heroic the tone of the lecturer as he cried: "Courage! courage! What matter so long as the Machine goes on? To it the darkness and the light are one." And though things improved again after a time, the old brilliancy was never recaptured, and humanity never recovered from its entrance into twilight. There was hysterical talk of "measures," of "provisional dictatorship," and the inhabitants of Sumatra were asked to familiarize themselves with the workings of the central power station, the said power station being situated in France. But for the most part panic reigned, and men spent their strength praying to their Books, tangible proofs of the Machine's omnipoence. There were gradations of terror—at times came rumors of hope—the Mending Apparatus was almost mended—the enemies of the Machine had been got under—new "nerve centers" were evolving which would do the work even more magnificently than before. But there came a day when, without the slightest warning, without any previous hint of feebleness, the entire communication system broke down, all over the world, and the world, as they understood it, ended.

Vashti was lecturing at the time, and her earlier remarks had been punctuated with applause. As she proceeded the audience became silent, and at the conclusion there was no sound. Somewhat displeased, she called to a friend who was a specialist in sympathy. No sound: doubtless the friend was sleeping. And so with the next friend whom she tried to summon, and so with the next, until she remembered Kuno's cryptic remark, "The Machine stops."

The phrase still conveyed nothing. If Eternity was stopping it would of course be set going shortly.

For example, there were still a little light and air—the atmosphere had improved a few hours previously. There was still the Book, and while there was the Book there was security.

Then she broke down, for with the cessation of activity came an unexpected terror—silence.

She had never known silence, and the coming of it nearly killed her—it did kill many thousands of people outright. Ever since her birth she had been surrounded by the steady hum. It was to the ear what artificial air was to the lungs, and agonizing pains shot across her head. And scarcely knowing what she did, she stumbled forward and pressed the unfamiliar button, the one that opened the door of her cell.

Now the door of the cell worked on a simple hinge of its own. It was not connected with the central power station, dying far away in France. It opened, rousing immoderate hopes in Vashti, for she thought that the Machine had been mended. It opened, and she saw the dim tunnel that curved far away toward freedom. One look, and then she shrank back. For the tunnel was full of people—she was almost the last in that city to have taken alarm.

People at any time repelled her, and these were nightmares from her worst dreams. People were crawling about, touching each other, vanishing in the dark, and ever and anon being pushed off the platform on to the live rail. Some were fighting round the electric bells, trying to summon trains which could not be summoned. Others were yelling for Euthanasia or for respirators, or blaspheming the Machine. Others stood at the doors of their cells fearing, like herself, either to stop in them or to leave them, and behind all the uproar was silence—the silence which is the voice of the earth and of the generations who have gone.

No—it was worse than solitude. She closed the door again and sat down to wait for the end. The disintegration went on, accompanied by horrible cracks and rumbling. The valves that restrained the Medical Apparatus must have been weakened, for it ruptured and hung hideously from the ceiling. The floor heaved and fell and flung her from her chair. A tube oozed toward her serpent fashion. And at last the final horror approached—light began to ebb, and she knew that civilization's long day was closing.

She whirled round, praying to be saved from this, at any rate, kissing the Book, pressing button after button. The uproar outside was increasing, and even penetrated the wall. Slowly the brilliancy of her cell was dimmed, the reflections faded from her metal switches. Now she could not see the reading stand, now not the Book, though she held it in her hand. Light followed the flight of sound, air was following light, and the original void returned to the cavern from which it had been so long excluded. Vashti continued to whirl, like the devotees of an earlier religion, screaming, praying, striking at the buttons with bleeding hands.

It was thus that she opened her prison and escaped—escaped in the spirit: at least so it seems to me, ere my meditation closes. That she escapes in the body—I cannot perceive that. She struck, by chance, the switch that released the door, and the rush of foul air on her skin, the loud throbbing whispers in her ears, told her that she was facing the tunnel again, and that tremendous platform on which she had seen men fighting. They were not fighting now. Only the whispers remained, and the little whimpering groans. They were dying by hundreds out in the dark.

She burst into tears.

Tears answered her.

They wept for humanity, those two, not for themselves. They could not bear that this should be the end. Ere silence was completed their hearts were opened, and they knew what had been important on the earth. Man, the flower of all flesh, the noblest of all creatures visible, man who had once made god in his image, and had mirrored his strength on the constellations, beautiful naked man was dying, strangled in the garments that he had woven. Century after century had he toiled, and here was his reward. Truly the garment had seemed heavenly at first, shot with the colors of culture, sewn with the threads of self-denial. And heavenly it had been so long as it was a garment and no more, so long as man could shed it at will and live by the essence that is his soul, and the essence, equally divine, that is his body.

The sin against the body—it was for that they wept in chief; the centuries of wrong against the muscles and the nerves, and those five portals by which we can alone apprehend—glozing it over with talk of evolution, until the body was white pap, the home of ideas as colorless, last sloshy stirrings of a spirit that had grasped the stars.

"Where are you?" she sobbed.

His voice in the darkness said, "Here."

"Is there any hope, Kuno?"

"None for us."

"Where are you?"

She crawled toward him over the bodies of the dead. His blood spurted over her hands.

"Quicker," he gasped, "I am dying—but we touch, we talk, not through the Machine."

He kissed her.

"We have come back to our own. We die, but we have recaptured life, as it was in Wessex, when Aelfrid overthrew the Danes. We know what they know outside, they who dwelt in the cloud that is the color of a pearl."

"But, Kuno, is it true? Are there still men on the surface of the earth? Is this—this tunnel, this poisioned darkness—really not the end?"

He replied:

"I have seen them, spoken to them, loved them. They are hiding in the mist and the ferns until our civilization stops. Today they are the Homeless—tomorrow—"

"Oh, tomorrow—some fool will start the Machine again, tomorrow."

"Never," said Kuno, "never. Hunanity has learned its lesson."

As he spoke the whole city was broken like a honeycomb. An airship had sailed in through the vomitory into a ruined wharf. It crashed downward, exploding as it went, rending gallery after gallery with its wings of steel. For a moment they saw the nations of the dead, and, before they joined them, scraps of the untainted sky.

The Mark Gable Foundation

by Leo Szilard

As soon as I saw the temperature of the rabbit come back to normal, I knew that we had licked the problem. It took twenty-four hours to bring his temperature down to one degree centigrade, injecting three grains of dorminol every ten minutes during that period. Sleep set in between the third and fourth hours, when the body temperature fell below twenty-six centigrade; and after twenty-four hours, at one centigrade, there was no longer any appreciable metabolic activity. We kept him at that low temperature for one day, after which time, having completed our measurements, we injected metaboline and allowed the temperature to rise to normal within one hour.

There was never any doubt in my mind that once we got this far, and got the temperature down to one centigrade, we could keep the rabbit "asleep" for a week, a year or a hundred years just as well as for a day. Nor had I much doubt that if this worked for the rabbit it would work for the dog; and that if it worked for the dog, it would work for man.

I always wanted to see what kind of place the world will be three hundred years hence. I intended to "withdraw from life" (as we proposed to call the process) as soon as we had perfected the method, and to arrange for being returned to life in 2260. I thought my views and sentiments were sufficiently advanced, and that I had no reason to fear I should be too much behind the times in a world that had advanced a few hundred years beyond the present. I would not have dared, though, to go much beyond three hundred years.

I thought at first that one year should be plenty for perfecting the process as well as for completing the arrangements; and that I should be in *statu dormiendi* before the year was over. As a matter of fact, it took only six months to get ready; but difficulties of an unforeseen kind arose.

A section of public opinion was strongly opposed to "withdrawal from life," and for a time it looked as though the Eighty-sixth Congress would pass a law against it. This, fortunately, did not come to pass. The A.M.A., however, succeeded in obtaining a court injunction against my "withdrawal" on the basis that it was "suicide," and suicide was unlawful. Since a man in *statu dormiendi* cannot of his own volition return to life—so the brief argued—from the legal point of view he is not living while in that state.

The ensuing legal battle lasted for five years. Finally Adams, Lynch and Davenport, who handled my case, succeeded in getting the Supreme Court to accept jurisdiction. The Supreme Court upheld the injunction, with three justices dissenting. Mr. Davenport explained to me that the ruling of the Supreme Court, though on the face of it unfavorable, was in reality a very fortunate thing for me because it removed all obstacles that might have stood in the way of my plans. The ruling of the Supreme Court, Mr. Davenport explained, established once and for all that a man is not legally living while in *statu dormiendi*. Therefore, he said, if I should now decide to act against the advice of his firm, disregard the court injunction and proceed to withdraw from life, no legal action could be taken against me under any statute until I was returned to life three hundred years hence, at which time my offense would come under the statute of limitations.

All arrangements have been completed in secrecy, and having named Adams, Lynch and Davenport as executors of my estate, I spent my last evening in the twentieth century at a small farewell party given to me by friends. There were about six of us, all old friends, but somehow we did not understand each other very well on this occasion. Most of them seemed to have the feeling that they were sort of attending my furneral, since they would not see me again alive; whereas to me it seemed that it was I who was attending their funeral, since none of them would be alive when I woke up.

According to the records, it took about two hours until sleep set in, but I do not remember anything that was said after the first hour.

The next thing I remember was the prick of a needle, and when I opened my eyes I saw a nurse with a hypodermic syringe in one hand and a microphone in the other.

"Would you mind speaking into the microphone, please?" she said, holding it at a comfortable distance from my face.

"We owe you an apology, as well as an explanation," said a well-dressed young man standing near my bed and holding a microphone in his hand. "I am Mr. Rosenblatt from Adams, Lynch, Davenport, Rosenblatt and Giannini. For reasons of a legal nature we deemed it advisable to return you to life, but if you wish to complete the three hundred years, which appears to be your goal, we hope we shall be able to make the necessary arrangements within one month. At least we shall try our best to do so.

"Now, before you say anything, let me explain to you that the gentleman sitting next to me is Mr. McClintock, the mayor of the city—a Democrat, of course. Subject to your approval, we have agreed that he may give you an interview which will be televised. The proceeds will go the the Senile Degeneration Research Fund. The broadcasting companies understand, of course, that it's up to you to agree to this arrangement, and they have an alternate program ready which can be substituted if you should object. If you agree, however, we shall go on the air in one minute. Naturally, the broadcasting companies are anxious to catch your first responses rather than have something rehearsed put on the air. I'm certain you'll appreciate their point of view."

"Before I answer this," I said, "would you mind telling me how long I've been asleep?"

"I should have told you this before," he said. "You were out ninety years."

"Then," I said after a moment's reflection, "I have no friends left from whom to keep any secrets. I have no objection to the broadcast."

As soon as the announcer finished with his somewhat lengthy introduction, the mayor came in. "As chairman of the Senile Degeneration Research Fund, I wish to express my thanks to you for having graciously consented to this interview. Senile degeneration is one of our most important diseases. One in eight die of senile degeneration, and more than half of those who reach the age of a hundred and five. Given ample funds for research, we cannot fail to discover the causes of this disease, and once the cause of the disease is known it will be possible to find a cure. But I know that I should not monopolize the air; there must be many things that you would want to know about our society. Please feel free to ask anything you like."

"Why was I returned to life?" I asked.

"I'm certain," the mayor said, "that Messrs. Adams, Lynch, Davenport, Rosenblatt and Giannini will want to give you a detailed explanation of that. It was their decision, and I have no doubt that it was a wise one in the circumstances. I'm not a lawyer, but I can tell you something about the political background of their decision. Politics—that's my field.

"I wonder whether you realize how much trouble your process of 'withdrawal from life' has caused the government. For a few years only a few persons followed your example, mostly political scientists and anthropologists. But then, all of a sudden, it became quite a fad. People withdrew just to spite their wives and husbands. And I regret to say that many Catholics who could not obtain a divorce chose this method of surviving their husbands or wives, to become widowed and to remarry, until this practice was finally stopped in 2001 by the papal bull 'Somnus Naturae Repugnans.'

"The Church did not interfere, of course, with the legitimate uses of the process. Throughout the latter part of the century doctors encouraged patients who suffered from cancer and certain other incurable diseases to withdraw from life, in the hope that a cure would be found in the years to come and that they could then be returned to life and cured. There were legal complications, of course, particularly in the case of wealthy patients. Often their heirs raised objections on the ground that withdrawal from life was not yet an entirely safe process; and equally often the heirs demanded that they too should be permitted to withdraw from life for an equal period of time, so that the natural sequence of the generations would be left undisturbed. There are about one million cancer patients at present in *statu dormiendi,* and half a million of their heirs."

"Then cancer is still not a curable disease?" I asked.

"No," the mayor said, "but with all the funds which are now available it can take at the most a few years until that problem is solved. The most important, even though a somewhat controversial, application of your process," he continued, "came about twenty-five years ago. That was when the present great depression started. It came as a result of seventy-five years of Republican mismanagement. Today we have a Democratic President and a Democratic Congress; but this is the first Democratic President since Donovan, and the first Democratic Congress since the Hundred and Fifth. As more and more of the Southern states began to vote Republican, our party was hopelessly outvoted, until gradually its voting strength began to rise again; and today, with a Democratic majority solidly established, we have nothing to fear from coming elections."

"So finally there's a truly progressive party in the United States?" I asked.

"Yes," the mayor said, "we regard ourselves as progressives. We have the support of the Catholic Church, and eighty per cent of the voters are Catholics."

"What brought about such mass conversions?" I asked.

"There were no mass conversions," the mayor said, "and we wouldn't want any. Families of Polish, Irish and Italian stock, having a stronger belief in the American way of life than some of the older immigrant stocks, have always given birth to more children; and so today we have a solid Catholic majority.

"Now that the Democratic Party is established in office, we're going to fight the depression by the proper economic methods. As I said before, there was a Republican Administration in office when the depression hit us twenty-five years ago. In the first year of that depression unemployment rose to ten million. Things looked pretty bad. There was no public-works program or unemployment relief, but Congress passed a law, the Withdrawal Act of 2025, authorizing the use of Federal funds to enable any unemployed who so desired to withdraw from life for the duration of the depression. Those unemployed who availed themselves of this offer had to authorize the government to return them to life when the government deemed that the labor market required such a measure.

"Seven out of ten million unemployed availed themselves of this offer by the end of the first year, in spite of the opposition of the Church. The next year unemployment was up another seven million, out of which five million were withdrawn from life. This went on and on, and by the time our party got into office, two years ago, there were twenty-five million withdrawn from life, with Federal support.

"Our first act in office was to make withdrawals from life unlawful; and the second was to institute a public-works program."

"What does your public-works program consist of?" I asked.

"Housing," the mayor said.

"Is there a housing shortage?" I asked. "No," the mayor said. "With twenty-five million unemployed in *statu dormiendi* there is, of course, no housing shortage."

"And will you now return these twenty-five million unemployed to life?" I asked.

"Only very gradually," the mayor replied. "The majority of the sleepers are non-Catholics and it would upset the political balance if they were returned to life all at once. Besides, operating the refrigerator plants of the public dormitories for twenty-five million sleepers is part of our public-works program.

"Incidentally," he added, "whether you yourself come under the Antiwithdrawal Act of 2048 is a controversial question. Your lawyers felt that you would not want to violate the law of the land, and they tried to get a court ruling in order to clear you; but the court refused to take the case, because you weren't legally alive; finally your lawyers decided to return you to life so that you may ask the court for a declaratory judgment. Even though there is little doubt that the court will rule in your favor, I personally hope that you'll find our society so pleasant, and so much more advanced than you would have expected, that you'll decide to stay with us in the twenty-first century."

"Thank you very much, Mr. Mayor," the announcer said. "This was beautiful timing. We're off the air," he said to me, thinking I needed more explanation.

The mayor turned to me. "If you feel well enough, I would like to take you home for dinner. It's a small party, four or five guests, my wife and my daughter Betty. The poor girl is brokenhearted. She has just called off her engagement, and I'm doing what I can to cheer her up. She's very much in love with the fellow."

"If she loves him so much, why did she break with him?" I asked.

"All her friends teased her about him because he wears teeth," the mayor said. "Of course, there's no law against it, it's just not done, that's all."

Something began to dawn upon me at this moment. The nurse, a pretty young girl, had no teeth, Mr. Rosenblatt had no teeth, and the mayor had no teeth. Teeth seemed to be out of fashion.

"I have teeth," I said.

"Yes, of course," the mayor replied, "and you wear them with dignity. But if you should decide to stay with us you'll want to get rid of them. They're not hygienic."

"But how would I chew my food, how do you chew your food?" I asked.

"Well," the mayor said, "we don't eat with our hands. We eat from plates—chewing plates. "They plug into sockets in the table and chew your food for you. We eat with spoons."

"Steaks, too?" I asked.

"Yes, everything," the mayor said. "But have no fear, we shall have knife and fork for you tonight, and flat plates such as you are accustomed to. My daughter kept them for her fiancé."

"I'm sorry that my second daughter will not be with us tonight," the mayor said as he was starting his car. "She's in the hospital. In college she's taking mathematics and chemistry. She could have talked to you in your own language."

"Nothing seriously wrong, I hope," I said.

"Oh, no!" the mayor said. "Just plastic surgery. She'll be out in a day or two."

"With a new nose?" I asked.

"Nothing wrong with her nose," the mayor said. "As a matter of fact, she has Mark Gable's nose. No, it's one of these newfangled operations. My wife and I don't approve of it, but this girl, she runs with the smart set. 'Esophagus bypass,' they call it. No longer necessary to watch your diet, you know. Eat as much as you please and switch it to the bypass—goes into a rubber container, of course. I tried to talk her out of it, but that girl has an answer for everything. 'Father,' she said, 'isn't there a food surplus in the world? If everybody ate twice as much, would that not solve the problem?' "

"Maybe she's right," I said, remembering with an effort that I always used to side with youth.

When we sat down at table I looked forward to the steak; I was pretty hungry by that time. But when it was served, after a few fruitless attempts with knife and fork I had to ask for a chewing plate.

"The choice cuts are always especially tough," my hostess explained.

"Tell me," I said, "when did people begin to discard their teeth, and why?"

"Well," the mayor said, "it started thirty years ago. Ford's chewing plates have been advertised over television for at least thirty-five years. Once people have chewing plates, what use do they have for teeth? If you think of all the time people used to spend at the dentist's, and for no good purpose, at that, you'll have to admit we have made progress."

"What became of all the dentists?" I asked.

"Many of them have been absorbed by the chewing-plate industry," the mayor explained, "Henry Ford VI gave preference over all categories of skilled workers. Others turned to other occupations. Take Mr. Mark Gable, for instance," the mayor said, pointing to a man sitting at my right, a man about fifty, and of great personal charm. "He had studied dentistry; today he is one of the most popular donors, and the richest man in the United States."

"Oh," I said. "What is his business?"

"Over one million boys and girls," the mayor said "are his offspring in the United States, and the demand is still increasing."

"That must keep you pretty busy, Mr. Gable," I said unable to think of anything else to say.

Apparently I had put my foot in it. Mrs. Gable blushed, and the mayor laughed.

"Mr. Gable is happily married," the mayor said. "He donated the seed when he was twenty-four years old. The stock should last indefinitely, although the demand may not. The Surgeon General has ruled that no seed donated by anyone above twenty-five may be marketed in the United States."

"Has there been legislation about this, giving the Surgeon General such authority?" I asked.

"No," the mayor said. "Legislation was blocked by filibuster in the Senate. But the Surgeon General takes action under the Pure Food and Drug Act."

"How can he do that?" I asked.

"There was a decision by the Supreme Court thirty years ago," the mayor said, "that all ponderable substance which is destined to enter through any orifice of the human body comes properly under that act. There was no legislation in this whole field whatsoever. Any woman who wishes to bear a child of her own husband is perfectly free to do so. Over fifteen per cent of the children are born in this manner; but most wives prefer to select a donor."

"How do they make a choice?" I asked.

"Oh," the mayor said, "the magazines are full of their pictures. You can see them on the screen at home and in the movies. There are fashions, of course. Today over seventy per cent of the 'donated' children are the offspring of the thirty-five most popular donors. Naturally, they're expensive. Today a seed of Mr. Gable's will bring a thousand dollars; but you can get seed from very good stock for a hundred. Fashions are bound to change, but long after Mr. Gable passes away his estate will still go on selling his seed to connoisseurs. It's estimated that for several decades his estate will still take in more than thirty million dollars a year."

"I have earned a very large sum of money," said Mr. Gable, turning to me, "with very little work. And now I'm thinking of setting up a trust fund. I want to do something that will really contribute to the happiness of mankind; but it's very difficult to know what to do with money. When Mr. Rosenblatt told me that you'd be here tonight I asked the mayor to invite me. I certainly would value your advice."

"Would you intend to do anything for the advancement of science?" I asked.

"No," Mark Gable said. "I believe scientific progress is too fast as it is."

"I share your feeling about this point," I said with the fervor of conviction, "but then why not do something about the retardation of scientific progress?"

"That I would very much like to do," Mark Gable said, "but how do I go about it?"

"Well," I said, "I think that shouldn't be very difficult. As a matter of fact, I think it would be quite easy. You could set up a foundation, with an annual endowment of thirty million dollars. Research workers in need of funds could apply for grants, if they could make out a convincing case. Have ten committees, each composed of twelve scientists, appointed to pass on these applications. Take the most active scientists out of the laboratory and make them members of these committees. And the very best men in the field should be appointed as charimen at salaries of fifty thousand dollars each. Also have about twenty prizes of one hundred thousand dollars each for the best scientific papers of the year. This is just about all you would have to do. Your lawyers could easily prepare a charter for the foundation. As a matter of fact, any of the National Science Foundation bills which were introduced in the Seventy-ninth and Eightieth Congresses could perfectly well serve as a model."

"I think you had better explain to Mr. Gable why this foundation would in fact retard the progress of science," said a bespectacled young man sitting at the far end of the table, whose name I didn't get at the time of introduction.

"It should be obvious," I said. "First of all, the best scientists would be removed from their laboratories and kept busy on committees passing on applications for funds. Secondly, the scientific workers in need of funds would concentrate on problems which were considered promising and were pretty certain to lead to publishable results. For a few years there might be a great increase in scientific output; but by going after the obvious, pretty soon science would dry out. Science would become something like a parlor game. Some things would be considered interesting, others not. There would be fashions. Those who followed the fashion would get grants. Those who wouldn't would not, and pretty soon they would learn to follow the fashion, too."

"Will you stay here with us?" Mark Gable said, turning to me, "and help me to set up such a foundation?"

"That I will gladly do, Mr. Gable," I said. "We should be able to see within a few years whether the scheme works, and I'm certain that it will work. For a few years I could afford to stay here, and I could then still complete the three hundred years which were my original goal."

"So you would want to go through with your plan rather than live out your life with us?" asked the mayor.

"Frankly, Mr. Mayor," I said, "before Mr. Gable brought up the plan of the foundation, with science progressing at this rapid rate I was a little scared of being faced with further scientific progress two hundred years hence. But if Mr. Gable succeeds in stopping the progress of science and gives the art of living a chance to catch up, two hundred years hence the world should be a livable place. If Mr. Gable should not go through with his project, however, I would probably prefer to live out my life with you in the twenty-first century. How about it, Mr. Mayor?" I said. "Will you give me a job if I decide to stay?" "You don't need a job," the mayor said. "You don't seem to realize that you're a very famous man."

"How does being famous provide me with a livelihood?" I asked.

"In more ways than one," the mayor said. "You could become a donor, for instance. Now that over half of our professional men are medical doctors, more and more wives want children with some measure of scientific ability."

"But, Mr. Mayor," I said, "I'm above twenty-five."

"Of course," the mayor said, "the seed would have to be marketed abroad. The rate of exchange is none too favorable," he continued, "but even so you should be able to earn a comfortable living if you decided to stay."

"I don't know, Mr. Mayor," I said. "The idea is a little novel for me; but I suppose I could get accustomed to it."

"I'm sure you could," said the mayor. "And incidentally, whenever you decide to get rid of that junk in your mouth, I shall be glad to get an appointment for you with Elihu Smith, the dental extractor. He took care of all our children."

"I appreciate your kindness very much, Mr. Mayor," I said, smiling politely and trying to hide a suddenly rising feeling of despair. All my life I have been scared of dentists and dental extractors, and somehow I suddenly became aware of the painful fact that it was not within the power of science to return me to the twentieth century.

The Enormous Radio

by John Cheever

Jim and Irene Westcott were the kind of people who seem to strike that satisfactory average of income, endeavor, and respectability that is reached by the statistical reports in college alumni bulletins. They were the parents of two young children, they had been married nine years, they lived on the twelfth floor of an apartment house in the East Seventies between Fifth and Madison Avenues, they went to the theatre on an average of 10.3 times a year, and they hoped someday to live in Westchester. Irene Westcott was a pleasant, rather plain girl with soft brown hair and a wide, fine forehead upon which nothing at all had been written, and in the cold weather she wore a coat of fitch skins dyed to resemble mink. You could not say that Jim Westcott, at thirty-seven, looked younger than he was, but you could at least say of him that he seemed to feel younger. He wore his graying hair cut very short, he dressed in the kind of clothes his class had worn at Andover, and his manner was earnest, vehement, and intentionally naïve. The Westcotts differed from their friends, their classmates, and their neighbors only in an interest they shared in serious music. They went to a great many concerts—although they seldom mentioned this to anyone—and they spent a good deal of time listening to music on the radio.

Their radio was an old instrument, sensitive, unpredictable, and beyond repair. Neither of them understood the mechanics of radio—or of any of the other appliances that surrounded them—and when the instrument faltered, Jim would strike the side of the cabinet with his hand. This sometimes helped. One Sunday afternoon, in the middle of a Schubert quartet, the music faded away altogether. Jim struck the cabinet repeatedly, but there was no response; the Schubert was lost to them forever. He promised to buy Irene a new radio, and on Monday when he came home from work he told her that he had got one. He refused to describe it, and said it would be a surprise for her when it came.

The radio was delivered at the kitchen door the following afternoon, and with the assistance of her maid and the handyman Irene uncrated it and brought it into the living room. She was struck at once with the physical ugliness of the large gumwood cabinet. Irene was proud of her living room, she had chosen its furnishings and colors as carefully as she chose her clothes, and now it seemed to her that the new radio stood among her intimate possessions like an aggressive intruder. She was confounded by the number of dials and switches on the instrument panel, and she studied them thoroughly before she put the plug into a wall socket and turned the radio on. The dials flooded with a malevolent green light, and in the distance she heard the music of a piano quintet. The quintet was in the distance for only an instant; it bore down upon her with a speed greater than light and filled the apartment with the noise of music amplified so mightily that it knocked a china ornament from a table to the floor. She rushed to the instrument and reduced the volume. The violent forces that were snared in the ugly gumwood cabinet made her uneasy. Her children came home from school then, and she took them to the Park. It was not until later in the afternoon that she was able to return to the radio.

The maid had given the children their suppers and was supervising their baths when Irene turned on the radio, reduced the volume, and sat down to listen to a Mozart quintet that she knew and enjoyed. The music came through clearly. The new instrument had a much purer tone, she thought, than the old one. She decided that tone was most important and that she could conceal the cabinet behind a sofa. But as soon as she had made her peace with the radio, the interference began. A crackling sound like the noise of a burning powder fuse began to accompany the singing of the strings. Beyond the music, there was a rustling that reminded Irene unpleasantly of the sea, and as the quintet progressed, these noises were joined by many others. She tried all the dials and switches but nothing dimmed the interference, and she sat down; disappointed and bewildered, and tried to trace the flight of the melody. The elevator shaft in her building ran beside the living-room wall, and it was the noise of the elevator that gave her a clue to the character of the static. The rattling of the elevator cables and the opening and closing of the elevator doors were reproduced in her loudspeaker, and, realizing that the radio was sensitive to electrical currents of all sorts, she began to discern through the Mozart the ringing of telephone bells, the dialling of phones, and the lamentation of a vacuum cleaner. By listening more carefully, she was able to distinguish doorbells, elevator bells, electric razors, and Waring mixers, whose sounds had been picked up from the apartments that surrounded hers and transmitted through her loudspeaker. The powerful and ugly instrument, with its mistaken sensitivity to discord, was more than she could hope to master, so she turned the thing off and went into the nursery to see her children.

When Jim Westcott came home that night, he went to the radio confidently and worked the controls. He had the same sort of experience Irene had had. A man was speaking on the station Jim had chosen, and his voice swung instantly from the distance into a force so powerful that it shook the apartment. Jim turned the volume control and reduced the voice. Then, a minute or two later, the interference began. The ringing of telephones and door-bells set in, joined by the rasp of the elevator doors and the whir of cooking appliances. The character of the noise had changed since Irene had tried the radio earlier; the last of the electric razors was being unplugged, the vacuum cleaners had all been returned to their closets, and the static reflected that change in pace that overtakes the city after the sun goes down. He fiddled with the knobs but couldn't get rid of the noises, so he turned the radio off and told Irene that in the morning he'd call the people who had sold it to him and give them hell.

The following afternoon, when Irene returned to the apartment from a luncheon date, the maid told her that a man had come and fixed the radio. Irene went into the living room before she took off her hat and her furs and tried the instrument. From the loudspeaker came a recording of the "Missouri Waltz." It reminded her of the thin, scratchy music from an old-fashioned phonograph that she sometimes heard across the lake where she spent her summers. She waited until the waltz had finished, expecting an explanation of the recording, but there was none. The music was followed by silence, and then the plaintive and scratchy record was repeated. She turned the dial and got a satisfactory burst of Caucasian music—the thump of bare feet in the dust and the rattle of coin jewelry—but in the background she could hear the ringing of bells and a confusion of voices. Her children came home from school then, and she turned off the radio and went to the nursery.

When Jim came home that night, he was tired, and he took a bath and changed his clothes. Then he joined Irene in the living room. He had just turned on the radio when the maid announced dinner, so he left it on, and he and Irene went to the table.

Jim was too tired to make even a pretense of sociability, and there was nothing about the dinner to hold Irene's interest, so her attention wandered from the food to the deposits of silver polish on the candlesticks and from there to the music in the other room. She listened for a few moments to a Chopin prelude and then was surprised to hear a man's voice break in. "For Christ's sake, Kathy," he said, "do you always have to play the piano when I get home?" The music stopped abruptly. "It's the only chance I have," the woman said. "I'm at the office all day." "So am I," the man said. He added something obscene about an upright piano, and slammed a door. The passionate and melancholy music began again.

"Did you hear that?" Irene asked.

"What?" Jim was eating his dessert.

"The radio. A man said something while the music was still going on—something dirty."

"It's probably a play."

"I don't think it is a play," Irene said.

They left the table and took their coffee into the living room. Irene asked Jim to try another station. He turned the knob. "Have you seen my garters?" a man asked. "Button me up," a woman said. "Have you seen my garters?" the man said again. "Just button me up and I'll find your garters," the woman said. Jim shifted to another station. "I wish you wouldn't leave apple cores in the ashtrays," a man said. "I hate the smell."

"This is strange," Jim said.

"Isn't it?" Irene said.

Jim turned the knob again. " 'On the coast of Coromandel where the early pumpkins blow,' " a woman with a pronounced English accent said, " 'in the middle of the woods lived the Yonghy-Bonghy-Bò. Two old chairs, and half a candle, one old jug without a handle . . . ' "

"My God!" Irene cried. "That's the Sweeneys' nurse."

" 'These were all his worldly goods,' " the British voice continued.

"Turn that thing off," Irene said. "Maybe they can hear *us.*" Jim switched the radio off. "That was Miss Armstrong, the Sweeneys' nurse," Irene said. "She must be reading to the little girl. They live in 17-B. I've talked with Miss Armstrong in the Park. I know her voice very well. We must be getting other people's apartments."

"That's impossible," Jim said.

"Well, that was the Sweeneys' nurse," Irene said hotly. "I know her voice. I know it very well. I'm wondering if they can hear us."

Jim turned the switch. First from a distance and then nearer, nearer, as if borne on the wind, came the pure accents of the

Sweeneys' nurse again: " 'Lady Jingly! Lady Jingly!' " she said,
" 'Sitting where the pumpkins blow, will you come and be my wife,
said the Yonghy-Bonghy-Bò . . .' "

Jim went over to the radio and said "Hello" loudly into the
speaker.

" 'I am tired of living singly,' " the nurse went on, " 'on this
coast so wild and shingly, I'm a-weary of my life; if you'll come
and be my wife, quite serene would be my life . . .' "

"I guess she can't hear us," Irene said. "Try something else."

Jim turned to another station, and the living room was filled
with the uproar of a cocktail party that had overshot its mark.
Someone was playing the piano and singing the Whiffenpoof
Song, and the voices that surrounded the piano were vehement
and happy. "Eat some more sandwiches," a woman shrieked.
There were screams of laughter and a dish of some sort crashed to
the floor.

"Those must be the Hutchinsons, in 15-B," Irene said. "I
knew they were giving a party this afternoon. I saw her in the
liquor store. Isn't this too divine? Try something else. See if you
can get those people in 18-C."

The Westcotts overheard that evening a monologue on salmon
fishing in Canada, a bridge game, running comments on home
movies of what had apparently been a fortnight at Sea Island, and
a bitter family quarrel about an overdraft at the bank. They
turned off their radio at midnight and went to bed, weak with
laughter. Sometime in the night their son began to call for a glass
of water and Irene got one and took it to his room. It was very
early. All the lights in the neighborhood were extinguished, and
from the boy's window she could see the empty street. She went
into the living room and tried the radio. There was a faint
coughing, a moan, and then a man spoke. "Are you all right,
darling?" he asked. "Yes," a woman said wearily. "Yes, I'm all
right, I guess," and then she added with great feeling, "But, you
know, Charlie, I don't feel like myself any more. Sometimes there
are about fifteen or twenty minutes in the week when I feel like
myself. I don't like to go to another doctor, because the doctor's
bills are so awful already, but I just don't feel like myself,
Charlie. I just never feel like myself." They were not young,

Irene thought. She guessed from the timbre of their voices that they were middle-aged. The restrained melancholy of the dialogue and the draft from the bedroom window made her shiver, and she went back to bed.

The following morning, Irene cooked breakfast for the family—the maid didn't come up from her room in the basement until ten—braided her daughter's hair, and waited at the door until her children and her husband had been carried away in the elevator. Then she went into the living room and tried the radio. "I don't want to go to school," a child screamed. "I hate school. I won't go to school. I hate school." "You will go to school," an enraged woman said. "We paid eight hundred dollars to get you into that school and you'll go if it kills you." The next number on the dial produced the worn record of the "Missouri Waltz." Irene shifted the control and invaded the privacy of several breakfast tables. She overhead demonstrations of indigestion, carnal love, abysmal vanity, faith, and despair. Irene's life was nearly as simple and sheltered as it appeared to be, and the forthright and sometimes brutal language that came from the loudspeaker that morning astonished and troubled her. She continued to listen until her maid came in. Then she turned off the radio quickly, since this insight, she realized, was a furtive one.

Irene had a luncheon date with a friend that day, and she left her apartment at a little after twelve. There were a number of women in the elevator when it stopped at her floor. She stared at their handsome and impassive faces, their furs, and the cloth flowers in their hats. Which one of them had been to Sea Island, she wondered. Which one had overdrawn her bank account? The elevator stopped at the tenth floor and a woman with a pair of Skye terriers joined them. Her hair was rigged high on her head and she wore a mink cape. She was humming the "Missouri Waltz."

Irene had two Martinis at lunch, and she looked searchingly at her friend and wondered what her secrets were. They had intended to go shopping after lunch, but Irene excused herself and went home. She told the maid that she was not to be disturbed; then she went into the living room, closed the doors, and switched on the radio. She heard, in the course of the afternoon, the halting conversation of a woman entertaining her aunt, the hysterical conclusion of a luncheon party, and a hostess briefing her maid about some cocktail guests. "Don't give the best Scotch to anyone who hasn't white hair," the hostess said. "See if you can get rid of that liver paste before you pass those hot things, and could you lend me five dollars? I want to tip the elevator man."

As the afternoon waned, the conversations increased in intensity. From where Irene sat, she could see the open sky above Central Park. There were hundreds of clouds in the sky, as though the south wind had broken the winter into pieces and were blowing it north, and on her radio she could hear the arrival of cocktail guests and the return of children and businessmen from their schools and offices. "I found a good-sized diamond on the bathroom floor this morning," a woman said. "It must have fallen out of that bracelet Mrs. Dunston was wearing last night." "We'll sell it," a man said. "Take it down to the jeweller on Madison Avenue and sell it. Mrs. Dunston won't know the difference, and we could use a couple of hundred bucks . . ." " 'Oranges and lemons, say the bells of St. Clement's,' " the Sweeneys' nurse sang. " 'Half-pence and farthings, say the bells of St. Martin's. When will you pay me? say the bells at old Baily . . .' " "It's not a hat," a woman cried, and at her back roared a cocktail party. "It's not a hat, it's a love affair. That's what Walter Florell said. He said it's not a hat, it's a love affair," and then, in a lower voice, the same woman added, "Talk to somebody, for Christ's sake, honey, talk to somebody. If she catches you standing here not talking to anybody, she'll take us off her invitation list, and I love these parties."

The Westcotts were going out for dinner that night, and when Jim came home, Irene was dressing. She seemed sad and vague, and he brought her a drink. They were dining with friends in the neighborhood, and they walked to where they were going. The sky was broad and filled with light. It was one of those splendid spring evenings that excite memory and desire, and the air that touched their hands and faces felt very soft. A Salvation Army band was on the corner playing "Jesus Is Sweeter." Irene drew on her husband's arm and held him there for a minute, to hear the music. "They're really such nice people, aren't they?" she said. "They have such nice faces. Actually, they're so much nicer than a lot of the people we know." She took a bill from her purse and walked over and dropped it into the tambourine. There was in her face, when she returned to her husband, a look of radiant melancholy that he was not familiar with. And her conduct at the dinner party that night seemed strange to him, too. She interrupted her hostess rudely and stared at the people across the table from her with an intensity for which she would have punished her children.

It was still mild when they walked home from the party, and Irene looked up at the spring stars. " 'How far that little candle throws its beams,' " she exclaimed. " 'So shines a good deed in a naughty world.' " She waited that night until Jim had fallen asleep, and then went into the living room and turned on the radio.

Jim came home about six the next night. Emma, the maid, let him in, and he had taken off his hat and was taking off his coat when Irene ran into the hall. Her face was shining with tears and her hair was disordered. "Go up to 16-C, Jim!" she screamed. "Don't take off your coat. Go up to 16-C. Mr. Osborn's beating his wife. They've been quarrelling since four o'clock, and now he's hitting her. Go up there and stop him."

From the radio in the living room, Jim heard screams, obscenities, and thuds. "You know you don't have to listen to this sort of thing," he said. He strode into the living room and turned the switch. "It's indecent," he said. "It's like looking in windows. You know you don't have to listen to this sort of thing. You can turn it off."

"Oh, it's so horrible, it's so dreadful," Irene was sobbing. "I've been listening all day, and it's so depressing."

"Well, if it's so depressing, why do you listen to it? I bought this damned radio to give you some pleasure," he said. "I paid a great deal of money for it. I thought it might make you happy. I wanted to make you happy."

"Don't, don't, don't, don't quarrel with me," she moaned, and laid her head on his shoulder. "All the others have been quarreling all day. Everybody's been quarrelling. They're all worried about money. Mrs. Hutchinson's mother is dying of cancer in Florida and they don't have enough money to send her to the Mayo Clinic. At least, Mr. Hutchinson says they don't have enough money. And some woman in this building is having an affair with the superintendent—with that hideous superintendent. It's too disgusting. And Mrs. Melville has heart trouble and Mr. Hendricks is going to lose his job in April and Mrs. Hendricks is horrid about the whole thing and that girl who plays the 'Missouri Waltz' is a whore, a common whore, and the elevator man has tuberculosis and Mr. Osborn has been beating Mrs. Osborn." She wailed, she trembled with grief and checked the stream of tears down her face with the heel of her palm.

"Well, why do you have to listen?" Jim asked again. "Why do you have to listen to this stuff if it makes you so miserable?"

"Oh, don't, don't, don't," she cried. "Life is too terrible, too sordid and awful. But we've never been like that, have we, darling? Have we? I mean we've always been good and decent and loving to one another, haven't we? And we have two children, two beautiful children. Our lives aren't sordid, are they, darling? Are they?" She flung her arms around his neck and drew his face down to hers. "We're happy, aren't we, darling? We are happy, aren't we?"

"Of course we're happy," he said tiredly. He began to surrender his resentment. "Of course we're happy. I'll have that damned radio fixed or taken away tomorrow." He stroked her soft hair. "My poor girl," he said.

"You love me, don't you?" she asked. "And we're not hypercritical or worried about money or dishonest, are we?"

"No, darling," he said.

A man came in the morning and fixed the radio. Irene turned it on cautiously and was happy to hear a California-wine commercial and a recording of Beethoven's Ninth Symphony, including Schiller's "Ode to Joy." She kept the radio on all day and nothing untoward came from the speaker.

A Spanish suite was being played when Jim came home. "Is

everything all right?" he asked. His face was pale, she thought. They had some cocktails and went in to dinner to the "Anvil Chorus" from "Il Trovatore." This was followed by Debussy's "La Mer."

"I paid the bill for the radio today," Jim said. "It cost four hundred dollars. I hope you'll get some enjoyment out of it."

"Oh, I'm sure I will," Irene said.

"Four hundred dollars is a good deal more than I can afford," he went on. "I wanted to get something that you'd enjoy. It's the last extravagance we'll be able to indulge in this year. I see that you haven't paid your clothing bills yet. I saw them on your dressing table." He looked directly at her. "Why did you tell me you'd paid them? Why did you lie to me?"

"I just didn't want you to worry, Jim," she said. She drank some water. "I'll be able to pay my bills out of this month's allowance. There were the slipcovers last month, and that party."

"You've got to learn to handle the money I give you a little more intelligently, Irene," he said. "You've got to understand that we won't have as much money this year as we had last. I had a very sobering talk with Mitchell today. No one is buying anything. We're spending all our time promoting new issues, and you know how long that takes. I'm not getting any younger, you know. I'm thirty-seven. My hair will be gray next year. I haven't done as well as I'd hoped to do. And I don't suppose things will get any better."

"Yes, dear," she said.

"We've got to start cutting down," Jim said. "We've got to think of the children. To be perfectly frank with you, I worry about money a great deal. I'm not at all sure of the future. No one is. If anything should happen to me, there's the insurance, but that wouldn't go very far today. I've worked awfully hard to give you and the children a comfortable life," he said bitterly. "I don't like to see all of my energies, all of my youth, wasted in fur coats and radios and slipcovers and—"

"Please, Jim," she said. "Please. They'll hear us."

"*Who'll* hear us? Emma can't hear us."

"The radio."

"Oh, I'm sick!" he shouted. "I'm sick to death of your apprehensiveness. The radio can't hear us. Nobody can hear us. And what if they can hear us? Who cares?"

Irene got up from the table and went into the living room. Jim went to the door and shouted at her from there. "Why are you so Christly all of a sudden? What's turned you overnight into a convent girl? You stole your mother's jewelry before they probated her will. You never gave your sister a cent of that money that was intended for her—not even when she needed it. You made Grace Howland's life miserable, and where was all your piety and your virtue when you went to that abortionist? I'll never forget how cool you were. You packed your bag and off to have that child murdered as if you were going to Nassau. If you'd had any reasons, if you'd any good reasons—"

Irene stood for a minute before the hideous cabinet, disgraced and sickened, but she held her hand on the switch before she extinguished the music and the voices, hoping that the instrument might speak to her kindly, that she might hear the Sweeneys' nurse. Jim continued to shout at her from the door. The voice on the readio was suave and noncommittal. "An early-morning railroad disaster in Tokyo," the loudspeaker said, "killed twenty-nine people. A fire in a Catholic hospital near Buffalo for the care of blind children was extinguished early this morning by nuns. The temperature is forty-seven. The humidity is eighty-nine."

The Finest Story in the World

by Rudyard Kipling

> "Or ever the knightly years were gone
> With the old world to the grave,
> I was a king in Babylon
> And you were a Christian slave."
> —*W.E. Henley.*

His name was Charlie Mears; he was the only son of his mother who was a widow, and he lived in the north of London, coming into the City every day to work in a bank. He was twenty years old and suffered from aspirations. I met him in a public billiard -saloon where the marker called him by his given name, and he called the marker "Bulls-eyes." Charlie explained, a little nervously, that he had only come to the place to look on, and since looking on at games of skill is not a cheap amusement for the young, I suggested that Charlie should go back to his mother.

That was our first step toward better acquaintance. He would call on me sometimes in the evenings instead of running about London with his fellow-clerks; and before long, speaking of himself as a young man must, he told me of his aspirations, which were all literary. He desired to make himself an undying name

177

chiefly through verse, though he was not above sending stories of love and death to the drop-a-penny-in-the-slot journals. It was my fate to sit still while Charlie read me poems of many hundred lines, and bulky fragments of plays that would surely shake the world. My reward was his unreserved confidence, and the self-revelations and troubles of a young man are almost as holy as those of a maiden. Charlie had never fallen in love, but was anxious to do so on the first opportunity; he believed in all things good and all things honorable, but, at the same time, was curiously careful to let me see that he knew his way about the world as befitted a bank clerk on twenty-five shillings a week. He rhymed "dove" with "love" and "moon" with "June," and devoutly believed that they had never so been rhymed before. The long lame gaps in his plays he filled up with hasty words of apology and description and swept on, seeing all that he intended to do so clearly that he esteemed it already done, and turned to me for applause.

I fancy that his mother did not encourage his aspirations, and I know that his writing-table at home was the edge of his wash-stand. This he told me almost at the outset of our acquaintance; when he was ravaging my bookshelves, and a little before I was implored to speak the truth as to his chances of "writing something really great, you know." Maybe I encouraged him too much, for, one night, he called on me, his eyes flaming with excitement, and said breathlessly:

"Do you mind—can you let me stay here and write all this evening? I won't interrupt you, I won't really. There's no place for me to write in at my mother's."

"What's the trouble?" I said, knowing well what that trouble was.

"I've a notion in my head that would make the most splendid story that was ever written. Do let me write it out here. It's *such* a notion!"

There was no resisting the appeal. I set him a table; he hardly thanked me, but plunged into the work at once. For half an hour the pen scratched without stopping. Then Charlie sighed and tugged his hair. The scratching grew slower, there was more erasures, and at last ceased. The finest story in the world would not come forth.

"It looks such awful rot now," he said, mournfully. "And yet it seemed so good when I was thinking about it. What's wrong?"

I could not dishearten him by saying the truth. So I answered: "Perhaps you don't feel in the mood for writing."

"Yes I do—except when I look at this stuff. Ugh!"

"Read me what you've done," I said.

He read, and it was wondrous bad, and he paused at all the specially turgid sentences, expecting a little approval; for he was proud of those sentences, as I knew he would be.

"It needs compression," I suggested, cautiously.

"I hate cutting my things down. I don't think you could alter a word here without spoiling the sense. It reads better aloud than when I was writing it."

"Charlie, you're suffering from an alarming disease afflicting a numerous class. Put the thing by, and tackle it again in a week."

"I want to do it at once. What do you think of it?"

"How can I judge from a half-written tale? Tell me the story as it lies in your head."

Charlie told, and in the telling there was everything that his ignorance had so carefully prevented from escaping into the written word. I looked at him, and wondering whether it were possible that he did not know the originality, the power of the notion that had come in his way? It was distinctly a Notion among notions. Men had been puffed up with pride by notions not a tithe as excellent and practicable. But Charlie babbled on serenely, interrupting the current of pure fancy with samples of horrible sentences that he purposed to use. I heard him out to the end. It would be folly to allow his idea to remain in his own inept hands, when I could do so much with it. Not all that could be done indeed; but, oh so much!

"What do you think?" he said, at last. "I fancy I shall call it 'The Story of a Ship.'"

"I think the idea's pretty good; but you won't be able to handle it for ever so long. Now I"—

"Would it be of any use to you? Would you care to take it? I should be proud," said Charlie, promptly.

There are few things sweeter in this world than the guileless, hot-headed, intemperate, open admiration of a junior. Even a woman in her blindest devotion does not fall into the gait of the man she adores, tilt her bonnet to the angle at which he wears his hat, or interlard her speech with his pet oaths. And Charlie did all these things. Still it was necessary to salve my conscience before I possessed myself of Charlie's thoughts.

"Let's make a bargain. I'll give you a fiver for the notion," I said.

Charlie became a bank-clerk at once.

"Oh, that's impossible. Between two pals, you know, if I may call you so, and speaking as a man of the world, I couldn't. Take the notion if it's any use to you. I've heaps more."

He had—none knew this better than I—but they were the notions of other men.

"Look at it as a matter of business—between men of the world," I returned. "Five pounds will buy you any number of poetry-books. Business is business, and you may be sure I shouldn't give that price unless"—

"Oh, if you put it *that way*," said Charlie, visibly moved by the thought of the books. The bargain was clinched with an agreement that he should at unstated intervals come to me with all the notions that he possessed, should have a table of his own to write at, and unquestioned right to inflict upon me all his poems and fragments of poems. Then I said, "Now tell me how you came by this idea."

"It came by itself." Charlie's eyes opened a little.

"Yes, but you told me a great deal about the hero that you must have read before somewhere."

"I haven't any time for reading, except when you let me sit here, and on Sundays I'm on my bicycle or down the river all day. There's nothing wrong about the hero, is there?"

"Tell me again and I shall understand clearly. You say that your hero went pirating. How did he live?"

"He was on the lower deck of this ship-thing that I was telling you about."

"What sort of ship?"

"It was the kind rowed with oars, and the sea spurts through the oar-holes and the men row sitting up to their knees in water. Then there's a bench running down between the two lines of oars and an overseer with a whip walks up and down the bench to make the men work.

"How do you know that?"

"It's in the table. There's a rope running overhead, looped to the upper deck, for the overseer to catch hold of when the ship rolls. When the overseer misses the rope once and falls among the rowers, remember the hero laughs at him and gets licked for it. He's chained to his oar of course—the hero."

"How is he chained?"

"With an iron band round his waist fixed to the bench he sits on, and a sort of handcuff on his left wrist chaining him to the oar. He's on the lower deck where the worst men are sent, and the only light comes from the hatchways and through the oar-holes. Can't you imagine the sunlight just squeezing through between the handle and the hole and wobbling about as the ship moves?"

"I can, but I can't imagine your imagining it."

"How could it be any other way? Now you listen to me. The long oars on the upper deck are managed by four men to each bench, the lower ones by three, and the lowest of all by two. Remember it's quite dark on the lowest deck and all the men there go mad. When a man dies at his oar on that deck he isn't thrown overboard, but cut up in his chains and stuffed through the oar-hole in little pieces."

"Why?" I demanded, amazed, not so much at the information as the tone of command in which it was flung out.

"To save trouble and to frighten the others. It needs two overseers to drag a man's body up to the top deck; and if the men at the lower deck oars were left alone, of course they'd stop rowing and try to pull up the benches by all standing up together in their chains."

"You've a most provident imagination. Where have you been reading about galleys and galley-slaves?"

"Nowhere that I remember. I row a little when I get the chance. But, perhaps, if you say so, I may have read something."

He went away shortly afterward to deal with booksellers, and I wondered how a bank clerk aged twenty could put into my hands with a profligate abundance of detail, all given with absolute assurance, the story of extravagant and bloodthirsty adventure, riot, piracy, and death in unnamed seas. He had led his hero a desperate dance through revolt against the overseas, to command of a ship of his own, and ultimate establishment of a kingdom on an island "somewhere in the sea, you know"; and, delighted with my paltry five pounds, had gone out to buy the notions of other men, that these might teach him how to write. I had the consolation of knowing that this notion was mine by right of purchase, and I thought that I could made something of it.

When next he came to me he was drunk—royally drunk on many poets for the first time revealed to him. His pupils were dilated, his words tumbled over each other, and he wrapped himself in quotations. Most of all was he drunk with Longfellow.

"Isn't it splendid? Isn't it superb?" he cried, after hasty greetings. "Listen to this—

" 'Wouldst thou,'—so the helmsman answered,
    'Know the secret of the sea?
    Only those who brave its dangers
    Comprehend its mystery.

By gum!
" 'Only those who brave its dangers
    Comprehend its mystery.' "

he repeated twenty times, walking up and down the room and forgetting me. "But I *can* understand it too," he said to himself. "I don't know how to thank you for that fiver. And this; listen—

" 'I remember the black wharves and the ships
    And the sea-tides tossing free,

And the Spanish sailors with bearded lips,
And the beauty and mystery of the ships,
And the magic of the sea.'

I haven't braved any dangers, but I feel as if I knew all about it."

"You certainly seem to have a grip of the sea. Have you ever seen it?"

"When I was a little chap I went to Brighton once; we used to live in Coventry, though, before we came to London. I never saw it,

" 'When descends on the Atlantic
     The gigantic
Storm-wind of the Equinox.' "

He shook me by the shoulder to make me understand the passion that was shaking himself.

"When that storm comes," he continued, "I think that all the oars in the ship that I was talking about get broken, and the rowers have their chests smashed in by the bucking oar-heads. By the way, have you done anything with that notion of mine yet?"

"No. I was waiting to hear more of it from you. Tell me how in the world you're so certain about the fittings of the ship. You know nothing of ships."

"I don't know. It's as real as anything to me until I try to write it down. I was thinking about it only last night in bed, after you had loaned me 'Treasure Island'; and I made up a whole lot of new things to go into the story."

"What sort of things?"

"About the food the men ate; rotten figs and black beans and wine in a skin bag, passed from bench to bench."

"Was the ship built so long ago as *that?*"

"As what? I don't know whether it was long ago or not. It's only a notion, but sometimes it seems just as real as if it was true. Do I bother you with talking about it?"

"Not in the least. Did you make up anything else?"

"Yes, but it's nonsense." Charlie flushed a little.

"Never mind; let's hear about it."

"Well, I was thinking over the story, and after awhile I got out of bed and wrote down on a piece of paper the sort of stuff the men might be supposed to scratch on their oars with the edges of their handcuffs. It seemed to make the thing more lifelike. It *is* so real to me, y'know."

"Have you the paper on you?"

"Ye-es, but what's the use of showing it? It's only a lot of scratches. All the same, we might have 'em reproduced in the book on the front page."

"I'll attend to those details. Show me what your men wrote."

He pulled out of his pocket a sheet of note-paper, with a single line of scratches upon it, and I put this carefully away.

"What is it supposed to mean in English?" I said.

"Oh, I don't know. Perhaps it means I'm beastly tired. It's great nonsense," he repeated, "but all those men in the ship seem as real as people to me. Do do something to the notion soon; I should like to see it written and printed.'"

"But all you've told me would make a long book."

"Make it then. You've only to sit down and write it out."

"Give me a little time. Have you any more notions?"

"Not just now. I'm reading all the books I've bought. They're splendid."

When he had left I looked at the sheet of note-paper with the inscription upon it. Then I took my head tenderly between both hands, to make certain that it was not coming off or turning round. Then . . . but there seemed to be no interval between quitting my rooms and finding myself arguing with a policeman outside a door marked *Private* in a corridor of the British Museum. All I demanded, as politely as possible, was "the Greek antiquity man." The policeman knew nothing except the rules of the Museum, and it became necessary to forage through all the houses and offices inside the gates. An elderly gentleman called away from his lunch put an end to my search by holding the note-paper between finger and thumb and sniffing at it scornfully.

"What does this mean? H'mm," said he. "So far as I can

ascertain it is an attempt to write extremely corrupt Greek on the part"—here he glared at me with intention—"of an extremely illiterate—ah—person." He read slowly from the paper, *"Pollock, Erckmann, Tauchnitz, Henniker"*—four names familiar to me.

"Can you tell me what the corruption is supposed to mean—the gist of the thing?" I asked.

"I have been—many times—overcome with weariness in this particular employment. That is the meaning." He returned me the paper, and I fled without a word of thanks, explanation, or apology.

I might have been excused for forgetting much. To me of all men had been given the chance to write the most marvelous tale in the world, nothing less than the story of a Greek galley-slave, as told by himself. Small wonder that his dreaming had seemed real to Charlie. The Fates that are so careful to shut the doors of each successive life behind us had, in this case, been neglectful, and Charlie was looking, though that he did not know where never man had been permitted to look with full knowledge since Time began. Above all he was absolutely ignorant of the knowledge sold to me for five pounds; and he would retain that ignorance, for bank-clerks do not understand metempsychosis, and a sound commercial education does not include Greek. He would supply me—here I capered among the dumb gods of Egypt and laughed in their battered faces—with material to make my tale sure—so sure that the world would hail it as an impudent and vamped fiction. And I—I alone would know that it was absolutely and literally true. I,—I alone held this jewel to my hand for the cutting and polishing. Therefore I danced again among the gods till a policeman saw me and took steps in my direction.

It remained now only to encourage Charlie to talk, and here there was no difficulty. But I had forgotten those accursed books of poetry. He came to me time after time, as useless as a surcharged phonograph—drunk on Byron, Shelley, or Keats. Knowing now what the boy had been in his past lives, and desperately anxious not to lose one word of his babble, I could not hide from him my respect and interest. He misconstrued both into respect for the present soul of Charlie Mears, to whom life was as new as

it was to Adam, and interest in his readings; and stretched my
patience to breaking point by reciting poetry—not his own now,
but that of others. I wished every English poet blotted out of the
memory of mankind. I blasphemed the mightiest names of song
because they had drawn Charlie from the path of direct narrative,
and would, later, spur him to imitate them; but I choked down
my impatience until the first flood of enthusiasm should have
spent itself and the boy returned to his dreams.

"What's the use of my telling you what *I* think, when these
chaps wrote things for the angels to read?" he growled, one evening. "Why don't you write something like theirs?"

"I don't think you're treating me quite fairly," I said, speaking
under strong restraint.

"I've given you the story," he said, shortly replunging into
"Lara."

"But I want the details."

"The things I make up about that damned ship that you call a
galley? They're quite easy. You can just make 'em up yourself.
Turn up the gas a little, I want to go on reading."

I could have broken the gas globe over his head for his amazing stupidity. I could indeed make up things for myself did I only
know what Charlie did not know that he knew. But since the
doors were shut behind me I could only wait his youthful pleasure and strive to keep him in good temper. One minute's want of
guard might spoil a priceless revelation: now and again he would
toss his books aside—he kept them in my rooms, for his mother
would have been shocked at the waste of good money had she
seen them—and launched into his sea dreams. Again I cursed all
the poets of England. The plastic mind of the bank-clerk had
been overlaid, colored and distorted by that which he had read,
and the result as delivered was a confused tangle of other voices
most like the muttered song through a City telephone in the
busiest part of the day

He talked of the galley—his own galley had he but known
it—with illustrations borrowed from the "Bride of Abydos." He
pointed the experiences of his hero with quotations from "The
Corsair," and threw in deep and desperate moral reflections from

"Cain" and "Manfred." expecting me to use them all. Only when the talk turned on Longfellow were the jarring cross-currents dumb, and I knew that Charlie was speaking the truth as he remembered it.

"What do you think of this?" I said one evening, as soon as I understood the medium in which his memory worked best, and, before he could expostulate, read him the whole of "The Sage of King Olaf!"

He listened open-mouthed, flushed, his hands drumming on the back of the sofa where he lay, till I came to the Song of Einar Tamberskelver and the verse:

"Einar then, the arrow taking
    From the loosened string,
Answered: 'That was Norway breaking
    'Neath thy hand, O King.' "

He gasped with pure delight of sound.

"That's better than Byron, a little," I ventured.

"Better? Why it's *true*! How could he have known?"

I went back and repeated:

" 'What was that?' said Olaf, standing
    On the quarter-deck,
'Something heard I like the standing
    Of a shattered wreck?' "

"How could he have known how the ships crash and the oars rip out and go *z-zzp* all along the line? Why only the other night. . . . But go back please and read 'The Skerry of Shrieks' again."

"No, I'm tired. Let's talk. What happened the other night?"

"I had an awful nightmare about that galley of ours. I dreamed I was drowned in a fight. You see we ran alongside another ship in harbor. The water was dead still except where our oars whipped it up. You know where I always sit in the galley?" He spoke haltingly at first, under a fine English fear of being laughed at.

"No. That's news to me," I answered, meekly, my heart beginning to beat.

"On the fourth oar from the bow on the right side on the upper deck. There were four of us at that oar, all chained. I remember watching the water and trying to get my handcuffs off before the row began. Then we closed up on the other ship, and all their fighting men jumped over our bulwarks, and my bench broke and I was pinned down with the three other fellows on top of me, and the big oar jammed across our backs."

"Well?" Charlies's eyes were alive and alight. He was looking at the wall behind my chair.

"I don't know how we fought. The men were trampling all over my back, and I lay low. Then our rowers on the left side—tied to their oars, you know—began to yell and back water. I could hear the water sizzle, and we spun round like a cockchafer and I knew, lying where I was, that there was a galley coming up bow-on, to ram us on the left side. I could just lift up my head and see her sail over the bulwarks. We wanted to meet her bow to bow, but it was too late. We could only turn a little bit because the galley on our right had hooked herself on to us and stopped our moving. Then, by gum! there was a crash! Our left oars began to break as the other galley, the moving one y'know, stuck her nose into them. Then the lower-deck oars shot up through the deck-planking, but first, and one of them jumped clean up into the air and came down again close to my head."

"How was that managed?"

"The moving galley's bow was plunking them back through their own oarholes, and I could hear the devil of a shindy in the decks below. Then her nose caught us nearly in the middle, and we tilted sideways, and the fellows in the right-hand galley un-hitched their hooks and ropes, and threw things on to our upper deck—arrows, and hot pitch or something that stung, and we went up and up and up on the left side, and the right side dipped, and I twisted my head round and saw the water stand still as it topped the right bulwarks, and then it curled over and crashed down on the whole lot of us on the right side, and I felt it hit my back, and I woke."

"One minute, Charlie. When the sea topped the bulwarks, what did it look like?" I had my reasons for asking. A man of my acquaintance had once gone down with a leaking ship in a still sea, and had seen the water-level pause for an instant ere it fell on the deck.

"It looked just like a banjo-string drawn tight, and it seemed to stay there for years," said Charlie.

Exactly! The other man had said: "It looked like a silver wire laid down along the bulwarks, and I thought it was never going to break." He had paid everything except the bare life for this little valueless piece of knowledge, and I had traveled ten thousand weary miles to meet him and take his knowledge, at second hand. But Charlie, the bank-clerk on twenty-five shillings a week, he who had never been out of sight of a London omnibus, knew it all. It was no consolation to me that once in his lives he had been forced to die for his gains. I also must have died scores of times, but behind me, because I could have used my knowledge, the doors were shut.

"And then?" I said, trying to put away the devil of envy.

"The funny thing was, though, in all the mess I didn't feel a bit astonished or frightened. It seemed as if I'd been in a good many fights, because I told my next man so when the row began. But that cad of an overseer on my deck wouldn't unloose our chains and give us a chance. He always said that we'd all be set free after a battle, but we never were; we never were." Charlie shook his head mournfully.

"What a scoundrel!"

"I should say he was. He never gave us enough to eat, and sometimes we were so thirsty that we used to drink salt-water. I can taste that salt-water still."

"Now tell me something about the harbor where the fight was fought."

"I didn't dream about that. I know it was a harbor, though; because we were tied up to a ring on a white wall and all the face of the stone under water was covered with wood to prevent our ram getting chipped when the tide made us rock."

"That's curious. Our hero commanded the galley, didn't he?"

"Didn't he just! He stood by the bows and shouted like a good 'un. He was the man who killed the overseer."

"But you were all drowned together, Charlie, weren't you?"

"I can't make that fit quite," he said with a puzzled look. "The galley must have gone down with all hands and yet I fancy that the hero went on living afterward. Perhaps he climbed into the attacking ship. I wouldn't see that, of course. I was dead, you know."

He shivered slightly and protested that he could remember no more.

I did not press him further, but to satisfy myself that he lay in ignorance of the workings of his own mind, deliberately introduced him to Mortimer Collins's "Transmigration," and gave him a sketch of the plot before he opened the pages.

"What rot it all is!" he said, frankly, at the end of an hour. "I don't understand his nonsense about the Red Planet Mars and the King, and the rest of it. Chuck me the Longfellow again."

I handed him the book and wrote out as much as I could remember of his description of the sea-fight, appealing to him from time to time for confirmation of fact or detail. He would answer without raising his eyes from the book, as assuredly as though all his knowledge lay before him on the printed page. I spoke under the normal key of my voice that the current might not be broken, and I know that he was not aware of what he was saying, for his thoughts were out on the sea with Longfellow.

"Charlie," I asked, "when the rowers on the gallies mutinied how did they kill their overseers?"

"Tore up the benches and brained 'em. That happened when a heavy sea was running. An overseer on the lower deck slipped from the centre plank and fell among the rowers. They choked him to death against the side of the ship with their chained hands quite quietly, and it was too dark for the other overseer to see what had happened. When he asked, he was pulled down too and choked, and the lower deck fought their way up deck by deck, with the pieces of the broken benches banging behind 'em. How they howled!"

"And what happened after that?"

"I don't know. The hero went away—red hair and red beard and all. That was after he had captured our galley, I think."

The sound of my voice irritated him, and he motioned slightly with his left hand as a man does when interruption jars.

"You never told me he was redheaded before, or that he captured your galley," I said, after a discreet interval.

Charlie did not raise his eyes.

"He was as red as a red bear," said he, abstractedly. "He came from the north; they said so in the galley when he looked for rowers—not slaves, but free men. Afterward—years and years afterward—news came from another ship, or else he came back"—

His lips moved in silence. He was rapturously retasting some poem before him.

"Where had he been, then?" I was almost whispering that the sentence might come gentle to whichever section of Charlie's brain was working on my behalf.

"To the Beaches—the Long and Wonderful Beaches!" was the reply, after a minute of silence.

"To Furdurstrandi?" I asked, tingling from head to foot.

"Yes, to Furdurstrandi," he pronounced the word in a new fashion. "And I too saw"— The voice failed.

"Do you know what you have said?" I shouted, incautiously.

He lifted his eyes, fully roused now. "No!" he snapped. "I wish you'd let a chap go on reading. Hark to this:

" 'But Othere, the old sea captain,
He neither paused nor stirred
    Till the king listened, and then
    Once more took up his pen
And wrote down every word.

" 'And to the King of the Saxons
In witness of the truth,
    Raising his noble head,
    He stretched his brown hand and said,
"Behold this walrus tooth." ' '

By Jove, what chaps those must have been, to go sailing all over
the shop never knowing where they'd fetch the land!
Hah!"

"Charlie," I pleaded, "if you'll only be sensible for a minute
or two I'll make our hero in our tale every inch as good as
Othere."

"Umph! Longfellow wrote that poem. I don't care about writing things any more. I want to read." He was thoroughly out of
tune now, and raging over my own ill-luck, I left him.

Conceive yourself at the door of the world's treasure-house
guarded by a child—an idle irresponsible child playing knuckle-
bones—on whose favor depends the gift of the key, and you will
imagine one-half my torment. Till that evening Charlie had
spoken nothing that might not lie within the experiences of a
Greek galley-slave. But now, or there was no virture in books, he
had talked of some desperate adventure of the Vikings, of
Thorfin Karsefne's sailing to Wineland, which is America, in the
ninth or tenth century. The battle in the harbor he had seen; and
his own death he had described. But this was a much more startling plunge into the past. Was it possible that he had skipped half
a dozen lives and was then dimly remembering some episode of a
thousand years later? It was a maddening jumble, and the worst
of it was that Charlie Mears in his normal condition was the last
person in the world to clear it up. I could only wait and watch,
but I went to bed that night full of the wildest imaginings. There
was nothing that was not possible if Charlie's detestable memory
only held good.

I might rewrite the Saga of Throfin Kalsefne as it had never
been written before, might tell the story of the first discovery of
America, myself the discoverer. But I was entirely at Charlie's
mercy, and so long as there was a three-and-six-penny Bohn
volume within his reach Charlie would not tell. I dared not curse
him openly; I hardly dared jog his memory, for I was dealing with
the experiences of a thousand years ago, told through the mouth
of a boy of today; and a boy of to-day is affected by every
change of tone and gust of opinion, so that he lies even when he
desires to speak the truth.

I saw no more of him for nearly a week. When next I met him it was in Gracechurch Street with a billbook chained to his waist. Business took him over London Bridge and I accompanied him. He was very full of the importance of that book and magnified it. As we passed over the Thames we paused to look at a steamer unloading great slabs of white and brown marble. A barge drifted under the steamer's stern and a lonely cow in that barge bellowed. Charlie's face changed from the face of the bank-clerk to that of an unknown and—though he would not have believed this—a much shrewder man. He flung out his arm across the parapet of the bridge and laughing very loudly, said:

"When they heard *our* bulls bellow the Skroelings ran away!"

I waited only for an instant, but the barge and the cow had disappeared under the bows of the steamer before I answered.

"Charlie, what do you suppose are Skroelings?"

"Never heard of 'em before. They sound like a new kind of seagull. What a chap you are for asking questions!" he replied. "I have to go to the cashier of the Omnibus Company yonder. Will you wait for me and we can lunch somewhere together? I've a notion for a poem."

"No, thanks. I'm off. You're sure you know nothing about Skroelings?"

"Not unless he's been entered for the Liverpool Handicap." He nodded and disappeared in the crowd.

Now it is written in the Saga of Eric the Red or that of Throfin Karlsefne, that nine hundred years ago when Karlsefne's galleys came to Leif's booths, which Leif had erected in the unknown land called Markland, which may or may not have been Rhode Island, the Skroelings—and the Lord He knows who these may or may not have been—came to trade with the Vikings, and ran away because they were frightened at the bellowing of the cattle which Throfin had brought with him in the ships. But what in the world could a Greek slave know of that affair? I wandered up and down among the streets trying to unravel the mystery, and the more I considered it, the more baffling it grew. One thing only seemed certain and that certainty took away my breath for the moment. If I came to full knowledge of anything at all, it would not be one life of the soul in Charlie Mears's body, but half a dozen—half a dozen several and separate existences spent on blue water in the morning of the world!

Then I walked round the situation.

Obviously if I used my knowledge I should stand alone and unapproachable until all men were as wise as myself. That would be something, but manlike I was ungrateful. It seemed bitterly unfair that Charlie's memory should fail me when I needed it most. Great Powers above—I looked up at them through the fog smoke—did the Lords of Life and Death know what this meant to me? Nothing less than eternal fame of the best kind, that comes from One, and is shared by one alone. I would be content—remembering Clive, I stood astounded at my own moderation,—with the mere right to tell one story, to work out one little contribution to the light literature of the day. If Charlie were permitted full recollection for one hour—for sixty short minutes—of existences that had extended over a thousand years—I would forego all profit and honor from all that I should make of his speech. I would take no share in the commotion that would follow throughout the particular corner of the earth that calls itself "the world." The thing should be put forth anonymously. Nay, I would make other men believe that they had written it. They would hire bull-hided self-advertising Englishmen to bellow it abroad. Preachers would found a fresh conduct of life upon it, swearing that it was new and that they had lifted the fear of death from all mankind. Every Orientalist in Europe would patronize it discursively with Sanskrit and Pali texts. Terrible women would invent unclean variants of the men's belief for the elevation of their sisters. Churches and religions would war over it. Between the hailing and re-starting of an omnibus I foresaw the scuffles that would arise among half a dozen denominations all professing "the doctrine of the True Metempsychosis as applied to the world and the New Era"; and saw, too, the respectable English newspapers shying, like frightened kine, over the beautiful simplicity of the tale. The mind leaped forward a hundred—two hundred—a thousand years. I saw with sorrow that men would mutilate and garble the story; that rival creeds would turn it upside down till, at last, the western world which clings to the dread of death more closely than the hope of life, would set it aside as an interesting superstition and stampede after some faith so long forgotten that it seemed altogether new. Upon this I changed the terms of the bargain that I would make with the Lords of Life and Death. Only let me know, let me write, the story with sure knowledge that I wrote the truth, and I would burn the manuscript as a solemn sacrifice. Five minutes after the last line was written I would destroy it all. But I must be allowed to write it with absolute certainty.

There was no answer. The flaming colors of an Aquarium poster caught my eye and I wondered whether it would be wise or prudent to lure Charlie into the hands of the professional mesmerist, and whether, if he were under his power, he would speak of his past lives. If he did, and if people believed him . . . but Charlie would be frightened and flustered, or made conceited by the interviews. In either case he would begin to lie, through fear or vanity. He was safest in my own hands.

"They are very funny fools, your English," said a voice at my elbow, and turning round I recognized a casual acquaintance, a young Bengali law student, called Girsh Chunder, whose father had sent him to England to become civilized. The old man was a retired native official, and on an income of five pounds a month contrived to allow his son two hundred pounds a year, and the run of his teeth in a city where he could pretend to be the cadet of a royal house, and tell stories of the brutal Indian bureaucrats who ground the faces of the poor.

Grish Chunder was a young, fat, fullbodied Bengali dressed with scrupulous care in frock coat, tall hat, light trousers and tan gloves. But I had known him in the days when the brutal Indian Government paid for his university education, and he contributed cheap sedition to *Sachi Durpan,* and intrigued with the wives of his school-mates.

"That is very funny and very foolish," he said, nodding at the poster. "I am going down to the Northbrook Club. Will you come too?"

I walked with him for some time. "You are not well," he said.

"What is there in your mind? You do not talk."

"Grish Chunder, you've been too well educated to believe in a God, haven't you?"

"Oah, yes, *here!* But when I go home I must conciliate popular superstition, and make ceremonies of purification, and my women will anoint idols."

"And hang up *tulsi* and feast the *purohit,* and take you back into caste again and make a good *khuttri* of you again, you advanced social Free-thinker. And you'll eat *desi* food, and like it all, from the smell in the courtyard to the mustard oil over you."

"I shall very much like it," said Grish Chunder, unguardedly. "Once a Hindu—always a Hindu. But I like to know what the English think they know."

"I'll tell you something that one Englishman knows. It's an old tale to you."

I began to tell the story of Charlie in English, but Grish Chunder put a question in the vernacular, and the history went forward naturally in the tongue best suited for its telling. After all it could never have been told in English. Grish Chunder heard me, nodding from time to time, and then came up to my rooms where I finished the tale.

"*Beshak,*" he said, philisophically. "*Lekin darwaza band hai.* (Without doubt, but the door is shut.) I have heard of this remembering of previous existences among my people. It is of course an old tale with us, but, to happen to an Englishman—a cow-fed *Malechh*—an outcast. By Jove, that is most peculiar!"

"Outcast yourself, Grish Chunder! You eat cow-beef every day. Let's think the thing over. The boy remembers his incarnations."

"Does he know that?" said Grish Chunder, quietly, swinging his legs as he sat on my table. He was speaking in English now.

"He does not know anything. Would I speak to you if he did? Go on!"

"There is no going on at all. If you tell that to your friends they will say you are mad and put it in the papers. Suppose, now, you prosecute for libel."

"Let's leave that out of the question entirely. Is there any chance of his being made to speak?"

"There is a chance. Oah, yess! But *if* he spoke it would mean that all this world would end now—*instanto*—fall down on your head. These things are not allowed, you know. As I said, the door is shut."

"Not a ghost of a chance?"

"How can there be? You are a Christi-an, and it is forbidden to eat, in your books, of the Tree of Life, or else you would never die. How shall you all fear death if you all know what your friend does not know that he knows? I am afraid to be kicked, but I am not afraid to die, becuase I know what I know. You are not afraid to be kicked, but you are afraid to die. If you were not, by God! you English would be all over the shop in an hour, upsetting the balances of power, and making commotions. It would not be good. But no fear. He will remember a little and a little less, and he will call it dreams. Then he will forget altogether. When I passed my First Arts Examination in Calcutta that was all in the cram-book on Wordsworth. Trailing clouds of glory, you know."

"This seems to be an exception to the rule."

"There are no exceptions to rules. Some are not so hard-looking as others, but they are all the same when you touch. If this friend of yours said so-and-so and so-and-so, indicating that he remembered all his lost lives, or one piece of a lost life, he would not be in the bank another hour. He would be what you called sack because he was mad, and they would send him to an asylum for lunatics. You can see that, my friend."

"Of course I can, but I wasn't thinking of him. His name need never appear in the story."

"Ah! I see. That story will never be written. You can try."

"I am going to."

"For your own credit and for the sake of money, of course?"

"No. For the sake of writing the story. On my honor that will be all."

"Even then there is no chance. You cannot play with the Gods. It is a very pretty story now. As they say, Let it go on that—I mean at that. Be quick; he will not last long."

"How do you mean?"

"What I say. He has never, so far, thought about a woman."

"Hasn't he though!" I remembered some of Charlie's confidences.

"I mean no woman has thought about him. When that comes; *bus—hogya*—all up!. . . . I know. There are millions of women here. Housemaids, for instance."

I winced at the thought of my story being ruined by a housemaid. And yet nothing was more probable.

Grish Chunder grinned.

"Yes—also pretty girls—cousins of his house, and perhaps *not* of his house. One kiss that he gives back again and remembers will cure all this nonsense, or else"—

"Or else what? Remember he does not know that he knows."

"I know that. Or else, if nothing happens he will become immersed in the trade and the financial specualtions like the rest. It must be so. You can see that it must be so. But the woman will come first, I think."

There was a rap at the door, and Charlie charged in impetuously. He had been released from office, and by the look in his eyes I could see that he had come over for a long talk; most probably with poems in his pockets. Charlie's poems were very wearying, but sometimes they led him to talk about the galley.

Grish Chunder looked at him keenly for a minute.

"I beg your pardon," Charlie said, uneasily; "I didn't know you had any one with you."

"I am going," said Grish Chunder.

He drew me into the lobby as he departed.

"That is your man," he said, quickly. "I tell you he will never speak all you wish. That is rot—bosh. But he would be most good to make to see things. Suppose now we pretend that it was only play"—I had never seen Grish Chunder so excited—"and pour the ink-pool into his hand. Eh, what do you think? I tell you that he could see *anything* that a man could see. Let me get the ink and the camphor. He is a seer and he will tell us very many things."

"He may be all you say, but I'm not going to trust him to your gods and devils."

"It will not hurt him. He will only feel a little stupid and dull when he wakes up. You have seen boys look into the ink-pool before."

"That is the reason why I am not going to see it any more. You'd better go, Grish Chunder."

He went, declaring far down the staircase that it was throwing away my only chance of looking into the future.

This left me unmoved, for I was concerned for the past, and no peering of hypnotized boys into mirrors and ink-pools would help me to that. But I recognized Grish Chunder's point of view and sympathized with it.

"What a big black brute that was!" said Charlie, when I returned to him. "Well, look here, I've just done a poem; did it instead of playing dominoes after lunch. May I read it?"

"Let me read it to myself."

"Then you miss the proper expression. Besides, you always make my things sound as if the rhymes were all wrong."

"Read it aloud, then. You're like the rest of 'em."

Charlie mouthed me his poem, and it was not much worse than the average of his verses. He had been reading his books faithfully, but he was not pleased when I told him that I preferred my Longfellow undiluted with Charlie.

Then we began to go through the MS. line by line; Charlie parrying every objection and correction with:

"Yes, that may be better, but you don't catch what I'm driving at."

Charles was, in one way at least, very like one kind of poet.

There was a pencil scrawl at the back of the paper and "What's that?" I said.

"Oh that's not poetry at all. It's some rot I wrote last night before I went to bed and it was too much bother to hunt for rhymes; so I made it a sort of blank verse instead."

Here is Charlie's "blank verse":

"We pulled for you when the wind was against us and the sails were low.
Will you never let us go?
We ate bread and onions when you took towns or ran aboard

quickly when you were beaten back by the foe.

The captains walked up and down the deck in fair weather singing songs, but we were below.

We fainted with our chains on the oars and you did not see that we were idle for we still swung to and fro.

Will you never let us go?

The salt made the oar handles like sharkskin; our knees were cut to the bone with salt cracks; our hair was stuck to our foreheads; and our lips were cut to our gums and you whipped us because we could not row.

Will you never let us go?

But in a little time we shall run out of the portholes as the water runs along the oarblade, and though you tell the others to row after us you will never catch us till you catch the oar-thresh and tie up the winds in the belly of the sail. Aho!

Will you never let us go?"

"H'm. What's oar-thresh, Charlie?"

"The water washed up by the oars. That's the sort of song they might sing in the galley, y'know. Aren't you ever going to finish that story and give me some of the profits?"

"It depends on yourself. If you had only told me more about your hero in the first instance it might have been finished by now. You're so hazy in your notions."

"I only want to give you the general notion of it—the knocking about from place to place and the fighting and all that. Can't you fill in the rest yourself? Make the hero save a girl on a pirate-galley and marry her or do something."

"You're a really helpful collaborator. I suppose the hero went through some few adventures before he married."

"Well then, make him a very artful card—a low sort of man—a sort of political man who went about making treaties and breaking them—a black-haired chap who hid behind the mast when the fighting began."

"But you said the other day that he was red-haired."

"I couldn't have. Make him black-haired of course. You've no imagination."

Seeing that I had just discovered the entire principles upon which the half-memory falsely called imagination is based, I felt entitled to laugh, but forbore, for the sake of the tale.

"You're right. *You're* the man with imagination. A black-haired chap in a decked ship," I said.

"No, an open ship—like a big boat."

This was maddening.

"Your ship has been built and designed, closed and decked in; you said so yourself," I protested.

"No, no, not that ship. That was open, or half decked because— By Jove you're right. You made me think of the hero as a red-haired chap. Of course if he were red, the ship would be an open one with painted sails."

Surely, I thought, he would remember now that he had served in two galleys at least—in a three-decked Greek one under the black-haired "politcal man," and again in a Vicking's open sea-serpent under the man "red as a red bear" who went to Markland. The devil prompted me to speak.

"Why, 'of course,' Charlie?" said I.

"I don't know. Are you making fun of me?"

The current was broken for the time being. I took up a note-book and pretended to make many entries in it.

"It's a pleasure to work with an imaginative chap like yourself," I said, after a pause. "The way that you've brought out the character of the hero is simply wonderful."

"Do you think so?" he answered, with a pleased flush. "I often tell myself that there's more in me than my mo—than people think."

"There's an enormous amount in you."

"Then, won't you let me send an essay on The Ways of Bank Clerks to *Tit-Bits,* and get the guinea prize?"

"That wasn't exactly what I meant, old fellow: perhaps it would be better to wait a little and go ahead with the galley-story."

"Ah, but I sha'n't get the credit of that. *Tit-Bits* would publish my name and address if I win. What are you grinning at? They *would.*"

"I know it. Suppose you go for a walk. I want to look through my notes about our story."

Now this reprehensible youth who left me, a little hurt and put back, might for aught he or I knew have been one of the crew of the Argo—had been certainly slave or comrade to Thorfin Kalsefne. Therefore he was deeply interested in guinea competitions. Remembering what Grish Chunder had said I laughed aloud. The Lords of Life and Death would never allow Charlie Mears to speak with full knowledge of his pasts, and I must even piece out what he had told me with my own poor inventions while Charlie wrote of the ways of bank-clerks.

I got together and placed on one file all my notes; and the net result was not cheering. I read them a second time. There was nothing that might not have been compiled at second-hand from other people's books—except, perhaps, the story of the fight in the harbor. The adventures of a Viking had been written many times before; the history of a Greek galley-slave was no new thing, and though I wrote both, who could challenge or confirm the accuracy of my details? I might as well tell a tale of two thousand years hence. The Lords of Life and Death were as cunning as Grish Chunder had hinted. They would allow nothing to escape that might trouble or make easy the minds of men. Though I was convinced of this, yet I could not leave the tale alone. Exaltation followed reaction, not once, but twenty times in the next few weeks. My moods varied with the March sunlight and flying clouds. By night or in the beauty of a spring morning I perceived that I could write that tale and shift continents thereby. In the wet, windy afternoons, I saw that the tale might indeed be written, but would be nothing more than a faked, false-varnished, sham-rusted piece of Wardour Street work at the end. Then I blessed Charlie in many ways— though it was no fault of his. He seemed to be busy with prize competitions, and I saw less and less of him as the weeks went by and earth cracked and grew ripe to spring, and the buds swelled in their sheaths. He did not care to read or talk of what he had read, and there was a new ring of self-assertion in his voice. I hardly cared to remind him of the galley when we met; but Charlie alluded to it on every occasion, always as a story from which money was to be made.

"I think I deserve twenty-five per cent, don't I, at least," he said, with beautiful frankness. "I supplied all the ideas, didn't I?"

This greediness for silver was a new side in his nature. I assumed that it had been developed in the City, where Charlie was picking up the curious nasal drawl of the underbred City man.

"When the thing's done we'll talk about it. I can't make anything of it at present. Red-haired or black-haired hero are equally difficult."

He was sitting by the fire staring at the red coals. "I can't understand what you find so difficult. It's all as clear as mud to me," he replied. A jet of gas puffed out between the bars, took light and whistled softly. "Suppose we take the red-haired hero's adventures first, from the time that he came south to my galley and captured it and sailed to the Beaches."

I knew better now than to interrupt Charlie. I was out of reach of pen and paper, and dared not move to get them lest I should break the current. The gas-jet puffed and whinnied, Charlie's voice dropped almost to a whisper, and he told a tale of the sailing of an open galley to Furdurstrandi, of sunsets on the open sea, seen under the curve of the one sail evening after evening when the galley's beak was notched into the centre of the sinking disc, and "we sailed by that for we had no other guide," quoth Charlie. He spoke of a landing on an island and explorations in its woods, where the crew killed three men whom they found asleep under the pines. Their ghosts, Charlie said, followed the galley, swimming and choking in the water, and the crew cast lots and threw one of their number overboard as a sacrifice to the strange gods whom they had offended. Then they ate sea-weed when their provisions failed, and their legs swelled, and their leader, the red-haired man, killed two rowers who mutinied, and after a year spent among the woods they set sail for their own country, and a wind that never failed carried them back so safely that they all slept at night. This, and much more Charlie told. Sometimes the voice fell so low that I could not catch the words, though every nerve was on the strain. He spoke of their leader, the red-haired man, as a pagan speaks of his God; for it was he who cheered them and slew them impartially as he thought best for their needs; and it was he who steered them for three days among floating ice, each floe crowded with strange beasts that "tried to sail with us," said Charlie, "and we beat them back with the handles of the oars."

The gas-jet went out, a burned coal gave way, and the fire settled down with a tiny crash to the bottom of the grate. Charlie ceased speaking, and I said no word.

"By Jove!" he said, at last, shaking his head. "I've been staring at the fire till I'm dizzy. What was I going to say?"

"Something about the galley."

"I remember now. It's 25 per cent of the profits, isn't it?"

"It's anything you like when I've done the tale."

"I wanted to be sure of that. I must go now. I've—I've an appointment." And he left me.

Had my eyes not been held I might have known that that broken muttering over the fire was the swan-song of Charlie Mears. But I thought it the prelude to fuller revelation. At last and at last I should cheat the Lords of Life and Death!

When next Charlie came to me I received him with rapture. He was nervous and embarrassed, but his eyes were very full of light, and his lips a little parted.

"I've done a poem," he said; and then, quickly: "it's the best I've ever done. Read it." He thrust it into my hand and retreated to the window.

I groaned inwardly. It would be the work of half an hour to criticise—that is to say praise—the poem sufficiently to please Charlie. Then I had good reason to groan, for Charlie, discarding his favorite centipede metres, had luanched into shorter and choppier verse, and verse with a motive at the back of it. This is what I read:

"The day is most fair, the cheery wind
    Halloos behind the hill,
Where he bends the wood as seemeth good,
    And the sapling to his will!

Riot O wind; there is that in my blood
    That would not have thee still!

"She gave me herself, O Earth, O sky;
    Grey sea, she is mine alone!
Let the sullen boulders hear my cry,
    And rejoice tho' they be but stone!
"Mine! I have won her O good brown
      earth,
    Make merry! 'Tis hard on Spring;
Make merry; my love is doubly worth
    All worship your fields can bring!
Let the hind that tills you feel my mirth
    At the early harrowing."

"Yes, it's the early harrowing, past a doubt," I said, with a dread at my heart. Charlie smiled, but did not answer.

"Red cloud of the sunset, tell it abroad;
    I am victor. Greet me O Sun,
Dominant master and absolute lord
    Over the soul of one!"

"Well?" said Charlie, looking over my shoulder.

I thought it far from well, and very evil indeed, when he silently laid a photograph on the paper—the photograph of a girl with a curly head, and a foolish slack mouth.

"Isn't it—isn't it wonderful?" he whispered, pink to the tips of his ears, wrapped in the rosy mystery of first love. "I didn't know; I didn't think—it came like a thunderclap."

"Yes. It comes like a thunderclap. Are you very happy, Charlie?"

"My God—she—she loves me!" He sat down repeating the last words to himself. I looked at the hairless face, the narrow shoulders already bowed by desk-work, and wondered when, where, and how he had loved in his past lives.

"What will your mother say?" I asked cheerfully.

"I don't care a damn what she says."

At twenty the things for which one does not care a damn should, properly, be many, but one must not include mothers in the list. I told him this gently; and he described Her, even as Adam must have described to the newly named beasts the glory and tenderness and beauty of Eve. Incidentally I learned that She was a tobacconist's assistant with a weakness for pretty dress, and had told him four or five times already that She had never been kissed by a man before.

Charlie spoke on, and on, and on; while I, separated from him by thousands of years, was considering the beginnings of things. Now I understood why the Lords of Life and Death shut the doors so carefully behind us. It is that we may not remember our first wooings. Were it not so, our world would be without inhabitants in a hundred years.

"Now, about that galley-story," I said, still more cheerfully, in a pause in the rush of the speech.

Charlie looked up as though he had been hit. "The galley—what galley? Good heavens, don't joke, man! This is serious! You don't know how serious it is!"

Grish Chunder was right. Charlie had tasted the love of woman that kills remembrance, and the finest story in the world would never be written.

The Shoddy Lands

by C. S. Lewis

Being, as I believe, of sound mind and in normal health, I am sitting down at 11 p.m. to record, while the memory of it is still fresh, the curious experience I had this morning.

It happened in my rooms in college, where I am now writing, and began in the most ordinary way with a call on the telephone. 'This is Durward,' the voice said. 'I'm speaking from the porter's lodge. I'm in Oxford for a few hours. Can I come across and see you?' I said yes, of course. Durward is a former pupil and a decent enough fellow; I would be glad to see him again. When he turned up at my door a few moments later I was rather annoyed to find that he had a young woman in tow. I loathe either men or women who speak as if they were coming to see you alone and then spring a husband or a wife, a fiancé or a fiancée on you. One ought to be warned.

The girl was neither very pretty nor very plain, and of course she ruined my conversation. We couldn't talk about any of the things Durward and I had in common because that would have meant leaving her out in the cold. And she and Durward couldn't talk about the things they (presumably) had in common because that would have left me out. He introduced her as Peggy and said

207

they were engaged. After that, the three of us just sat and did social patter about the weather and the news.

I tend to stare when I am bored, and I am afraid I must have stared at that girl, without the least interest, a good deal. At any rate I was certainly doing so at the moment when the strange experience began. Quite suddenly, without any faintness or nausea or anything of that sort, I found myself in a wholly different place. The familiar room vanished; Durward and Peggy vanished. I was alone. And I was standing up.

My first idea was that something had gone wrong with my eyes. I was not in darkness, nor even in twilight, but everything seemed curiously blurred. There was a sort of daylight, but when I looked up I didn't see anything that I could very confidently call a sky. It might, just possibly, be the sky of a very featureless, dull, grey day, but it lacked any suggestion of distance. 'Non-descript' was the word I would have used to describe it. Lower down and closer to me, there were upright shapes, vaguely green in colour, but of a very dingy green. I peered at them for quite a long time before it occurred to me that they might be trees. I went nearer and examined them; and the impression they made on me is not easy to put into words. 'Trees of a sort,' or, 'Well, trees, if you call *that* a tree,' or, 'An attempt at trees,' would come near it. They were the crudest, shabbiest apology for trees you could imagine. They had no real anatomy, even no real branches; they were more like lamp-posts with great, shapeless blobs of green stuck on top of them. Most children could draw better trees from memory.

It was while I was inspecting them that I first noticed the light: a steady, silvery gleam some distance away in the Shoddy Wood. I turned my steps towards it at once, and then first noticed what I was walking on. It was comfortable stuff, soft and cool and springy to the feet; but when you looked down it was horribly disappointing to the eye. It was, in a very rough way, the colour of grass; the colour grass has on a very dull day when you look at it while thinking pretty hard about something else. But there were no separate blades in it. I stooped down and tried to find them; the closer one looked, the vaguer it seemed to become.

It had in fact just the same smudged, unfinished quality as the trees: shoddy.

The full astonishment of my adventure was now beginning to descend on me. With it came fear, but, even more, a sort of disgust. I doubt if it can be fully conveyed to anyone who has not had a similar experience. I felt as if I had suddenly been banished from the real, bright, concrete, and prodigally complex world into some sort of second-rate universe that had all been put together on the cheap; by an imitator. But I kept on walking towards the silvery light.

Here and there in the shoddy grass there were patches of what looked, from a distance, like flowers. But each patch, when you came close to it, was as bad as the trees and the grass. You couldn't make out what species they were supposed to be. And they had no real stems or petals; they were mere blobs. As for the colours, I could do better myself with a shilling paintbox.

I should have liked very much to believe that I was dreaming, but somehow I knew I wasn't. My real conviction was that I had died. I wished—with a fervour that no other wish of mine has ever achieved—that I had lived a better life.

A disquieting hypothesis, as you see, was forming in my mind. But next moment it was gloriously blown to bits. Amidst all that shoddiness I came suddenly upon daffodils. Real daffodils, trim and cool and perfect. I bent down and touched them; I straightened my back again and gorged my eyes on their beauty. And not only their beauty but—what mattered to me even more at that moment—their, so to speak, honesty; real, honest, finished daffodils, live things that would bear examination.

But where, then, could I be? 'Let's get on to that light. Perhaps everything will be made clear there. Perhaps it is at the centre of this queer place.'

I reached the light sooner than I expected, but when I reached it I had something else to think about. For now I met the Walking Things. I have to call them that, for 'people' is just what they weren't. They were of human size and they walked on two legs; but they were, for the most part, no more like true men than the Shoddy Trees had been like trees. They were indistinct. Though

they were certainly not naked, you couldn't make out what sort
of clothes they were wearing, and though there was a pale blob at
the top of each, you couldn't say they had faces. At least that
was my first impression. Then I began to notice curious exceptions. Every now and then one of them became partially distinct; a
face, a hat, or a dress would stand out in full detail. The odd
thing was that the distinct clothes were always women's clothes,
but the distinct faces were always those of men. Both facts made
the crowd—at least, to a man of my type—about as uninteresting
as it could possibly be. The male faces were not the sort I cared
about; a flashy-looking crew—gigolos, fripoons. But they seemed
pleased enough with themselves. Indeed they all wore the same
look of fatuous admiration.

I now saw where the light was coming from. I was in a sort of
street. At least, behind the crowd of Walking Things on each side,
there appeared to be shop-windows, and from these the light
came. I thrust my way through the crowd on my left—but my
thrusting seemed to yield no physical contacts—and had a look at
one of the shops.

Here I had a new surprise. It was a jeweller's, and after the
vagueness and general rottenness of most things in that queer
place, the sight fairly took my breath away. Everything in that
window was perfect; every facet on every diamond distinct, every
brooch and tiara finished down to the last perfection of intricate
detail. It was good stuff too, as even I could see; there must have
been hundreds of thousands of pounds' worth of it. 'Thank Heaven!' I gasped. 'But will it keep on?' Hastily I looked at the next
shop. It *was* keeping on. This window contained women's frocks.
I'm no judge, so I can't say how good they were. The great thing
was that they were real, clear, palpable. The shop beyond this one
sold women's shoes. And it was still keeping on. They were real
shoes; the toe-pinching and very high-heeled sort which, to my
mind, ruins even the prettiest foot, but at any rate real.

I was just thinking to myself that some people would not find
this place half as dull as I did, when the queerness of the whole
thing came over me afresh. 'Where the Hell,' I began, but immediately changed it to 'Where on earth'—for the other word seemed,
in all the circumstances, singularly unfortunate—'Where on earth

have I got to? Trees no good; grass no good; sky no good; flowers no good, except the daffodils; people no good; shops, first class. What can that possibly mean?'

The shops, by the way, were all women's shops, so I soon lost interest in them. I walked the whole length of that street, and then, a little way ahead, I saw sunlight.

Not that it was proper sunlight, of course. There was no break in the dull sky to account for it, no beam slanting down. All that, like so many other things in that world, had not been attended to. There was simply a patch of sunlight on the ground, unexplained, impossible (except that it was there), and therefore not at all cheering; hideous, rather, and disquieting. But I had little time to think about it; for something in the centre of that lighted patch—something I had taken for a small building—suddenly moved, and with a sickening shock I realized that I was looking at a gigantic human shape. It turned round. Its eyes looked straight into mine.

It was not only gigantic, but it was the only complete human shape I had seen since I entered that world. It was female. It was lying on sunlit sand, on a beach apparently, though there was no trace of any sea. It was very nearly naked, but it had a wisp of some brightly coloured stuff round its hips and another round its breasts; like what a modern girl wears on a real beach. The general effect was repulsive, but I saw in a moment or two that this was due to the appalling size. Considered abstractly, the giantess had a good figure; almost a perfect figure, if you like the modern type. The face—but as soon as I had really taken in the face, I shouted out.

'Oh, I say! There you are. Where's Durward? And where's this? What's happened to us?'

But the eyes went on looking straight at me and through me. I was obviously invisible and inaudible to her. But there was no doubt who she was. She was Peggy. That is, she was recognizable; but she was Peggy changed. I don't mean only the size. As regards the figure, it was Peggy improved. I don't think anyone could have denied that. As to the face, opinions might differ. I would hardly have called the change an improvement myself. There was no more—I doubt if there was as much—sense or kindness or honesty in this face than in the original Peggy's. But it was certainly more regular. The teeth in particular, which I had noticed as a weak point in the old Peggy, were perfect, as in a good denture. The lips were fuller. The complexion was so perfect that it suggested a very expensive doll. The expression I can best describe by saying that Peggy now looked exactly like the girl in all the advertisements.

If I had to marry either I should prefer the old, unimproved Peggy. But even in Hell I hoped it wouldn't come to that.

And, as I watched, the background—the absurd little bit of sea-beach—began to change. The giantess stood up. She was on a carpet. Walls and windows and furniture grew up around her. She was in a bedroom. Even I could tell it was a very expensive bedroom though not at all my idea of good taste. There were plenty of flowers, mostly orchids and roses, and these were even better finished than the daffodils had been. One great bouquet (with a card attached to it) was as good as any I have ever seen. A door which stood open behind her gave me a view into a bathroom which I should rather like to own, a bathroom with a sunk bath. In it there was a French maid fussing about with towels and bath salts and things. The maid was not nearly so finshed as the roses, or even the towles, but what face she had looked more French than any real Frenchwoman's could.

The gigantic Peggy now removed her beach equipment and stood up naked in front of a full-length mirror. Apparently she enjoyed what she saw there; I can hardly express how much I didn't. Partly the size (it's only fair to remember that) but, still more, something that came as a terrible shock to me, though I suppose modern lovers and husbands must be hardened to it. Her body was (of course) brown, like the bodies in the sunbathing advertisements. But round her hips, and again round her breasts, where the coverings had been, there were two bands of dead white which looked, by contrast, like leprosy. It made me for the moment almost physically sick. What staggered me was that she could stand and admire it. Had she no idea how it would affect ordinary male eyes? A very disgagreeable conviction grew in me that this was a subject of no interest to her; that all her clothes and bath salts and two-piece swimsuits, and indeed the voluptuousness of her every look and gesture, had not, and never had had, the meaning which every man would read, and was intended to read, into them. They were a huge overture to an opera in which she had no interest at all; a coronation procession with no Queen at the centre of it; gestures, gestures about nothing.

And now I became aware that two noises had been going for a long time; the only noises I ever heard in that world. But they were coming from outside, from somewhere beyond that low, grey covering which served the Shoddy Lands instead of a sky. Both the noises were knockings; patient knockings, infinitely remote, as if two outsiders, two exluded people, were knocking on the walls of that world. The one was faint, but hard; and with it came a voice saying, 'Peggy, Peggy, let me in.' Durward's voice, I thought. But how shall I describe the other knocking? It was, in some curious way, soft; 'soft as wool and sharp as death,' soft but unendurably heavy, as if at each blow some enormous hand fell on the outside of the Shoddy Sky and covered it completely. And with that knocking came a voice at whose sound my bones turned to water: 'Child, child, child, let me in before the night comes.'

Before the night comes—instantly common daylight rushed back upon me. I was in my own rooms again and my two visitors were before me. They did not appear to notice that anything unusual had happened to me, though, for the rest of that conversation, they might well have supposed I was drunk. I was so happy. Indeed, in a way I was drunk; drunk with the sheer delight of being back in the real world, free, outside the horrible little prison of that land. There were birds singing close to a window; there was real sunlight falling on a panel. That panel needed repainting; but I could have gone down on my knees and kissed its very shabbiness—the precious real, solid thing it was. I noticed a tiny cut on Durward's cheek where he must have cut himself saving that morning; and I felt the same about it. Indeed anything was enough to make me happy? I mean, any Thing, as long as it really was a Thing.

Well, those are the facts; everyone may make what he pleases of them. My own hypothesis is the obvious one which will have occurred to most readers. It may be too obvious; I am quite ready to consider rival theories. My view is that by the operation of

some unknown psychological—or pathological—law, I was, for a
second or so, let into Peggy's mind; at least to the extent of
seeing her world, the world as it exists for her. At the centre of
that world is a swollen image of herself, remodelled to be as like
the girls in the advertisements as possible. Round this are grouped
clear and distinct images of the things she really cares about.
Beyond that, the whole earth and sky are a vague blur. The
daffodils and roses are especially instructive. Flowers only exist
for her if they are the sort that can be cut and put in vases or sent
as bouquets; flowers in themselves, flowers as you see them in the
woods, are negligible.

As I say, this is probably not the only hypothesis which will
fit the facts. But it has been a most disquieting experience. Not
only because I am sorry for poor Durward. Suppose this sort of
thing were to become common? And how if, some other time, I
were not the explorer but the explored?

Afterword

by Harry Harrison

Within the small world of science fiction there is a tendency to be more than a little chauvinistic about our special and apart status. Many readers and, alas, some writers, enjoy the fact that we are ignored by what might be called the 'mainstream' establishment.

They are all wrong, both inside and out. There is no longer that small world of science fiction except in attitude. Commercially, science fiction is a going and important part of the publishing scene. It is becoming more and more a part of the academic world of letters. There is no chance that the unique qualities of science fiction may be swallowed up in the greater field of general fiction, nor—thank goodness—is there any hope that SF will engulf all of English literature. What *is* possible is that America will follow Great Britain and other parts of the world in admitting that science fiction is what it is, a specialized corner of literature.

SF has too long been invisible to the world of letters, like H. G. Wells' invisible man shivering naked in the snow and looking through the window at the warmth and plenty within. Cut off from the larger world of literature SF has suffered from cultural inbreeding—while at the same time it has denied the larger world of letters its particular benefits. The visible and the invisible have both been deprived.

Inside science fiction we have been deprived of reviews, greater sales potential, larger markets, as well as in many smaller ways. (A chapter of one of my novels was once selected for anthology use in a college level rhetoric reader—until one of the two English professors editing the book discovered that the extract was *science fiction* and could therefore not be used. What is invisible must remain that way.) The greater world of letters has missed some very fine work. There are writers, like Brian W. Aldiss, who are major authors and who just happen to do most of their work in this medium. If their books did not have the stigmata of SF on their covers they would undoubtedly have brought a certain fame and reward to their authors, while enriching more readers at the same time.

Science fiction is penetrating academia. There are a number of courses in high schools and universities around the country; I recently taught one myself at San Diego State College. Here is a living literature that relates to our times—and is fun to read as well. It appears that the time is close when the union will at last be joined. I hope that this anthology will do something to effect that union.

The stories here are good. They are science fiction. They were written by authors who are not considered, either by themselves or the critics, to be practicing science fiction writers. But they are authors who have both reputation and respect. And once one begins digging it is amazing to discover just how many good stories of this kind there are. The main problem, as James Blish mentions in his introduction, is in weeding out the overly familiar. To do this I have leaned most heavily on the judgement and advice of Norbert Slepyan, who was not just the publisher's editor for this book but more like a collaborator at times. James Blish was a tower of strength and aid, while a special note of thanks must go to Dr. Willis E. McNelly of California State College at Fullerton for suggestions and advice.

Harry Harrison